ENTERTAINING MONA LISA

PHILIPPE DE FELICE

GW00602747

SCRIPTUS BOOKS

First published in 2015 in Great Britain by
Scriptusbooks Ltd
46 Murray Road
London SW19 4PE

Scriptusbooks.com

Printed by printondemand-worldwide.com
Cover designed by Barbara Loxton Design
ISBN 978-0-9564466-4-0

ENTERTAINING MONA LISA

For Hilary with love

CONTENTS

Preface

All these stories are based on historical fact and are presented in chronological order, starting with the 20th Century and ending with the Roman period. Some readers have expressed interest in the sources on which they are based and brief notes are provided at the end of the book.

Philippe de Felice

London, 1st December 2015

THE CONVERSION OF HANS FRANK

THE CONVERSION OF HANS FRANK

Nuremberg, 15th October 1946

Dear Father Johannes,

You have always been my guide. To you I owe my call to the priesthood. Above all, you taught me how to pray.
To you I now turn for help.

***

The war is over and Hitler is dead. For six years, we've lived in the shadow of death. Every time I close my eyes, I hear the mad shouts of cheering crowds, I see endless ranks of soldiers parading the streets, I feel the heat of burning cities... Our daily lot as Catholic priests has been to witness cruelties and injustices beyond description. But our faith was not shaken and we held firm. Throughout these long years, you and I prayed together and felt that God was near us, that Christ was also suffering on His Cross with us. Didn't Our Lord promise: *'Whenever two or three gather together in my name, then I am in the midst of them'*?
Germany now lies in ruins. The rest of Europe is starting to breathe again. Everywhere there is new hope.

But not for me.
For me, the shadows are lengthening... When I close my eyes and pray, all I feel is silence and emptiness. It is only now, after all that suffering, that I understand a faith can die, just as a body may decay and die.
They say God has a purpose for us all, but haven't I suffered enough? Why should I be selected as the priest to minister to these monsters?
I pleaded with Bishop Andreas, I did everything to make him understand that there are things even a priest cannot bring himself to do. But he was immovable. My orders were to go to

11

Nuremberg and turn the other cheek. I begged him to release me from my vows, I threatened to appeal to Rome itself: I nearly broke down and shouted in front of the others. Why should I, of all the thousands whom they could have selected, be the priest ordered to offer forgiveness?

As I lay on my bed in the American army hostel I couldn't pray. Outside, I could hear the sounds of the deserted city. An occasional shout in the night, the distant cry of a patrol challenging someone breaking the curfew, then silence. The Allied bombers have left so little of Nuremberg standing that the wind howls ceaselessly through the half-broken buildings, their torn facades making fantastic shapes in the darkness. Sometimes, the bombs have left the side of a building still standing, its piping somehow hanging suspended at impossible angles, high up over the streets. There they hang, rattling in the wind, like demonic jesters clamouring for attention. The strangest sound is that moan, that persistent cry of the wind whistling through broken windows, through gaping roofs, like a perpetual accusation.

I lay still and cold for many hours, my mind a blank: I couldn't even decide who to pray for. For the countless dead lying strewn across Europe? For the survivors, so that their grief may be alleviated by grace? My clumsy words seemed a particularly grotesque way of helping them.

***

30th August 1946

I have done my duty according to my vows of obedience.
I met the other priests assigned to give spiritual guidance to the accused. The priest in charge is Father Siktus O'Connor, an American from New York, the sort of large heavily-built man you see in Hollywood films. He welcomed us warmly and spoke enthusiastically about the power of the Holy Spirit: four of the

defendants have apparently returned to the Faith: Von Pappen, Kaltenbrunner, Seyss-Inquart and Frank. It seems that the Lutherans have done even better than we Catholics. Their pastor, Father Gerecke (another American, this time from Missouri) has apparently managed to 'net' -as he puts it- the majority of the accused, holding services in a chapel constructed out of two cells. There you can hear Von Ribbentrop, Field-Marshall Keitel, Admiral Dönitz, Von Schirach and Speer, all lustily singing their hymns and reciting their prayers in unison. Even Goering is there, but at least he has the honesty to admit that he only goes to church to get out of his cell...

The only ones who stubbornly refuse are Hess, Rosenberg and Streicher. I must admit that I have a secret admiration for those three, steadfastly rejecting the possibility of redemption and resolutely facing damnation. But Father O'Connor says he still prays for them every day.

We've each been assigned one of the Catholics. Father O'Connor will minister to Kaltenbrunner, the former head of the Gestapo. ("I'm keeping the worst to myself", he said with a hearty laugh). Father Herenfeld is in charge of Seyss-Inquart, Father Michaelis has Von Pappen and I've been assigned Hans Frank, the butcher of the Poles. Apparently, Frank is the most unstable of the four: his moods swing wildly from tortured guilt to defiant arrogance. For some reason, Father O'Connor decided I have the necessary compassion to coax him back to salvation.

***

5th September 1946

I met Herr Frank for the first time today. He turns out to be surprisingly likeable. He immediately stood up and welcomed me when I came into his cell. He is a little shorter than me but

13

immaculately dressed in the suits his wife brings him to wear-
isn't it odd how we humans insist on our outward dignity? On
first meeting, he is the archetypal German lawyer: correct, polite,
serious- the sort of man who'd think it a stain on his moral
standing if a letter went unanswered for more than a week.
Unlike some of the other accused, he is a man of considerable
culture. We talked about the glories of German civilisation. He
spoke enthusiastically about Goethe, Caspar David Friedrich
and Brückner. He spoke feelingly about his walks in the
Schwarzwald reciting his beloved Rilke! Then the pictures of
Auschwitz and Treblinka came to my mind. Then I
remembered that these indescribable horrors happened in
Poland, where he was Governor-General, while he enveloped
Poland in a shroud of darkness...

As our discussions continued, I somehow tried to persuade
myself I could feel some compassion for this despicable
monster. But every time I began to feel a sense of peace, the
thought of his heinous crimes surged up, like an overflowing
cesspit. I saw his bloated innocent face, I remembered his small
hunched figure in Courtroom 600, sitting between Keitel and
Speer, darting little furtive looks around him, as if asking for
approval for the horrors for which he was responsible. Looking
at him again, I was filled with a sense of such utter loathing that
it terrified me.
Please, Johannes, please pray that I may save my faith...

***

9th September 1946

The reason why Nuremberg was chosen to host the trials of the
Nazi leaders is not for any symbolic value or because Hitler held
his rallies here. The reason is more banal: it is the only town in
Germany where a large courtroom has been left standing at a
reasonable distance from a capacious hotel. And Nuremberg's

Palace of Justice has the added advantage of having enough underground cells to house all the twenty-three accused in one place. There is something almost comical in the existence of the two buildings, the courtroom and the hotel, standing almost miraculously intact in a landscape of utter desolation- as if providence has somehow spared those two heavy late nineteenth century buildings for a purpose.

Things have now settled down to a routine. We start the day with Mass at the Sebalduskirche - unless the weather makes it impossible to use the ruined church, in which case we use the American army barracks. Afterwards, we go to the trial, sitting in the row at the back, with the other priests.

It is interesting how each nationality is reflected by its legal traditions: the chief Judge, Lord Lawrence, embodies a British sense of fair play- Olympian and slightly ironic as he presides over the trial, sometimes cajoling a witness or reining back a particularly aggressive line of questioning. The Soviets are brutally pragmatic: Major-General Nikitchenko makes it perfectly obvious that he's getting increasingly impatient at the whole lengthy procedure: for him, the trial should simply list the crimes of the accused and march them off to a firing squad. The French go to great lengths to establish the trial's theoretical justification, with wonderful flows of Cartesian rhetoric. The Americans imitate the British, only more aggressively and without the same poise. As for the German defence lawyers, they sit impassively, insisting on the observance of the most minute details of procedure. Their arguments are predictable: the trial has no legal basis, the accused merely obeyed the laws of the Third Reich, the whole thing is a dangerous precedent of retrospective justice... They don't have the nerve to accuse the Allies of indulging in victor's revenge: only Goering has done that, probably realising that he has nothing to lose, as he's bound to be executed anyway.

Gradually, the trial is turning into a routine. Even the daily revelations of new horrors become part of it. As the wheels of justice laboriously turn towards their inevitable conclusion, I often catch the accused looking bored or even falling asleep... At first, the guards tried to maintain decorum by nudging the defendants with their truncheons whenever they doze off in the heat of the overcrowded courtroom, but by now even they have given up and the whole grotesque charade grinds on day after day.

But today things were different.
Today, they showed a film that chilled the blood in my veins. The lights were dimmed and the courtroom became a vast hall of shadows. The screen slowly lit up and started showing the nightmarish discoveries Allied troops made when they reached Auschwitz and Belsen. A hush descended over the whole courtroom and only the distant whir of the projector could be heard from somewhere behind me. They showed us everything: the chambers, the ovens, all the paraphernalia of murder turned into an industrial process... But it was the faces of the survivors that tore into our minds: faces where the eyes bulged out, where the eyes had no trace of life, staring at us accusingly.
At that very moment, a soft band of light from the screen illuminated the expressions of the accused: Goering's bloated face, Von Ribbentrop looking arrogant, Hess obviously quite mad and lost in some deep private meditation. Each of them was transfixed in the cold bluish light of the film, like creatures from another world. They claimed they knew nothing of what went on in the camps, but now their reactions were there for everyone to see. I watched their faces gradually change from bored indifference to horror as the film showed the mass graves where bulldozers rolled countless corpses into the pits, like great waves of putrefying flesh. At that moment, most of the audience held their breath, some even crouched down unable to bear what they were being shown. Truly we were witnesses to depths of evil greater than at any point in human history: even

Dante never imagined the unspeakable horrors of Auschwitz. He could never have imagined them for the simple reason that his was a naïve age which believed that suffering is always linked to guilt. This is why the Nazis were uniquely evil: they proved man's deepest sense of justice wrong, they inflicted untold suffering on people who were entirely innocent, whose only 'crime' was being alive in a form of humanity they were determined to exterminate.

Something forced me to go on looking at the accused. I saw Goering pursing his lips until they were drained of blood. Keitel covered his eyes with hands that shook uncontrollably. Admiral Dönitz- the Führer's chosen successor for the last days of the Reich- lowered his head in shame. Then I saw Hans Frank, collapsing in convulsive sobs, but none of his companions seemed to notice, so engrossed were they by the horrors before their eyes.

Since this film, I've begun to feel myself capable of the gravest of sins: despair or- more precisely- of doubts that Christ's incarnation and sacrifice were of any use at all. Auschwitz proves we humans are truly fallen creatures. The accused sitting on those heavily guarded benches were not mad, they were perfectly capable of normal thought. Hans Frank is the model of the polite and industrious provincial lawyer. But when I think what he did, then I feel shadows darkening in my mind... I'm finding it intolerable to be alone.

***

10th September 1946

The next day, I made my daily visit to Herr Frank.

At first, we sat in silence but I could tell he wanted me to be the one to start talking. Instead, I merely watched him- God forgive me!- almost enjoying the sight of him writhing in front of me, guilt tearing him inside like an acid.

He stood up and paced up and down, smoking cigarette after cigarette nervously. I did nothing but merely watched him, filled with a loathing deeper than I can describe.
But it was his turn to surprise me.
'Father ', he said, 'why exactly are you here?'
His question hit me like a knife. Suddenly all the gospel passages of forgiveness, of our duty to love and pray for our enemies flooded my mind. I remembered Christ inviting the Pharisees to cast the first stone, saying that he'd come to find sinners rather than the virtuous, Christ sacrificing himself on the Cross so that there could be redemption. What had *I* done to live by this example? What had I done but to act in a way contrary to everything that Christ stood for?
I've no idea whether my face reflected my inner turmoil, but Hans Frank stopped and looked at me with a curious expression, carefully placing yet another cigarette in his ivory holder.
I could not look at him without thinking of that film of Auschwitz and then remembering the Parable of the Prodigal Son. I was like one of those medieval sculptures of a man flanked by a demon and an angel, each whispering advice into his ears... I remembered those corpses stacked high and immediately afterwards the image of Christ on a stained glass window, hatred surging inside me while, above, I glimpsed the pure light of heaven...
'I am here to help you', I said simply.
'How can you help *me*?', he asked immediately. 'Haven't I done everything to ensure God will reject me?'
'God never rejects anyone', I replied, perhaps a little too mechanically. 'It is always *we* who chose to reject His love'.
'Are you really saying that there can be hope, even for someone like me?'

I looked at him, standing in his neatly-cut grey suit: urbane, suave but also somehow terribly vulnerable.

'Yes', I began to reply, grateful that the Catholic Church provides us with ready-made formulas, 'the salvation of the Church is offered to every sinner'. Then I quoted the Catechism: ' *There is no-one, however wicked and guilty, who may not confidently hope for forgiveness, provided his repentance is honest. The gates of forgiveness should always be open to anyone who turns away from sin.*'

There was a long silence. He drew on his cigarette and inhaled deeply. Then he looked outside at the grey autumn day through the bars of his cell. He seemed to want to say something but then changed his mind at the last moment. I felt privileged to be a witness to his inner struggle: before my very eyes, I was watching a soul deciding its own fate.

I wondered whether I should intervene- whether it was my duty to say some words of encouragement. But I am ashamed to confess I couldn't bring myself to do so: as I watched him struggle within himself, those images of Auschwitz came surging up again, and I -a Christian priest of fifteen years' standing- I with all the venom that my heart could muster- I *hoped* for his damnation. I yearned for him to refuse, I longed for him to turn round and demand that I leave his cell- like Rosenberg or Streicher contemptuously refusing the attentions of the priests assigned to the care of their souls. At that moment, I passionately wanted him to reject me, to shut the door to salvation and plunge headfirst into the lowest pit of Hell.

'Even I, Father?', he said suddenly.
I looked up at him, startled out of my thoughts by his question.
'Father, do you really mean that if I asked you to hear my confession and I was sincere, I could receive the sacraments?'
I could not help myself twisting the knife:
'If your repentance was sincere'.
'How could you know that?'

'You can always tell', I replied simply.
Without saying another word, I handed him my Rosary and left.

***

12th September 1946

Two days later, I had my first pastoral meeting with Herr Frank.
I let him talk and he unburdened his soul, his rambling words
fluctuating violently from extreme arrogance to abject despair.
There were impassioned rants about the vanished glories of the
Reich followed by convulsive sobs, as the horror of his crimes
overwhelmed him.
He spent a great deal of time talking about Hitler. For him, the
Führer answered Frank's craving for certainty. His presence
cancelled doubt: he had almost become a god. Hitler was
selflessly devoted to the German *Volk*, completely free of
personal greed compared to the fawning and corrupt rabble
around him... Whenever he felt disgusted by some atrocity, the
Führer would be there, gazing at him from his portrait on his
desk and the doubts would melt. At such moments, he would
look at his idol and realise that he was only being a weakling,
that shedding blood was necessary to create a better world, that
it was his lot to live through the times when Europe's
purification must take place. In centuries to come, they would
look upon his generation as heroes, those who had ushered in
the New Order. As he spoke, I imagined Hans Frank in his
palace in Krakow, surrounded by his terrified Polish servants- all
praying they might get out alive while their new master
harangued them about the glories of the Third Reich.
The Führer had a mesmeric hold on all his followers were
transfixed by him, subjugating their consciences and willingly
surrendering their free will to that demon. A true German- a
true National Socialist- should always place himself in the
position of the Führer, Hans Frank insisted. His duty was to
imitate Adolf Hitler, in every act and in every thought.

20

Führerworte haben Geseztkraft: the words of the Führer have the force of law! He even quoted me a lecture he once delivered on Aryan Law: *'Say to yourselves at every decision which you make: 'How would the Führer decide in my place?' This unity of your will with the will of Adolf Hitler will endow you with the authority of the Third Reich!'*

As he ranted, I remembered the words Saint Teresa. *'Christ has no body now on Earth but yours, no hands but yours, no feet but yours. Yours are the eyes through which Christ's compassion looks at the world. Yours are the hands through which he now blesses'...* That incomparable saint and that repulsive man had each modelled themselves on another being but with what vastly different results! Truly it is we mortals who chose our salvation or decide to be damned.

His confession went on. He described his life of luxury and splendour while Poland starved. His governor's residence was not in Warsaw but in Wavel Castle, a Renaissance palace on the hills overlooking Krakow. From there he ruled over Poland, the Lord of life and death, intoxicated by the thrill of his power over the millions of men who cowered at his feet. He smiled suddenly 'Some even quipped that with me, Hans Frank, in power Poland had become *'Frank-Reich'*...'

'I loved the Wavel', he said, remembering the cool breezes that fanned the surrounding gardens during the hot summer months. He pillaged old masters from the Royal Palace in Warsaw. His wife, Brigitte, now the mistress of a wonderfully grand establishment, hugely enjoyed her time in Poland. There she indulged in her fantasy life of style and luxury, even going out shopping in the Jewish ghetto 'because they turned out such gorgeous lace...'

His wildest ambitions were now fulfilled. He was now Governor of Poland, he the small lawyer from Karlsrühe, who had shocked his elders and betters at the Munich Bar by joining the nascent Nazi movement, even taking part in the Beer Hall Putsch. He was particularly proud of that: *he* was an 'Alter Kampfer', one of the old fighters who had been 'in the movement' from the beginning. I think he was proud of this mainly because it proved that he wasn't the weakling which, deep down, he considered himself to be.

To keep his subordinates in control, Hitler used to encourage rival factions within the Third Reich. In Poland, a parallel S.S. administration competed with Frank's civil government, each outdoing the other in brutality to gain the Führer's approval. It became a mad race of murder and cruelty for its own sake: whenever the SS hanged a hundred Poles or Jews, Frank would order even greater numbers to the scaffold. He even confessed to envying these men of violence. He secretly longed to be as ruthless as the S.S., to be as free from the constraints of humanity as they were.

Standing on the balcony of his private apartments, he would look at Krakow beneath his feet, admiring the old streets and spires stretching below, feeling like a god. Everything around him belonged to *him*: he could switch between magnanimity and brutality as the whim took him. The whole process was immensely exciting, even intoxicating. At this point he smiled disarmingly: 'It was like a drug, Father. The power and the certainty of being able to use force without any resistance is the sweetest and most noxious poison that can be introduced into a ruler's mind.'

And so came a slow but deadly transformation. Gradually, he began to lose his fear of divine retribution, he began to feel liberated, as if suddenly placed beyond the reach of good and evil. He would look up defiantly at the starlit sky and know there was nothing above him. No God. No punishment and no reward. His earthly existence had only as much meaning as his thoughts were capable of giving to it. Whether he ordered someone's death that day was of no more consequence than if he ordered a merciful delivery of food to the ghetto: ultimately, it did not matter for both acts were of equal insignificance. The day he understood that, he said, he knew he had transcended the limitations of petty humanity, like an eagle soaring in the sky: he had truly become a man!

I listened to him hour after hour, as he paced up and down his cell. I tried to think of something else, but I could only feel an overwhelming sense of disgust. I have sometimes doubted the dogma of Hell, even the existence of Satan. But that evening, as I listened to him ranting about the Führer, about the vanished glories of what Germany might have been, I felt I was in the presence of pure evil, as if Hitler's very presence was conjured back into the little cell where we sat.

Suddenly he stopped. Then with terrible slowness, he knelt down in front of me, asking for my benediction.

'It tortures me now to think how far I strayed from God', he said.

I couldn't find words to express my nausea and revulsion. In fifteen years as a priest I've heard terrifying sins in the confessional, but never before have I been confronted by pure evil. I looked at him and he looked at me.

Suddenly I could stand it no longer and rushed out of the cell.

***

14th September 1946

Today, I was not required to visit Herr Frank. I was immensely relieved…

It was a fine crisp morning, with a freshness in the air. The sky was so blue it momentarily helped me forget the degradation around me, the daily horrors revealed in Courtroom 600. My thoughts soared upwards and I went out, deciding to go to the city parks, where I hoped the rich autumnal colours would remind me that there was still beauty in the world.

The people of Nuremberg are in a desperate state. As I walked to the tram station, there was a commotion in the street in front of me: a carthorse had fallen into a bomb crater and the driver was badly hurt. Luckily for him, a patrol of soldiers was nearby and he was driven off to hospital. But the crowds had their own reasons for wanting him out of the way: as soon as the army truck had turned the corner, a policeman put the horse out of its misery and the crowd got to work. Like a swarm of flies, they flocked to the carcass producing butcher's knives and cleavers out of their pockets: with much shouting, arguments and even the occasional fight, the horse was swiftly dismembered, the blood of the poor beast splashing everywhere on the clothes of the respectable housewives.

I watched the whole spectacle with horrified fascination, reflecting on how odd it was that, only a few hundred yards away, we were confining a few dozen men and keeping them well fed and housed until the day of their execution, while all around us there were children and old people almost dying of hunger.

My tram stopped at Dutzendteich Park, where Hitler once held his rallies. The arena was still there, with its endless rows of seats, filled with an eerie silence. The Americans have tried to destroy the huge slabs of concrete, but in vain. The strongest charges of dynamite cannot dent the titanic structures spawned by the Thousand Year Reich, so now they leave the whole area as an empty memorial. Just one year after the war has ended, vegetation is already spreading all over the concrete structures and birds have made their nests under the cavernous arches.

I sat down and my thoughts inevitably returned to Hans Frank, that odious and repulsive man sitting in his cell, waiting for the hangman but also waiting for me to save his soul. For days, I had been fighting against such thoughts, but I knew what my faith, my God and my entire calling meant. However much I rebelled against the thought I knew that if I couldn't 'save' him, if Christian forgiveness couldn't stretch even to a Hans Frank, then we are all doomed. The greatest saints in history considered themselves appalling sinners- and they were right.

Even Saint Teresa was a sinner, her life filled with imperfections and not just because of the lofty standards she applied to herself. She was a mere human and therefore could never achieve purity. Perhaps the cruellest result of the Fall, I understood, is mankind's ability to conceive of perfection without being able to achieve it! Like the stars in the firmament, these absolutes shine above our heads, to taunt and inspire us. This is why Saint Teresa suffered, why she was right to kneel and beg God for grace and salvation.

I stood up and started walking energetically across the vast arena. Perhaps it was fitting that such thoughts should have come to me in such a monstrous place, but I now suddenly understood how I could offer Hans Frank absolution. He would have to earn it by finding the self-disgust and, yes, the courage to take the hand of forgiveness which was being held out to him.

***

16th September 1946

Perhaps it is the boredom of prison or perhaps it is the lawyer in him, but, in the last week, Herr Frank has been particularly insistent that we should discuss theological points.

It is a bit like debating with a medieval scholastic. He constantly asks questions like: 'Can grace be varied according to the needs of the individual soul?' or 'Are there different types of grace to match the circumstances of each individual?' Herr Frank finds new questions to ask me on every visit, as if trying to learn a whole procedural system, as if theology were a science reducible to a few set formulas.

I try to make him understand that religion is not simply a set of rules, that the Holy Spirit shines through every moment of our lives, radiating the presence of God through our human imperfections, that dogma is only shorthand to express mystical experience, but I am not sure he really understands me.

I comfort myself with the thought that he is, at least, inquiring about the Faith, that this is a beginning, that something is happening in the depths of his being. As if a very, very dry plant is beginning to come back to life.

Herr Frank's mind is better trained than mine. He often finds holes in my explanations. But he is keen to learn and pretends not to be too concerned when my arguments are less than watertight: perhaps he has at last begun to understand that faith is beyond reason because it is based on a deeper reality, that faith is beyond logic and beyond the arid limitations of the human mind.

But, deep down, I find his questions irritating, mere word games while, all around us, the reality of transcendence whispers in the background. If there could be a cast-iron definition of God, if one could find an incontrovertible proof for the existence of God, it would have been found by now. How glad I am that no such proof has ever been produced! I prefer a hidden God than a God who forces his creatures to believe in him by the sheer majesty of his divine presence.

***

20th September 1946

Today, Herr Frank asked me to hear his confession. I was so taken aback that I immediately agreed to do so, without thinking about what I was committing myself to do. He immediately began to recite the confessional opening formula, saying it off pat, as if he had been practising for this moment for some time. And before I knew what I was doing, he was kneeling to my left and began to recite his sins, as if this was the most natural thing in the world: in an instant, the man responsible for the horrors of wartime Poland, was listing his crimes in a matter of fact tone, like an inventory.

At the Seminary, we were taught to shut our eyes while hearing confessions, so as better to see the inner soul of the repentant sinner. But this time, I not only opened my eyes, but I positively ogled the confessant kneeling before me. Was it really the power of the Holy Spirit that I was witnessing, shining through this list of appalling crimes or was he a consummate actor, playing his part to diabolic perfection?

As I listened to his monstrous list, I looked at him, I stared at the bald crown of his head, at his sober and respectable suit. No, I would not- I could not- allow this to pass as an act of contrition and open the gateway to Heaven so easily. Something inside me urged me to make him suffer longer. I wanted to see the torturing guilt really come to the surface: I convinced myself that it was my duty to test the sincerity of his 'conversion'. Most of all, I wanted him to crawl before me and grovel for forgiveness, to clutch my legs with desperation like all the countless victims he had sent to their deaths. It never entered my mind that I might be being seduced by a particularly subtle and dangerous temptation.

Solemnly, I told him to think again. To look into the depths of his heart and only then to ask for God's forgiveness. I knew - God forgive me!- that this was totally unjustified, that here was a truly repentant sinner before me- but I not only wanted him to suffer, I wanted to *see* him suffering.

I rose quickly and left him shaking on the cold floor of his cell.

***

24th September 1946

My next visit was scheduled three days later.

Those intervening days were a terrible torment for me. I kept being haunted by the memory of seeing him kneeling on the floor of his cell, confessing his crimes in that precise, soft voice of his. Of course I knew perfectly well that I had abused my powers as a priest: I had deliberately refused absolution, I had violated my vows of charity, I had offered a stone to the one who had begged me for bread...

If Hans Frank died now, he would die unforgiven and would be damned for Eternity -unless it was theologically correct that an act of late repentance is sufficient to earn divine forgiveness *in extremis*. But that would only happen if he was truly repentant at the exact time of his death: should he die without absolution, if my deliberate refusal had turned him against God, if the fragile shoot of contrition had been killed off by my act of cruelty, then his soul would be damned forever. His lost soul would be on my conscience for the rest of my life, however much he might have deserved eternal damnation.

How I wrestled with my conscience during these three days! One moment, a surge of guilt would make me want to race over to give him absolution. But then I'd remember what he'd done in Poland and my heart would be filled with such loathing that I almost knelt down to pray that he might be thrown into the lowest pit of Hell. Once I was almost on the point of demanding to be driven to the cells but I then reflected that there was no guarantee that- at the point when I would arrive- Hans Frank would be in a state disposed to receive absolution. My sudden arrival would then have no purpose and might even provoke a *false* act of contrition... To grant absolution in response to false contrition would be even worse than letting God's unfathomable mercy respond to a deathbed conversion... And so the whole cycle of guilt, doubt, followed by rationality would begin again.

I began to think that it was *I* who was being driven mad.

***

Hans Frank stood up as I came in and greeted me with a slight bow. His face looked untroubled. It suddenly dawned on me that perhaps he had accepted my refusal to grant him absolution as something perfectly normal- as part of the usual process of 'earning' one's salvation. I found him polite and even strangely submissive, as if he had become convinced that, provided he did as he was told, then he would achieve his objective. I have said before that Frank strikes me as a fundamentally weak man and that his is the sort of personality that needs to anchor itself on a strong outside influence. The irony was not lost on me that if it was Adolf Hitler who once dominated his mind and cancelled all doubt, now a mere twelve months after his idol's death, it was I -or rather Christ through me- who now performed the same function!

We discussed the reading I had given him. He said he'd been particularly comforted by the quotation from Isaiah: *'I live, says the Lord, ready to help and comfort you more than ever, if you will trust Me and call on Me with devotion'*. He spoke feelingly about his yearning for penance, quoting the words of St. Thomas à Kempis: *'I desire no consolation that would deprive me of contrition'*. He declared that this was 'the key': it proved to him he would have to suffer- and be willing to embrace suffering- to achieve true peace.

He never mentioned Poland again, as if he was now removed from his past and even from his present. He knew the trial would continue, that he was almost certain to be sentenced to death- after all, he had pleaded guilty to all charges against him. All that interested him was to prepare himself for death.

And so, I was privileged to witness the Holy Spirit at work, saving a man and claiming him back from the edge of the abyss.

***

27th September 1946

Today I received a call from the prison to come urgently. I set off immediately, arriving in Herr Frank's cell expecting the worse. But he had not slashed his wrists and I wasn't called upon to administer extreme unction.

As I entered his cell, he stood up, looking at me with a matter of fact expression. Then he asked very politely whether I would hear his confession again. We proceeded with the sacrament at once and I watched my hands making the sign of the Cross. It was thus that I finally heard myself reciting the ritual words that cleansed away the deliberate murder of millions of nameless Jews...

***

1st October 1946

The court has handed down its sentence: like most of the defendants, Hans Frank is condemned to death by hanging. The executions will take place the following week, on the evening of the 14th October.

***

12th October 1946

Frank had a 'blessed night' yesterday: that is his term for a night when he isn't tormented by his guilt and can bring himself to believe that God has accepted his repentance. He said he was suddenly seized by a feeling of immense peace when he recited the end of the Hail Mary: *'pray for us sinners, now and at the hour of our death'*...

It was when I talked to him that I understood why the Church always teaches that the worse sin is not lack of belief. It is despair. Nothing can be worse than rejecting God's love and losing hope. Although the words burn in my throat, even if I feel a sense of utter repulsion at the thought of this man receiving forgiveness for his crimes, I know in my heart of hearts that Salvation means nothing if it excludes a Hans Frank.

Sometimes I have doubts about his contrition: is it more based on the terror of eternal punishment than a genuine conversion? Is it therefore a true rejection of the horrors of his past life? If the Nazis were miraculously brought back to power and he was released, would he revert to his abominable crimes? Either he is a consummate liar and an actor of genius, or somehow the Holy Spirit has genuinely began to work in him. But it is not for us priests to cast out but to welcome sinners instead.

Even so, I began to hate Hans Frank far more for what he was doing to my priestly vocation than for his unspeakable crimes in Poland. I knew that my own soul was being corroded by his presence and that the sooner he was dead the better it would be for me. A few more months of this tortured, contradictory inner turmoil and I would no longer feel able to administer the sacraments, I would no longer be able to function as a priest. Desperately, while he knelt down and prayed at my side, looking genuinely all a truly repentant sinner should be, I would try to fill my mind with something else than loathing and contempt. I tried to occupy my thoughts with the Rosary, reciting the sequence of prayers again and again, but after a while my fingers ended up just fingering the beads mechanically, my mind a complete void.

Christ have mercy on me.

***

13/14th October 1946

The final day before the executions arrived and the atmosphere of the cells changed dramatically. They would not tell us who would go to the scaffold first, but only that all would be hanged by two o'clock in the morning.

Everyone could hear the noise of the US Army sappers putting up the scaffold, but strangely no-one commented on the noise of the saws cutting wood or the sound of the nails being hammered in.

Extra security measures were introduced to prevent any of the condemned men from committing suicide: all the accused were forced to wear handcuffs at all times, daily exercise was forbidden and they slept with the lights on to detect any suspicious movements.

The accused were allowed to take Communion at about midday, while the afternoon was left for them to prepare themselves and for those with families to see them once more.

***

I gave Hans Frank the last rites just before 10pm. That would leave him about two hours to prepare himself for the final moment. We recited a few prayers together- the Credo, the Pater Noster and the Ave Maria- and then I laid hands on him. Afterwards I anointed his forehead and hands.

I felt exhausted by the emotions of the last few days. But as I knelt and rather mechanically prayed for his soul, a strange sense of peace came over me. The long process had now come to its fitting end and felt an odd lack of emotion at the thought that the man who I had guided back into the Faith was about to die.

I have often had to give extreme unction to the sick and the dying, but this was the first time that I had administered the sacrament to a healthy man. As I laid my hands and felt the slight warmth of his head, it felt terribly strange to know that this speaking and breathing man would not see the dawn in the morning, that in a few hours he would be dead. I was being allowed to watch a man making that awesome transition from the living to the dead.

***

A little after midnight, the executions began. We were not the first to be called upon but had to wait for at least an hour.

We didn't say much to each other, and I simply sat in the cell, ready to be called upon if he needed me. I felt calm, and oddly I did not expect him to flinch at the last moment and suddenly reject Christ. I didn't really pray but somehow blankly concentrated on the pattern made by the brickwork on the back wall.

Finally the doors opened and four soldiers came in, one from each of the Occupying Powers. The officer in charge of the executions, an American called Colonel Anders, read out the Court's sentence once again and led Herr Frank out the cell. I followed the platoon a few steps behind.

We walked quickly along the corridors lit by the crude and rather clinical light of neon strips. The soldiers marched in step, with Frank in the middle, arms tied in front by handcuffs. As I walked, I could not help myself observing the way his legs and hips moved. It was then that I was struck by the full absurdity of the killing that was about to take place. With great solemnity, we were about to put to death a perfectly fit man, a man who was presently breathing the same air as we were breathing, who was seeing exactly the same things that we were seeing, whose legs walked as quickly as mine. The difference was that, in a few minutes, with a sudden snap of a rope around his neck, he would be dead and we would be alive. In ten minutes from now, he would no longer be part of the same world. In ten minutes, he would know whether there was life after death, whether centuries of prayer and devotion had a purpose.

We had now reached the place of execution. There was a small crowd of people in the room, representatives of Britain, France, America and Russia, as well as two German observers and a few journalists. The scaffold stood in the centre of the large hall, draped in a black cloth.

Beside me, I could hear Hans Frank mumbling a prayer softly, over and over again, but the sound started to irritate me. I suddenly desperately wanted him to die as quickly as possible, I began to loathe him again.

Hans Frank was led to the scaffold, his body beginning to sag as he started to be overcome with exhaustion. I blessed him as quickly as I could and watched him go up the steps to the execution platform. An American sergeant put the rope round his neck, and, just before he put the hood over his head, I caught a glimpse of Hans Frank's face, looking straight in front of him. It was a strange expression, calm and empty, as if he had suddenly regained his strength at his final moments: afterwards, I could not decide whether his last expression was one of resignation or of ironic defiance.

The sergeant gave a little signal that all was ready.

I shut my eyes at that moment and all I heard was the trap door suddenly opening and a dull thud as his body reached the end of its fall.

There was a short silence and two doctors went under the scaffold to certify the fact of death. As with all the executed Nazi leaders, his body would then be put in a wooden coffin, the rope still round his neck with a small label for official identification. Tomorrow the bodies would be cremated and their ashes thrown in a river to prevent any martyrs' shrines being erected.

Afterwards, when all the condemned had been executed, I was invited back to the officers' mess where we were offered Bourbon by Colonel Anders and Cognac by a French officer whose name I can't remember. We all talked rather louder than usual, as if we needed to fill a silence. I found that I was laughing quite loudly, and that everyone was laughing as well. Someone offered a few biscuits which I ate greedily, feeling the warmth of the Bourbon going down inside me. A Russian officer handed round cigarettes, explaining that they were American contraband, and everyone laughed loudly at the joke. We all chatted and laughed, Soviet and American, British and French, all together exchanging pleasantries amicably.

I remember lifting my eyes to the dawn just beginning to emerge on the horizon. I looked at the skyline now breaking slowly with a thin but dazzling strip of light. It was then that I realised that the shadows were still crowding in my mind, that I could still hear the soft whispering of damnable thoughts.

PLAYING POKER WITH BERIA

PLAYING POKER WITH BERIA

MOSCOW, 1938

I

Evgeny Varga looked out of the window: the grey roofscape of
Moscow receded into the distance under an equally grey winter
sky. In the streets, crowds of monochrome people went about
their business with expressionless faces, huddled under grey
coats, trying not to slip on the sludge-covered pavement. The
only splash of colour was a huge mural in blood-red letters
exhorting Muscovites to ever greater efforts in the fight against
the enemies of Socialism.

Varga swivelled in his chair and contemplated his book-lined
study. He was one of the fortunate few, with a studio flat to
himself, a fairly easy-going job as the economic adviser to the
Hungarian People's Party Government in exile. His flat was
warm, he was reasonably well-fed and, above all, he was still
alive.

The same could not be said of Bukharin, of Zinoviev, of
Kamenev... all the glittering cast of the First International, now
exposed by the vigilant efforts of the NKVD as a nest of
traitors, spies, saboteurs, Trotskyites and terrorists, all in the pay
of the secret services of America, England, France, Fascist
Germany, Fascist Italy, Fascist Spain and Fascist God only knew
where else.

Except that God couldn't possibly have an opinion on the
matter for the simple reason that he could neither exist nor have
a role in a world that Man had built with his unaided and fertile
imagination. A man-made world it might be, Varga reflected
with a sardonic smile, but it certainly was also a profoundly
fallible world: there seemed to be no end to the list of traitors in
their midst, to the capacity of the enemies of Socialism to
infiltrate the inner sanctum of World Communism. Every day,
the working masses of the Soviet Union were called upon to

clench their fists at a new batch of traitors who grovellingly admitted their guilt and treachery in the full glare of cameras.

And now they had even started unmasking traitors in the midst of the KOMINTERN, at the heart of the Communist International, among Comrades who had devoted their entire lives to the creation of a better world. Had it had not been proved beyond a shadow of a doubt that the exiled Communists Parties who had taken refuge in the Soviet Union from Hitler's Germany, Franco's Spain, Salazar's Portugal, Mussolini's Italy or Antonescu's Rumania were riddled with agent-provocateurs and capitalist spies? And now, the plague of treachery had apparently spread even to his native Hungarians, spawning a swarm of traitors within the ranks of his own Comrades. Those who had been at his side since the Great War, ever since the short-lived Hungarian Soviet Republic of 1919. If what the NKVD said was true, there were Fascist spies even among those he had hidden with in the rat-infested cellars of Budapest, trying to escape from Admiral Hórthy's secret police. Bokany, Magyar, Münnich, Gerö, even Béla Kun- they all turned out to have been spies and traitors.

Yes, even that inspirational Communist Béla Kun, the leader of the Hungarian Soviet of 1919 and Comrade Stalin's faithful follower: hadn't he also abjectly confessed that he had been a German spy since 1916, a Rumanian spy since 1919 (and therefore *during* the Soviet uprising which he had led!), a double agent for the Hungarian police since 1920 (to save his own skin) and a British spy since 1936. As befits a man capable of spying for no less than four imperialist powers at the same time, Béla Kun had been shot.

That had been yesterday.

Varga laughed hollowly, trying to imagine what absurd lies they would concoct against him when his turn came to confess abjectly in front of huge crowds of seething Comrades. No doubt that would be after days of relentless torture in the darkest cellars of the Lubyanka. He hoped that he would die of the 'treatment' quickly- (the doctors had told him he had a weak heart) - or at least that they would shoot him quickly.

He looked out of the window again. He was on the eighth floor. If they knocked on the door, he could jump of course. That would be a quick and effective way of avoiding the whole ghastly charade.

In Moscow, the winter night started early and it was already getting dark outside. He opened the draw of his desk and took out a well-worn pack of playing cards. Tonight he would try to teach Beria 'Texas Hold 'Em'. Beria liked high stakes and the version of 'Hold 'Em' he had learned from American dockworkers in Houston was about the most high-risk version of poker around.

II

Beria learned quickly, laughing like a schoolboy as he raked the chips towards him with a greedy sweep of the hand.

Lebedev dealt the cards again, two face down for each player. Beria was in a buoyant mood and opened the bidding with 30 roubles.

'30', said Kaganov with a grunt.

Avram Yakovlev glanced at his opponents and visibly did a quick mental calculation. He had lost badly that night, well over 200 roubles and, as a relatively junior NKVD officer, his salary could not hope to keep pace with Beria's or Malerian's *penchant* for high stakes. He lit a cigarette and puffed at it philosophically. Then he looked round.

'30', he said in a decisive voice.

Beria smiled approvingly.

'30', said Malerian, brushing back his mesh of dark hair with a mechanical wave of the hand, as was his habit when deep in thought.

Varga had also lost badly. At least 120 roubles so far. But that had been deliberate. He knew that it was important for Beria to win a few rounds. After all, it was probably was the only thing that kept him out of the clutches of the Chekhists.

'30', he said.

'30', said Lebedev.

They looked at their cards, each responding in character. Beria smiled, Malerian brushed his hair back again, Yakovlev tried to look impassive like in the American cowboy movies he had seen and Lebedev sighed and picked up his glass of vodka.

Varga had a 10 ♥ and a Q♦.

Lebedev dealt out the 'Flop': the three cards on the table were Q♠, 7♣ and 10♣. Varga's spirits lifted. It could have been worse: at least he had the makings of a 'straight'. But it was a marginal hand, and he probably would have to bid cheaply to stay in. Alternatively, he could combine the Q♦ in his hand with the Q♠ and the 10 ♥ with the 10♣: combining the cards in his hands with those in the Flop, he would then have two Pairs. That worked to his advantage, as the likelihood of Beria also having a matching pair of Queens or 10s was slim. He would raise Beria and claw back some of his earlier losses.

'30', said Beria.

Varga immediately smiled back at Beria, acknowledging the low cunning of the man. He was lulling the others into a state of self-confidence by bidding low. Perhaps he had a K♥ and a 9♣? There were already a Q♠ and a 10♠ in the Flop: that would mean that he was near to a 'straight' K♠ down to 9♠ if the J♠ turned up when the 'Fourth Street' or 'Fifth Street' cards were dealt out. Or perhaps Beria's series started from the Q♠ or even the 10♠.

'30', said Kaganov quietly.

'Fold', said Yakovlev, turning his cards on the table, and downing his glass of vodka. The upturned cards were 2♥ and 6♣. A miserable hand. He had been right to cut his losses and quit.

'Fold', said Malerian with a broad grin, turning up a J♦ and a 2♠.

'30', said Lebedev.

'30', said Varga and stared impassively across the table at Lebedev and Beria.

Lebedev dealt out the 'Fourth Street' card. It was a 8♠. That only increased the chances of Beria having a 'straight'. Although he had little chance of beating Beria, he determined to bluff it out.

The great thing about poker, Varga always maintained, was that players communicated through their cards or through the chips they slammed on the table. It was their 'body language', to use the expression used by those fashionable modern psychologists. In chess, the player who wins is the one who 'sees' further than his opponent, although both are presented with exactly the same display of pieces on the board. In poker, you only saw *some* of the cards and the game was won or lost through the subtle and deadly struggle of bid and counter-bid, bluff and counter-bluff. 'You can ask some pretty cruel questions with those chips', the old Texan dock worker who had taught him poker was always fond of saying, (usually as he swept back towards him a mound of coins and garishly coloured counters…)

Varga considered the position again. He had two doubles. Beria was almost certain not to have also got two Queens and two 10s: his only real hope would be a straight starting with the Ace ♠ or the K♠, or perhaps starting from the Q♠.

The overhead lamp hung low over the table and gave the room an oddly intense atmosphere. Outside, the street was silent except for the occasional burst of wind in the birch trees and the sound of the NKVD guards outside trying to keep warm. Varga looked round at his opponents around the table. Their faces looked whiter and more puffy in the crude light of the single bulb and the cigarette smoke. Lebedev's face had a homely quality to it, a large generous peasant's face, with strong jaws and wide glasses, like a friendly village elder. His dark uniform did not suit him, only emphasising the contrast between the rather fatherly figure and the cold-blooded executioner he was by day. His hands were large and slightly podgy, and he held his cards delicately as if they were they were fragile: Varga could hardly imagine them torturing the mangled body of his victims.

'Raise 40', said Beria.

'40', said Lebedev.

Varga decided to take the plunge: 'Raise 50'.

Beria looked at him with a hard stare that did not suit his rather cherubic features. Varga lit a cigarette and placed his two cards neatly on the table one next to the other, face down. Then he waited to see what would happen. That made 430 roubles on the table: equal to a factory worker's monthly salary. He worked out that he only had 200 roubles of his KOMINTERN allowance left, so that winning the pot would be essential to make ends meet.

Beria poured himself half a glass of vodka with mannered precision, as if he was measuring out medicine. It was terribly quiet in the room as he sipped his glass. Then, slowly, he put it down.

'50', he said.

'Fold', said Kaganov, throwing down a K♣ and a J♥.

Beria nodded to Lebedev who dealt out the 'Fifth Street' card. It was a J♣.

'Fold', said Beria suddenly, throwing down his cards: a K♠ and a 9♠. Varga had been right: Beria had been tantalisingly close to a 'straight'. He said nothing, but simply put his cards onto the table, showing his two pairs. Beria's face did not register any emotion. Varga calmly collected the 430 roubles on the table and poured himself a generous helping of vodka.

III

The Hotel Lux still stands on Gorky Street, except that it has recently been renamed the Hotel Tsentralnaïa and the street is now called Tverskaïa Street. This constant change of names hardly bothers the average Muscovite, who now cheerfully ignores the current rather Pharisaic trend to expunge all traces of a Communist world which, until recently, everybody applauded to the last hurrah.

The Hotel Lux was no ordinary hotel during the reign of the

44

Red Tsar. You could not ring up and book a room at the Hotel Lux and ordinary Russians never went there- except, that is, when they were wearing the sombre green uniform of the Soviet People's Police or the even more anonymous long grey coats of the NKVD.

In fact, the Hotel Lux was not a real hotel at all. Instead, it was home to a veritable zoological assembly of the different species and sub-species of World Communism. For there, in the overcrowded rooms and suites of the now rather dingy Tsarist hotel, had collected the flotsam and jetsam of World Communism and its numberless failed revolutions. The Hotel Lux's guests were German, Italian, French, Chinese, Vietnamese and there was even a sprinkling of earnest Americans and Englishmen, all taking refuge in the safety of the One True Workers' State on Earth. The rooms and suites of the Hotel Lux thus became the headquarters of a series of revolutionary governments in exile, each waiting for the chance to lead their countrymen to the Socialist Nirvana or to be sent on missions of subversion by Comrade Stalin. A visitor casually walking the corridors of the Hotel Lux would have met all the great names of 1930 Communism: Klement Gottwald, Heinz Neumann, Palmiro Togliatti, Dolores Ibarruri- yes, even the great 'La Passionara' of the Spanish Civil War- they could all be seen under one roof...

The NKVD found the whole arrangement very convenient: having all these foreigners in one place made it much easier to watch their every movement. It also made their arrest and purging that much simpler to organise.

Casually flashing his KOMINTERN identification card, Varga walked past the NKVD guards and went inside the Hotel Lux. It was very late, as his session of poker with Beria had lasted until after 2 am, but lights were still on in the sets of rooms occupied by the Hungarians.

He knocked on the door and went straight in. Ferenc Laszlo

and Peter Dohanyi were talking in a haze of tobacco smoke over a bottle of red wine. They stopped as soon as he came in. Ferenc got up and walked towards Varga. He looked pale and highly agitated. He shook Varga's hand nervously and quickly blurted out something about the NKVD having 'raided the Lux' earlier that evening. Shots had been fired upstairs where the Poles were and several NKVD men had been shot before Wyzinsky had been overpowered. He had been dragged fighting and screaming down the stairs to a waiting car. The fact that people had guns in the Lux would only give 'them' another excuse for further raids.

'Wasn't Wyzinsky a friend of yours?', Varga asked.

'Yes'. Ferenc looked away. 'He often came down here. To practice his Hungarian. He had lived in Budapest as a child, you see.'

'What on earth was that idiot doing having a gun in the Lux?', Varga said.

Varga looked at Ferenc with a sudden infinite compassion. Ferenc was one of the best of the Party' new blood. He had been only a boy during the 1919 uprising. Ferenc had recently told him his boyhood memories, seeing the defeated revolutionaries being hounded by Admiral Hórthy's police. His admiration for their hopeless heroism had driven him to join the underground while at University. He had accomplished several dangerous missions under the very noses of the secret police before inevitably being unmasked by an informer. He had only just managed to escape with his life to swell the throngs of revolutionaries taking refuge in Moscow.

Varga studied Ferenc's face closely. He had the expressions of the true ascetic. With his short dark hair and gaunt, stubbly face, he could almost have come out of the portraits of those ardent Counter-Reformation Jesuits missionaries, all passionately seeking their martyrdom. But now all that idealism, all that unquestioning energy and devotion would be snuffed out like a candle in the deepening darkness. Wyzinsky would be tortured, of course, and he would yell out all the names of anyone he had ever met in Moscow in the sound-proofed cells of the Lubyanka. That would certainly include Ferenc. The NKVD would therefore arrest him as well, if only to ensure that they could not be accused of neglecting their quota.

There was a fragile innocence about Ferenc that made his impending annihilation all the more monstrous. A lesser man would have allowed his emotions to get the better of him, but Varga had witnessed too many reversals of fortune, he had experienced too many of History's cruelties and ironies to do that. In a sense, Varga reflected as they talked, Ferenc was not only insignificant but he was even expendable. Varga had seen many better men die since those heady days of the 1919 uprising and its savage crushing at the hands of the Whites. He had fought in the Soviet Civil War and he had witnessed the horrors of enforced collectivisation in the Ukraine. He had learned to contemplate human suffering with a stoical hardness that could easily pass for indifference. But it was not indifference: it was simply that men had to learn through suffering that individual tragedy is unimportant against the March of History. As Comrade Stalin himself had remarked, with his characteristic gift for pithy aphorisms: 'When a man dies it is a tragedy, but when a hundred thousand men die it is a national statistic'.

Secretly he despised Stalin as a murderous brute but he had to admit that the monster had forged the Soviet Union into a force to be reckoned with. England and France had simply watched helplessly as Hitler swallowed up the Sudetenland and Austria. The USSR was probably now the only bulwark against Fascism. Ferenc's approaching destruction was an irrelevance against the rising tide of insanity sweeping over Europe. The fight against these new barbarians made everything else insignificant. In a world of Hitlers and Francos, idealists like Ferenc were at best useful fools, young flesh to be sacrificed on the altar of twentieth century madness.

IV

The NKVD duly arrested Ferenc the next day. People said that he had gone quietly, putting on his winter coat and following the grey-suited men down the stairs without saying a word. The whole thing was over in a few minutes.

V

The morning light was unusually clear with the vast orb of the winter sky stretching over the city like a lid of cold steel. The sun was bright but without warmth.

Varga walked quickly, oblivious to his surroundings, his breath steaming in the frosty air. He walked up to the University Park, and, in the distance, he could see the cold facade of the recently completed University buildings, with the central spire crowned by a huge red star. Row upon row of concrete blocks of flats spread out in the distance, without any trace of individuality or colour. This, surely, was the price of kneading the thick clay of humanity into a new force: the individual did not matter. The mass was the only unit of measurement modern man understood. He looked up, feeling suddenly atomised by the vastness of the sky, the sheer scale of the functional buildings that lined the streets, the immensity of the force that was relentlessly crushing them all one by one.

The paths had been cleared of snow and his boots crunched the frosty gravel as he walked. A group of squat women wrapped in many layers of scarves and coats were shuffling the snow into huge mounds, intoning a mournful and repetitive song as they worked. Beyond, children were playing and throwing snowballs at each other with shrieks of delight. He could see their Red Pioneer scarves through their thick coats. The mothers looked tired and worn, even fearful, but the children -poorly dressed and badly fed as they obviously were- looked happy and full of energy. One threw a snowball in his direction and Varga threw one back, provoking a chorus of delighted giggles. The other children immediately pelted him until stopped by their mothers, snatching them from Varga's path, evidently taking him for an important Party official because of the quality of his winter coat. Varga laughed and walked on.

They would kill Ferenc, soon they might kill him as well, but they could not slaughter the whole of humanity. There would always be that irrepressible energy, that sheer lust for life would eventually defeat tyranny…

VI

Beria gave a full, hearty chuckle as he swept his winnings back towards him. He was having an extraordinary run of luck that evening. First he had been dealt triple Aces, followed by a Straight led from the K♣, and now he had just had two Kings and two Queens. He sat back with a boyish grin, his side of the table positively covered with coins and notes.

Beria was in a splendid mood. Rumour had it that Yezhov was being quickly elbowed out. Although he had mysteriously fallen from Stalin's favour, he was still formally in charge of the Water Transport Commission, clinging on to that sinecure for dear life: but as each of his supporters were being systematically arrested and shot, it was only a matter of time before he was himself purged and Beria's success complete. Very soon he would be the head of the NKVD.

As Beria bid for ever higher stakes and collected his rich harvest of coins, Varga reflected on the insane logic of the blood-letting unleashed by Yezhov, Beria and their kind. Every NKVD interrogator was duty-bound to demand a list of all his victim's accomplices: once these were extracted, it would then be suicidal negligence not to arrest each and every person denounced by the defendant screaming with pain on the floor of his cell. The other night, Lebedev had got the worse for vodka and had started to talk freely, as if suddenly desperate to unburden his heart to someone. The NKVD, Lebedev explained, was gradually getting trapped by the diabolic system it had created: everybody was denouncing everybody else. Mathematically, the whole population of Moscow would soon be incriminated. Lebedev then told him about a man they had recently arrested who had a prodigious memory: he had implicated each of the 212 scientists in the Research Institute where he worked. He had even cleverly included members of the NKVD in the list of his accomplices. His tormentors thus found themselves trapped by their own mechanism: they could not torture him any further because he had confessed and they could hardly investigate themselves. The matter was referred to the senior NKVD officer in charge, who promptly ordered an end to the interrogation. Of course, the trick had not saved the wretched man from being sent off to the GULAG for the standard 25 year term. Lebedev told him the story with loud guffaws that only seemed to emphasise his obvious fears about his own position.

'Raise 50', said Beria, beaming with pleasure at the sight of the cards he had been dealt with.

VII

The NKVD raided the Lux again that night

Like some specie of night predators, the NKVD only came in the dead of night, preferably between three and four o'clock in the morning. They had followed their familiar pattern. First, the soft sound of the convoy of cars and trucks approaching the Lux in the dead of night. Then, an occasional shout somewhere in the darkness outside and the piercing beam of headlights on the walls of the building. Finally, the clatter of boots up the stairs, the agonizing wait to know which floor and which corridor the thudding footsteps had selected this time.

All the inhabitants of the Lux would sit up and listen in the darkness. Varga could hear his neighbour, Anton Gyorgos, a fat man rather prone to copious sweating, getting out of his bed and drawing back the curtains. Gyorgos was a fatalist, keeping by his bedside a small suitcase containing the few personal belongings the regulations apparently allowed those arrested to take with them. Rather superstitiously, Varga had never dared to ask him what he had selected to take with him, but the suitcase had become the object of rather ghoulish jokes among the Hungarians in the Lux.

This time Gyorgos' fatalism proved correct. The footsteps stopped on the third floor and the corridor on the right. The whole building waited to hear the expected knock on the door. First there was silence, then a muffled order shouted from the bottom of the stairwell. Another silence, then a loud repeated knock. It was all over quickly and efficiently. Gyorgos meekly opened the door, ready with his suitcase. Varga heard him follow the NKVD men down the stairs, and then the trucks moved off with a soft crunching of gravel, gradually fading away.

At first there was complete silence as the inhabitants of the Lux gathered their courage again. Then Varga heard the first sound of opening doors, as hushed enquiries where the raid had happened began to fill the dead silence. People could be heard announcing that 'it' had happened on the third floor. Already there were exaggerated claims that three, no five, had been taken away, that they had been Hungarians and Bulgarians. There was an immediate counter claim shouted from one floor to the next, as people congregated in the stairwell to discuss the night's events as if the tally of those taken away were a score in a macabre kind of sport. Varga heard the sounds of the arguments, the swearing and the cursing in the stairwell with a mounting sense of anger and helplessness.

He got up and pulled a draw in his desk. There was a small packet of photographs bound together by an elastic band. He started looking through them. There was Ernö Gerö, sitting comfortably on a wicker chair wearing a summer hat; that must have been on the Black Sea, perhaps at one of the Party's summer *dachas*. There was a group photograph of him with Béla Kun and Detcho Bokany, posing with their wives. Next there was a picture of Ferenc Lazslo, toasting the camera with a broad grin on his face. There were also pictures of Lajos Magyar, of Szanto (who had subsequently denounced Béla Kun), of Matyas Rakosi who now looked set to take over from Béla Kun, of George Lukács...

He looked at each face- the faces of those who had vanished and were now probably dead. He took out the picture of Ferenc, setting it carefully on the side of his desk lamp. Then he tore up the rest of the photos and threw them into the dustbin.

VIII

They had been playing for nearly two hours now: the air was filled with the acrid smoke of the heavy cigarettes which Kaganov smoked incessantly. Beria had been losing heavily, with Varga out bluffing him consistently throughout the evening. A large pile of notes were strewn in front of Varga, like a thick carpet of multi-coloured leaves.

Beria downed a swig of vodka with an irritated flick of the hand and proposed that they switch to 'Draw Poker'. He grandly declared that 'Texas Hold 'Em' was a game of pure bluff and therefore inferior. He much preferred Draw Poker because each player kept his cards completely hidden from the others: there was none of this combining of hands with communal cards exposed on the table. Draw Poker was 'a game of psychological insight', he declared. The art was to second-guess the opponent from the way he bid.

Varga readily agreed: by a happy coincidence, Draw Poker was something of a speciality for him and he was in no mood to show mercy.

Lebedev dealt the cards nonchalantly. Malerian's face froze while Yakovlev twitched nervously in his chair: he had had another disastrous night the previous week, and Varga was sure that he would have had to borrow from friends to be in on the game tonight.

Varga looked at his five cards. He had a J♥, J♦, 8♦, 6♠ and 3♣. It wasn't too bad: at least with the pair of Jacks, he could discard the minor cards at the draw and improve his hand. The chances of having a third Jack was high.

Kaganov checked and passed to Beria. Beria bid 100 Roubles immediately. Varga tried to repress a smile: Beria was losing his legendary self-control and bidding too high. Varga hesitated whether he should bid: he had the requisite two Jacks or above to be allowed to bid but he decided to check and not bid: although he had two Jacks of his own, there was no point in joining in the bidding as Beria must have at least the same as his hand or higher. It would be better to increase the psychological pressure by passing on bidding and keeping Beria guessing as to the strength of his hand. Naturally, he was taking a risk: if he stayed in the game with only two Jacks, he was almost certain to be beaten by the pair of Jacks or higher that Beria must have in order to have opened the bidding. He was therefore putting all his chances on drawing a third Jack in exchange for the three cards he would discard, but he reckoned that he could out bluff Beria on a showdown.

'Check', he said and helped himself to a generous glass of vodka.

'Check', said Lebedev, looking increasingly dispirited.

'Raise 110', said Yakovlev with sudden enthusiasm.

'Check', said Malerian.

Kaganov, Lebedev and Malerian folded. It would therefore be a three cornered fight between Beria, Yakovlev and him. Malerian got up and walked round the table, looking at the cards of each remaining player without showing any reaction to what he saw.

'Raise 120', said Beria in a flat, expressionless voice.

'140', said Varga calmly, staring at Beria across the table. He had deliberately upped the ante to put him on the defensive.

Yakovlev looked increasingly uncomfortable. He obviously had a strong hand, or he would not have risked so much of the money had borrowed on one throw. For him to lose now would make him be in debt for two month's wages at least, but the others evidently must also have strong hands. There was now nearly 800 roubles in the pot, including the antes bid before the cards were dealt. The sum would easily restore Yakovlev's fortunes.

'150', he said with commendable bravery.

They then started to discard. Either Beria had a very strong hand or he was bluffing: he discarded only one card, indicating that he had either a four of a kind or two pairs. Varga decided to string him along. He discarded two cards, to make Beria and Yakovlev think that he had a three of a kind. He threw down the 6♠ and the 3♣. Slowly he picked up his two new cards: a 10♥ and a 5♦. That meant certain disaster, since even if Beria had only two Jacks as well, he would be almost bound to have higher three other cards than his miserable Queen, 10 and 8.

Yakovlev threw down two cards and picked up his replacement cards with visible excitement.

The bidding resumed. Varga decided to force out Yakovlev and make Beria win this massive hand only to clean him out in the later part of the game. To see Yakovlev bankrupted would not inspire the slightest twinge of pity: Varga had expected him to show at least *some* residual deference to his Hebraic origins, but the man was an amoral swine who had persecuted Jews and Russians with a total absence of racial prejudice, such was his devotion to Stalin and the ghastly regime he had created.

'200', said Beria, with a brutal tone of triumph.

Varga thought for a while. He quickly calculated how much he would lose in the process of bankrupting Yakovlev before conceding to Beria. He looked at Yakovlev, stirring uncomfortably in his chair, looking increasingly desperate at the huge sum slipping from his grasp.

'210', he said and looked at Yakovlev with a deliberate smile of triumph.

Yakovlev's eyes darted from Beria to Varga and back again suspiciously. Then a huge cloud of despair covered his face as he realised that he could not afford to keep up with such high stakes. Varga almost laughed as Yakovlev dejectedly threw down his cards and walked away from the table.

Beria stared at Varga, holding his cards prominently, like a shopkeeper making a proposition.

'220', he said.

Varga waited for a few theatrical moments, savouring the effect his deliberate hesitation was having on the others. Then, very calmly, as if the small fortune on the table were coffee beans or toy marbles, he threw down his cards without saying a word.

Beria only just managed to suppress a cry of triumph and hurriedly raked back his mountain of notes with a scything movement of the hand.

'Another round?', he said with a cheerful boyish expression. He was obviously expecting Varga to refuse.

Varga lit a cigar slowly.

'By all means', he replied, 'your luck cannot last forever'.

The implied slur on Beria's poker playing skills had the desired effect. Lebedev understood that Beria wished to resume play immediately and dealt out five cards to each player. Even Yakovlev understood that this was not the moment to flinch in the face of duty and he sat down manfully at the table, resigning himself to add to the borrowed fortune which he had already squandered away.

Lebedev yawned loudly and apologised. Varga looked at his watch and thought of Ferenc and Gyorgos. It was just coming up to 2 a.m. That was the time when they normally started the night shift of interrogations in the Lubyanka and hauled their victims out of their cells: few men are brave in the dead of night.

An oppressive feeling of uselessness swept over him. He felt completely powerless in front of Beria and his despicable gang of thugs. He was at their mercy, his own life meant as little to them as the cards they played with and discarded. He felt a deep loathing for Beria and the degenerate crowd of hangers-on that surrounded him, but he felt even an even deeper loathing for himself, at the way he had allowed them to humiliate him, at his despicable cowardice buying a precarious survival by playing cards with his executioners. Somewhere in the Lubyanka, they were inflicting unimaginable suffering on their infinite supply of victims: meanwhile, there he was, like a court jester, playing poker with the very men who had created this world of terror. Had he had a gun at that moment, he would have taken the greatest of pleasure in shooting them one by one, without a shred of mercy, taking care to reserve the final bullet for himself to deny the NKVD the satisfaction of torturing him in revenge. But that would be impossible: the guards always gave visitors a thorough body search before allowing anyone into Beria's *dacha*.

He looked at Beria, sitting across the table, with his well-fed and cheerful face. He looked round at the others fawning on his every word. How he loathed them then! It was only by an immense effort of self-control that he stopped himself from lurching across the table and throttling Beria with his bare hands.

Gradually, he managed to bring his raging emotions under control and produce an affable smile, as he examined the cards Lebedev had dealt him.

Suddenly a mad, insane plan dawned on him. Yes, it was truly an insane plan. Only a man certain of his own imminent death would dream up something like that. A vast strength welled up inside him, a sudden feverish energy, the passion of a condemned man with only a few hours to live and no concern for the future. As he visualised what he would do, he knew the scheme was sheer madness but a feeling of immense peace and determination came over him.

He smiled affably at the others and the game began.

Immediately, they started bidding for astronomically high stakes.

'100', said Yakovlev, hardly being able to suppress his excitement at the quality of the cards he had picked up.

'Check', said Lebedev.

'110', said Malerian.

'Check', said Kaganov.

Varga and Beria faced each other in the silence.

'120', said Beria with icy precision.

Varga didn't even bother to look at his cards again. He knew that he had a pair of Jacks, a 10, an 8 and a 7. That gave him a near flush or almost a four of a kind.

'130', he said calmly. This time he would break him. He would raise him until Beria was forced to put all the money he had won that evening back on the table. And then he would strike.

IX

Twenty minutes later, the pile of coins and notes across the table had become absurdly high.

'250', said Varga, throwing in his last reserves.

Varga waited to see how Beria would match that last bid. He could see that Beria had only 150 roubles left in front of him and could not match Varga. He looked round anxiously at his henchmen, as if expecting them to come to his aid with a loan. Varga could not suppress a smile of triumph.

'The last bid was 250 roubles', he said, ramming home the point that Beria did not have enough money to match him. He knew Beria had a very good hand, otherwise he would not have doggedly matched his bids, higher and higher, until he had exhausted his reserves.

Varga then threw caution to the winds.

'May I offer a way out of your...difficulties?' Varga said with as much insolence as his boiling hatred could manage.

Beria merely stared at him blankly.

'Ferenc Laszlo', he said. 'I'll accept Ferenc Laszlo and 150 roubles'.

Beria's eyebrows rose in puzzled surprise.

'Your men arrested him yesterday', Varga explained.

Slowly, Varga pulled his wallet out of his pocket and took out the picture of Ferenc. Then he tossed it on top of the pile of coins and notes on the table.

Beria gave him an odd look, at first not recognising the innocent and care-free face on the photograph. And then he understood and roared with good-natured laughter. It was a full-bodied, honest guffaw, his whole body shaking so much that the others started to laugh as well, but nervously, not understanding the joke but laughing all the same, out of suddenly released tension.

'Of course, of course', Beria said, hardly being able to speak the words out properly, as he was laughing so much. 'How terribly amusing.'

The others froze into silence as they watched Varga and Beria fighting over Ferenc Lazslo's fate.

Varga knew perfectly well that he had probably signed his own death warrant. For some reason, he did not even consider the absurdity of his self-sacrifice: if Ferenc was not dead by now he very soon would be. Varga's impulsive act of defiance would not save Ferenc and it would probably kill him in the process as well. Nobody would be there to applaud his dazzling courage in standing up to Beria: it was like an act of the purest heroism performed on board a plane crashing towards the ground. But he went on, as if driven by a higher force. Had he believed in a god, he could at least have comforted himself that his martyrdom would be rewarded in a celestial tribunal. But it was an act done simply for its own sake. A cry of defiance in the darkness. When his death came, he hoped that it would be quick and that the end of consciousness would be instantaneous, an enveloping shadow painlessly snuffing out his mind.

'Very well', said Beria, '150 roubles *and* Ferenc Laszlo', pronouncing the Hungarian name with mannered deliberation.

Varga looked at the photograph of his young friend, lying rather absurdly on the top of the pile of notes and coins. Beria discarded two of his cards, slowly taking them out of his hands as if they were gloves and then placed them face down on the table. Lebedev dealt him out the two replacement cards: if they had improved his hand, Beria's face certainly showed no reaction.

Varga decided to keep the two Jacks and to discard the 10, 8 and 7.

Everyone waited in total silence as Lebedev picked three cards out of the pack and dealt them to Varga. He took his time to pick them up, one by one. Without a third Jack, he was lost.

The first card was a 10♦ and Varga cursed himself for having discarded the other 10, as the two pairs would have given him a chance of winning. The clock in the entrance hall struck the half hour: the interrogations would be well under way by now in the Lubyanka. He snatched the second card nervously: a K♥. He looked up. The last card lay on the table, its cheap laminated back reflecting the low lamp over the table. His heart pounded but he tried to look as calm as possible. Varga picked up the card, sensing that everyone was watching his every movement.

The grinning face of a Jack of Spades stared at him from the card.

Slowly, he put the five cards down and looked straight at Beria. Then he picked up his glass and had a little sip of vodka, savouring the fiery liquid as it rolled on his tongue.

Beria looked as impassive as stone.

There was a long silence as the two men faced each across the table.

Then, all of a sudden, Beria's face relaxed.

'Show?', he said, with an engaging smile.

59

Varga nodded.

Beria turned up his cards: a pair of Aces and a pair of 4s. Varga calmly turned up his three Jacks and Beria roared with laughter.

As if in a dream, Varga watched Beria convulsed with laughter, getting out a pen and a piece of paper. Then he wrote down a few lines, his hand shaking with each chortle, passing the note to Varga with an ironic little bow.

To whom it may concern:
I hereby order the release of Ferenc Lazlo, citizen of Hungary and resident at the Hotel Lux, Moscow.
Signed: Lavrenti Pavlovich Beria, Director, People's Commissariat for Internal Affairs, Moscow, 12th November 1938'.

As Varga looked up, Beria roared with laughter again and wrote down a telephone number. Hardly able to get the words out, as he was laughing so much, he asked Lebedev to dial the number and to order the immediate release of Ferenc Laszlo.

'Gentleman's word of honour', he said, turning to Varga, as he brought his laughter under control. 'A gentleman should always honour his debts'.

He reached across the table and shook Varga's hand with genuine warmth.

'My congratulations on a most enjoyable evening', he said, rising from the table.

Varga piled his winnings into neat piles of bank notes and coins, hearing Lebedev on the telephone in the hall giving the order for Ferenc's release. Apparently there was some resistance or disbelief at the other end, as Lebedev had to read out Beria's order again. Then there was a pause and he saw Lebedev put the receiver down.

'A most entertaining game', Beria said. 'I had a pair of Queens as well as a pair of Aces. But I let greed get the better of me and decided to play double or quits. Like a fool, I decided to discard the Queens and go for three Aces. As luck would have it, I only got a pair of 4s back'.

Beria laughed again and patted him on the back, with genuine affection.

Varga looked at him with astonishment. It suddenly dawned on him that Beria had deliberately thrown away a winning hand.

THE ISLANDS OF DESOLATION

THE ISLANDS OF DESOLATION

TO HIS EXCELLENCY, THE DUC DE CROŸ, FROM HIS HUMBLE SERVANT, M. DE ROCHEGUDE, LIEUTENANT OF HIS MAJESTY'S NAVY AND CHEVALIER DE L'ORDRE DE SAINT-LOUIS.

Paris, the 1st March 1774

Your Excellency,

You have done me the honour of requesting my account of the events surrounding the two expeditions to the Southern Oceans led by the Chevalier de Kerguelen.

Inasmuch as I was a witness to these tragic events, I now present my testimony for Your Excellency: being a plain seaman, I write without pretence of literary art and grace, and I beg Your Excellency's indulgence for the infelicities of my style. I can, however, solemnly pledge that what I have written is the truth, so far as my own eyes witnessed it.

My opinion of the history of our explorations are perhaps superfluous now that the court martial His Majesty has been pleased to appoint has delivered its judgment on M. de Kerguelen. It is, of course, not for me to presume to substitute my own judgment from that of superior officers, particularly naval officers as distinguished as the Comte d'Aché, M. d'Orvillers or the Capitaine de Ville-Blanche. Nevertheless, compassion and loyalty make it necessary for me to confess that I deplore the cruel fate that has befallen our mutual friend and explorer. No man is free of vice but equally no man is devoid of virtue. While we Frenchmen are locked in a desperate struggle against the English and the Hollanders to conquer new worlds, History decreed that M. de Kerguelen was to be born out of time, to come at the end of an illustrious procession of explorers who have dispersed the darkness of our world: Marco Polo, Columbus, Magellan, Torres, Tasman... Indeed, the cruellest fact is that, by the time M. de Kerguelen set out for the Southern Oceans, there were no lands of any importance left to discover. The Great Southern Continent we strove so earnestly to discover proved to be as much of a delusion as the mirages that haunt the minds of desert explorers. Instead of lush forests and abundant pastures, we found only wild and bleak islands set in the icy seas of the Antarctic, quite barren of vegetation and inhabited by monstrous creatures.

Your Excellency has been widely praised for your enlightened patronage of scientific endeavour. Indeed you were one of those at Court who gave unstinting support for our adventures. If anyone deserves to know the full truth, it is Your Excellency. You have instructed me to write a report explaining how it was that our explorations ended in abject failure: I have therefore tried to obey your commands as faithfully as I can. 'To understand all is to forgive all' states the proverb, and the short account that I now present Your Excellency seeks to narrate the truth and to explain the conduct of those who took part in our adventures.

Vice coexists with greatness and frailty often lives in the same breast as bravery: my aim has therefore been to explain rather than to condemn. If I have judged men harshly and praised others unjustly, my only defence is that this is where truth and honesty directed my pen.

***

There have been many exaggerated accounts of our first landing. These I will now try to put right. It was my privilege to be selected for the landing party that claimed the islands for the Crown of France under the command of M. de Boiheugenneuc, and I am confident that he would confirm the accuracy of my account.

For several days we had received indications of approaching land: seagulls and shoals of dolphins accompanied our two ships as we sailed due south in the Indian Ocean, past the 40th parallel towards thick cloud on the horizon. No men had gone further south in these unknown seas and M. de Kerguelen promised twenty Louis d'Or to the first man who saw land.

On the third day, we glimpsed the first outlying islands, tantalisingly shrouded in a thick mist. We spent the night on board in growing excitement imagining what the marvels the next morning would bring. At first light the entire crew was on deck and, by a stroke of fortune, the seas which howling winds had tormented throughout the night suddenly calmed: the clouds briefly parted and revealed a wondrous spectacle of snow-crowned peaks and undulating country stretching as far as the eye could see. The land was covered with a green of such luminous intensity that it seemed that paradise was opening its gates before us. Every man on board shouted with joy and it must have been a strange sight to see our two ocean clippers, sails filled with wind with the flag of France unfurled, advancing over the icy grey waters, firing three rounds of canon shot by way of celebration.

As is so often the case in M. de Kerguelen's Islands, a vision of ethereal beauty vanishes as quickly as it appears: the Ancients would have certainly declared the islands to be inhabited by sirens and demons rather than angels. As if to tantalise our imagination, the spell of calm weather was quickly dispelled by one of the sudden storms which the Islands create as if by the whims of the gods. In the passing of a few seconds, war was declared in the heavens: with astonishing speed, dark clouds enveloped our beatific vision and a roar of wind rushed across the sky. I was reminded of the vision in the Apocalypse: '*And the temple of God was opened in heaven, and there was seen in his temple the ark of testament: and there were lightnings, and voices, and thunderings, and an earthquake, and great hail*'. A titanic war now started between sea and sky: huge waves were lifted up by howling gales and we hurriedly put out to deeper seas for fear of being dashed against the rocks.

The tempest raged for the whole day and continued unabated for the next. M. de Boiheugenneuc was undeterred, however, and volunteered to lead a landing party as soon as the storms had spent their fury.

Eventually we were able to set down a small boat to row to the unknown shore. We climbed down into the little craft, having each been blessed and taken the Sacraments, every man conscious of the momentous events in which he was about to take part. M. de Kerguelen stood on deck, saluting our little party as it went out to claim a hitherto unknown continent for the Catholic Church and the King of France.

As I have already said, M. de Kerguelen's Islands are filled with the most wondrous sights: as we advanced towards the shore through a thick fog and surging waves, our little boat was confronted with an arch of rock, towering above us a thousand feet high, a huge construction fashioned by centuries of winds and raging seas. It soared above us like a vast dome, as if the entry to an enchanted castle, and even our sea-hardened sailors stared at it with awe.

Gradually, we negotiated our way towards the land. Our six oarsmen heaved the boat on the black sand and M. de Boiheugenneuc leapt into the icy water, raising his sword. We were accompanied by four soldiers, carrying muskets should there be any inhabitants minded to resist our landing. I am sure that if any were observing us, advancing in full dress uniform and triform hats, we must have looked as outlandish as the strange beasts we encountered on the shore.

For a moment we simply stood on the windswept beach, feeling a little like sacrilegious intruders. Then M. de Boiheugenneuc ordered the flag of France to be raised and we all took heart when we saw the Fleur de Lys unfurling in the air. There was a break in the clouds and the sun caught the gold braid of the weaving in a momentary burst of sunlight. Our spirits lifted and M. de Boiheugenneuc took possession in the name of His Majesty King Louis XV, ordering our men to cry 'Long Live the

King'. We sent off three discharges of musket shot, the reports of our guns echoing among the rocks, making a peculiar wailing sound as the shots faded away in the distance. We then made a cairn of loose rock and buried inside it a bottle containing a piece of parchment with the solemn words:

' Ludovico XV Galliarium
Rege et d. de Boynes
Regis a Secretis ad res
Maritimas annis 1772 et 1773'.

I looked around. The bay and the flat lands around us were covered with moss and a type of wild cress. The soil itself was deep black from which I deduced it was volcanic ash. The whole area was soaked with recent rain and icy pools of molten snow. Everywhere there were birds and sea-lions, those huge placid monsters of the Southern Oceans, with their grotesque protuberances in the place of a nose and their clumsy gargantuan waddling movement. The ease with which we approached these wild animals who looked at us without fear suggested to me that these Islands could not be inhabited.

I abandoned my companions and went for a solitary exploration of the surrounding hills. After a steep climb on hard, black rock I reached the summit of a not inconsiderable promontory. I sat on a stone and gazed around me, searching for signs of civilisation- a fire or a path in the dark green vegetation that covered the ground as far as the eye could see. On landing, M. de Boiheugenneuc had thought he could discern some trees in the far distance, but I did not have my eyeglass and can neither confirm nor deny his claim.

I sat in the complete silence, perhaps as far from humanity as a man has been before.

My mind retains two dominant images from the Islands: the wind and the black volcanic rock. The wind whistles incessantly like a demon, as if sneering at the foolish alien invaders who have dared to intrude this solitary bleakness. I shut my eyes and listened: as the winds howled through the crevasses in the rocks, unknown noises filled the air like plaintive songs of exultation or pain, like sighs or low groans, like a cry that never quite becomes free. The wind completely dominates this wild landscape which I was now sure had never been seen by human eyes before me. The sounds of the wind were like an oppressive recitation, an insistent echo from the bowels of the Earth. The wind of these islands is unique in Creation. It does not whistle and roar like in our countries, where it must swish through leaves and brush through the grass. Here it finds nothing but rock and stone: it does not so much whistle as groan, a deep low diapason, incessant and elemental, like the strange choruses of phantasmagorical monks. Only in these Islands did I understand why the wind is the image of God, why Genesis speaks of the Earth being without form, darkness upon the face of the deep and why the Apocalypse speaks of the voice of God rushing like unfurling clouds in the sky. Our barren islands are a land where Creation stopped on the third day, when only sea, air and earth had been created.

Over the centuries, the rocks have been cut into nightmarish shapes by the constant gales and storms. They stand in the icy air like huge, gnarled fingers of solidified lava, raised like so many hands exclaiming to the heavens a cry of despair carried by the howling winds.
At length, the solitude and the silence made me yearn desperately for the comfort of human speech. I felt a strange aura of menace surrounding me. Soon it became unbearable and I ran down the hill as fast as I could, as if driven by an undefined, half-conscious terror.
I must have spent a longer than I thought in my solitary explorations, as I found my companions anxious as to my whereabouts: the weather had suddenly deteriorated, with strong gusts of wind and hail sweeping down from the mountains. In the far distance, I could see our ships tacking the winds to stay clear of the treacherous rocks. At length, we heard three canon

shot warning us to return aboard. We put to sea hurriedly as thick mists unfurled across the bay.

**

That was to be our first and only glimpse of the Islands. The weather worsened and our mast was broken in one of the most violent storms it has been my misfortune to endure. Further explorations were out of the question. With a heavy heart, M. de Kerguelen decided to return to our base in Mauritius. It must have been a painful decision for him to make, particularly as he had been denied the chance of even setting foot on the lands he had discovered. But our ship was badly in need of repair and our crew woefully unprepared for the approaching winter. It was safer to return with a better equipped fleet, especially as we now had some idea of the terrain and the weather conditions.

And so, we sailed back to France to report our discoveries.

**

There has been much speculation in minds greater than my own concerning the existence of a large Southern Continent. As Your Excellency is aware, geographers of universal renown have held that the continents of the Northern Hemisphere must, of necessity, be counterbalanced by an equivalent mass of southern continents. Illustrious explorers have plied the oceans from China to India and to the Americas in search of those lands, and yet the precise whereabouts of this Southern Continent remained unknown. Instead, all these explorers have only found a vast emptiness between China and the Americas in which a few islands are sprinkled like so many grains of sand. The science of our century is unanimous: such a void, a veritable watery chasm, is an impossibility. I have it on the greatest authority that the Great Southern Continent is not Australia, nor that of the two large islands west of it, as their combined land masses would be quite insufficient to counterbalance China, India, Europe and the Americas. Consequently, the Unknown Continent must lie either in an area south of India or must be situated in one of the vast empty areas of the Pacific Ocean which we have not yet explored. This explains M. de Kerguelen's decision to sail due south from Mauritius, and to proceed much further south than any seafarer had yet dared to venture.

It has to be admitted that we did not find anything to prove that we had found the Southern Continent or at least its extremities. Nevertheless, I am moved by the thought that the Islands we discovered lie at the same latitude as Tasman's strange island, which I read to be full of bizarre hopping animals, creatures which have both beaks and fur and which carry their young after birth in pouches: if anything, that fact alone makes me believe that there exists an entirely unexplored Antipodean continent populated by creatures quite different from those that we see in our Hemisphere. But time, Your Excellency, is running out, as the Hollanders and the English are hot on our trail. Indeed, I greatly fear that the Dutch will have stolen a march on us again, and that they are preparing further voyages of exploration. It is perhaps worthy of mention that whereas we Frenchmen broadcast our failure to the outside world, publicising the verdict of M. de Kerguelen's court martial, the Burghers of Amsterdam have kept the log-books and diaries of Tasman and Rooggeven a closely guarded secret. These Dutchmen are not spurred by a love for science. Unlike us, their explorations are only inspired by one motive: greed.

***

Within a week of our return to Paris, we were summoned by M. de Boynes, the Minister for Naval Affairs, to give an account of our discoveries before the most distinguished members of the Académie Française. Everywhere we were treated like returning heroes from a famous battle. It was with a growing despair that

72

I saw all around us projecting their imaginative fantasies on what we had discovered. People were not interested in truth: they were only interested in hearing whether we had found gold or whether we had discovered Noble Savages. The reality was that we had stumbled upon a bleak, wind-torn archipelago. I could not form any opinion as to whether we had in fact found the tip of a huge Continent, or sufficient new lands to compensate France for the Canadian colonies which we had recently lost to the English. But all Paris had made up its mind: we had found something which would make the Dutch and the Spaniards froth at the mouth with envy and nothing we said or did could dispel those delusions.

Our first evening, we had the honour of being invited by a distant relative of M. de Kerguelen from Brittany, Madame de Carnavaillac, to an evening at her illustrious salon. I was honoured to be introduced to all that was noble and brilliant Parisian society: Bouffon, de Rochemont, the Duc de Cunéron, M. de Maupertuis and countless others who are now but a sea of powdered wigs in my memory... Mme de Carnavalliac's Hotel de Ville struck my uncouth mariner's mind as an almost paradisiac vision of glittering decoration, wealth, ornate and sumptuous paintings. But most wonderful of all to me - and I know Your Excellency will surely smile at my naivety- everywhere there was an overwhelming abundance of fresh wholesome food. Those who have not experienced the privations of a sea voyage will find it impossible to imagine the effect of mountains of food on our minds. There was an profusion of fresh fruit, of colour, of mingled scents from cooked meats and finely spiced preparations. Your Excellency will easily guess what dreams were inspired in the mind of a man whose only food for months on end had been salted meat, stale biscuits and fetid water! My chief memory is not the elegant discourses that followed between the Abbé de Rougemont and the Duc de Barreyres as to the moral qualities of the inhabitants of 'Kerguelen's Islands': no, my chief memory is the abundance of fresh fruits on the tables, piled high in extraordinary pyramids and cascades of luxuriant colours which my still-scurvied mouth could not resist. While the rooms resounded with an intense debate on the natural propensity towards evil or goodness in mankind, I can only recall the startling freshness of the grapes which I ate in great bunches, the sweet taste of the first plums, the way even cherries tingled the pasty skin of my palate and deliciously stung the exposed gums around my teeth.

M. de Cunéron joined the battle against the Abbé with all the relish of a disciple of Voltaire. He roundly declared that the inhabitants of the Islands, being so far from any known land, must of necessity be both uncorrupted by superstition *and* noble in spirit. The Abbé, predictably, rejoined that nobility could not come from our unaided human lights: to believe that man is innately good is pure vanity, the sort of pride that can only lead to damnation. Our Lord's gospel could not have reached the southerly latitudes of the Islands and the inhabitants must therefore share in Adam's sin. The Duc de Cunéron replied with a loud guffaw that if the Islanders had been spared superstition by virtue of their happy isolation, then they could hardly avoid being nobler than us. The Abbé answered that all living things decay and die and that mankind was no exception: it thus followed that mankind could not be perfect. The Duc retorted that death, of itself, did not abase mankind, that Montaigne had taught us that to philosophise is to learn how to die and that only superstition makes our physical imperfections degrading... M. de Maupertuis, who had listened to the whole debate with growing impatience, roundly declared that he would prefer to spend one hour conversing with one of our islanders than with the finest mind in Europe. He then left the table to take the air of the gardens. Mme de Carnavalliac came to the rescue by leading us to dinner, during which the finest delicacies were served in her elegant dining hall.

***

The next day we had the honour of being granted an audience by His Majesty.

It was a splendid July morning and Versailles glowed in all its radiance under a pure azure sky. After the roughness of our sailors' attire, it felt awkward and strange to ascend the steps of the Palace in wig, ruffs, doublets and all the refined extravagance of full court dress. Kerguelen himself looked grave and composed. His face had the same hardness as when he stood on the foredeck in heavy seas. He spoke little as we approached the Audience Chamber, but made some ironic remark that he was marching to his appointment with fame and destiny.

As the first Officer to have landed on the Islands, the Chevalier de Boiheugenneuc led the way. All eyes were on us as the King received us graciously. He even stood up to greet us despite his great age, as we completed our ceremonial bows.

His Majesty appeared passionately interested in the description of the lands we had discovered and our conversation cantered on the culture of the inhabitants of the Islands, (some courtiers having put it in our Sovereign's mind that the Islands were inhabited). I felt an urge to point out that we had only made the briefest of landings and that the archipelago showed every sign of being devoid of human settlements but I noticed that Kerguelen did not contradict His Majesty and, in deference to my commander, I kept my counsel.

The courtiers around us could hardly contain their excitement at the thought of vast new lands being added to the French Crown and much anxiety was expressed at the need to secure the Islands against the rapacious English with an appropriate garrison. The King declared that he had a particular wish that his rapidly advancing years and his failing health would not prevent him seeing the Islanders become loyal subjects of the Catholic Kings of France. His Majesty was therefore pleased to

75

command that no time should be lost to return to the Southern Oceans: M. de Kerguelen was honoured to receive the Order of Saint-Louis as well as a generous sum to mount a well-equipped expedition to map and colonise the new Continent.

***

Your Excellency has instructed me to be honest and truthful in my account of our voyages and veracity thus bids me to express my anxiety, if not surprise at the description which M. de Kerguelen produced for His Majesty. Truth should always be its own sufficient reason and a loyal subject should never have to fear telling his Sovereign the truth rather than what he wants to hear. I shall limit myself to quoting the following passage from M. de Kerguelen report presented at Court:

'The Lands which I have had the good fortune to discover seem to constitute the central mass of the continent- the fifth continent of the world- and the region which I have named South France is situated in such a manner as to dominate India, the Moluccas, China and the South Seas. It extends East North East and offers varying temperatures and climates for settlement by our compatriots... South France will henceforth give a new existence to our possessions in Réunion and Mauritius. It will increase their commerce and wealth threefold and provide the settlers in those tropical islands with the provisions and products to which they were accustomed in their native climate and which they cannot do without. There is no doubt that we shall find in the new Continent timber, mines, diamonds, rubies, semi-precious stones, marble... An isolated Continent which has never been in communication with the rest of the world should be able to throw a wonderful light on the process of evolution on our globe. Even if we do not find there men of a different species to our own, we shall at least find natural human beings living in a primitive state, free from defiance and remorse and ignorant of the artifices of civilised man. In fact South France will furnish a wonderful exhibition of moral and physical specimens.'

In truth, I cannot explain the extravagance of this description, so divorced as it is from the realities which I saw. Was M. de

Kerguelen forced to state such patent fantasies or was he a gambler, staking his all on the chance that his dreams might come true?

Soon afterwards we set off for Brest to examine the ships that might be available for our return to the Southern Oceans.

***

The command of His Majesty was that we should set out for the Southern Oceans with all speed and this we obeyed as diligently as we could. Nevertheless, if Your Excellency will allow me to do so in these private pages, I must express my severest doubts at the wisdom of our Monarch's command: our departure was made without the normal elementary precautions of those setting out in such dangerous waters. We arrived in Brest as fast as the horses of the Royal Guard could carry us, and the Comte d'Estaing, the Commander of His Majesty's Navy, gave us every possible assistance. To fulfil the King's command we were forced to embark on the first suitable ship and M. de Kerguelen quickly accepted the '*Roland*', a new vessel fresh out of the shipyards of La Rochelle. The *Roland* was fitted out with the greatest speed, a third of its cannons being removed to make room for the supplies we would need: soon the ship was turned into a veritable Ark, filled to the brim with wood for building the houses of our settlement, crammed with food in abundance and even making room for a small herd cattle which was housed in deplorably cramped conditions in the rear of the vessel. There was so little space on board that the crew had to sleep above barrels in hammocks, under tables or wherever they could squeeze. We officers lived stacked together, like ordinary crew members: to give ourselves some illusion of privacy, we hitched up sheets across the few rooms allotted to us.

Our crew was chosen in great haste. Everybody wanted to join the expedition and the selection of our officers owed more to Parisian intrigues than to seafaring experience. I was personally honoured by M. de Kerguelen's invitation to accompany him on

77

his return journey to the Islands. Sadly, the Chevalier de Boiheugenneuc received a handsome commission in the Indies and was not able to join us on this second voyage. Would that he had been able to, as his place was taken by M. de Cheyron, of whose unspeakable character and propensity to intrigue I shall have ample occasion to describe.

**

It was as if our voyage was doomed from the start. No sooner had we set out that a fever spread round the crew. Every day, men fell sick and the smell of illness hung in the air. To compound our misery, my worst fears began to be realised: the ship being brand new, the young wood of the planks began to sweat and damp invaded our food stores. Within weeks, our putrefying rations ravaged the crew with disease. Soon the narrow corridors below deck became a fetid labyrinth, the dark air echoing with the groans of the sick, the passage ways littered with vomit or bowls of excrement.

The pestilential atmosphere on board was exacerbated by the rifts that quickly emerged amongst the officers. I record with regret that several of the young officers did their utmost to undermine the authority of their Captain. This cabal was of course led by M. de Cheyron, a young man whose outrageous insolence was only matched by his egregious ambition. I surmise that his dislike for M. de Kerguelen must have originated from his jealousy at his commanding officer's meteoric advancement at Court: Your Excellency will recall that M. de Kerguelen was promoted over some ninety five officers of the equal rank. Throughout our voyage, he and his fellow officers did not lose a single occasion for subtle insubordination or sly rumour-mongering. Had I had the command of the ship, I should have ordered M. de Cheyron to shore duties at the earliest opportunity.

Unusually for a voyage on a military ship, we also had a few civilians on board. The Abbé de Cure was on his way to preach the Word of God to the savages of Madagascar, and M. de Gautier was travelling to join the staff of the Governor of Mauritius. But they were not our only guests: Your Excellency will imagine our stupefaction when, on the first evening around the officers' table, next door to our Captain's private quarters, we glimpsed the soft hue of pink silk and heard the laughter of a woman's voice. A ship is an austere universe created solely by men and the presence of the fair sex on board is only permitted when calling at a port, as the virile discipline that is necessary to confront the seas would easily dissolve if our sailors were allowed to be accompanied by their womenfolk.

To our consternation, the doors opened and M. de Kerguelen ushered in a young woman of most pleasing looks, no more than eighteen years of age, her headdress and attire making it evident that she was a lady of some rank. Our Captain introduced her to us as Mlle. Louise Seguin, explaining that he had been asked to take her under his guardianship and protection until we reached Mauritius. He declared that chivalry required that she should enjoy the privacy of the Captain's own quarters: he would use his chaise-longue as a sleeping couch, gallantly devoting his sleeping quarters to her. M. de Kerguelen never explained to us who it was that had asked him to place her under his protection, and, while I am sure that his conduct towards her was beyond reproach, all manner of calumnies and rumours soon swarmed about him, the slanders being well orchestrated by M. de Cheyron and the young officers. Inevitably, her presence dominated every conversation and the lowest sailors competed for a glimpse of her graceful figure: for them she was an object of veneration, but to me she was a Siren, enticing us to our destruction, her very presence subtly permeating our lives with voluptuous dreams and longings for the comforts of the shore.

***

We reached Mauritius in a pitiful state.

The immediate impression of a traveller arriving in the Indian Ocean is one of languor, of an exquisite lethargy. Luxuriant vegetation is bathed in the heavy air of the tropics and even the waves roll on the beaches with a generous undulating movement. As we disembarked, we could immediately smell the soft, overripe scents of the tropical forest blowing from the hills mingling with the salty air. The quayside was filled with Negro slaves unloading the ships, and it was a stirring sight to see the flag of France flying on the fortress of Port-Louis and orderly lines of the sugar plantations receding in the distance.

Our urgent task was to make our ship sea-worthy for the rigours of the southern oceans and replenish our damaged supplies. Your Excellency, it is here my duty to record publicly that we encountered nothing but opposition and obstruction from those in Port-Louis. As I have said before, M. de Kerguelen's swift promotion made him many enemies: this poisonous envy spread even to our Colonies, infecting the minds of the authorities with rumours and prejudice.

Your Excellency will readily appreciate that our possessions in the Indian ocean are so far from France that all manner of irregularities can happen there without being seen by the King's Governor. As it happens, the Governor is, in my estimate, of a nature too easily disposed to indulgence and without the firmness that would suffice to suppress intrigue. The cabal against M. de Kerguelen was led by M. Maillart du Mesle, the Governor's Intendant. He had heard countless calumnies against the Chevalier and he lost no time to express the opinion that explorers were worthless if they could not bring back spice plants to grow in competition with the Dutch. Too many of the ships which had ventured out in the southern oceans had returned with diseased crews or storm-battered ships: they were a waste of scarce resources and when they were captained by upstarts who had leapt through the ranks of the Navy like M. de Kerguelen, they had to be taught a lesson.

It goes without saying that M. de Cheyron and his fellow

officers gleefully fanned the flames.

We asked for materials to repair our mast and tar to line the hold of the ship, but each time we were expecting the necessary supplies to arrive, a new ship would berth and be given priority. We asked for fresh meat to salt and provisions to store in expectation of our long journey: we were only offered the carcasses of diseased animals and generally impeded at every turn. The final insult came when we requested men to replace our fever-ridden crew: we were merely told to enquire 'at the Fortress'. Your Excellency must understand what that meant: we were obliged to populate our ship with the scum of the island, to recruit men from those who had committed such misdeeds that they had been branded and condemned to moulder in its dungeons. So desperate were they to escape their fate that this *canaille* eagerly competed for any chance leave the islands and earn their passage back to France.

Thus was our ship doomed to sail unfit for the savage seas that lay ahead of us. Our provisions were of such inferior quality they were bound to ravage our men with scurvy and our crew was now mainly composed of the lowest dregs of humanity. The rage of M. de Kerguelen knew no bounds as it was obvious his enemies had succeeded in destroying his chances of success.

But if the cabal thought that they had defeated the Chevalier de Kerguelen, they did not count on his courage -I almost wrote 'his pride'. They had placed him on the horns of an impossible dilemma: to turn back and abandon the voyage would have risked incurring the King's displeasure. There was also the risk that the Dutch or the English would claim the putative Continent for themselves. On the other hand, to set sail with such a dreadfully inadequate crew with supplies already rotting in the hold was next to madness.

What drove M. de Kerguelen to defy his enemies and set sail regardless? A preference to die gloriously in the service of his King or a damnable obstinacy? An uncontrollable ambition to rise above the wiles of his enemies and conquer greatness? Better to be engulfed by the raging oceans than to languish for the rest of his days in disgrace... Perhaps he might indeed discover the untold riches he had so rashly promised to his King! Perhaps he might even find lush forests from which to build new ships, returning in triumph laden with tribute from the King's new subjects, confounding his enemies?

***

From the moment we set sail due south, I knew all my premonitions of disaster would prove true. M. de Kerguelen acted with great haste, as if fired by a passion. I found him distant, almost cold, living in a world remote from all of us. He would occasionally emerge from his quarters, wherein he kept his 'Louison' (as he now affectionately called Mlle. Seguin). He would pace up and down the deck like a caged animal, giving curt orders to the men and eyeing the skyline anxiously, as if somehow dreading what would appear over the horizon. Relations with the young officers were, if anything, even worse than before, with M. de Cheyron now openly courting the attentions of Mlle. Seguin: as the English say, there is no smoke without fire, and his attentions were, I am sure, at least encouraged by our coquettish 'guest' on the rare occasions when she emerged from her incarceration. The mealtimes of the officers were an occasion for the most subtle but malicious warfare, streams of venom flowing under the formal politeness of our conversations.

At length, we approached the area of our first discovery and began searching for the islands. Once again, there were the signs of approaching land: the weather grew mistier and albatrosses could be seen gliding aside our ship with that graceful floating movements of their huge wings. Skuas and petrels were sighted, gulls landed on deck and the seas became lighter. But most memorable of all was the magnificent sight of a veritable herd of whales, the sun catching their glistening backs as they plunged up and down majestically in the icy waters. Even our most experienced sailors swore that they had never seen such an abundance of the beasts and I predict future generations of whalers will find much profit in these waters.

Finally, we sighted land. To tantalise us, the thick clouds parted and we were treated to the glorious sight of a range of towering peaks covered in ice, as if giants had laid out table cloths for an Olympian feast. The crew shouted their hurrahs and M. de Kerguelen ordered a salvo of canon to be fired.

But as we approached land the weather deteriorated, heavy rain turning to snow and hail stones the size of musket shot. Even the hardened criminals in the crew were cowed by the monstrous waves that suddenly surged up and lashed the sides of our little ship. The crew froze at their posts and I heard one of these ruffians cursing the day he had left his dungeon. Slowly, we used the currents to approach the land as close as we dared. M. de Kerguelen knew my enthusiasm for exploration and promised me the honour of leading the landing party. For the next three days, we tacked the wind and looked for a suitable place to land our first settlers once the weather had settled.

By now I was increasingly concerned at M. de Kerguelen's strange behaviour. He appeared suddenly seized by an odd listlessness, an apathy born of some inner melancholia that seemed to devour his energy. I would have expected him to be overjoyed at the prospect of returning to the lands he had discovered, to be fired by the same enthusiasm that made me burn to stand on those dark and ashen beaches. Instead, he withdrew further in his private quarters, where Mlle. Seguin had also mysteriously retired, as if content to drown himself into a voluptuous oblivion. When he emerged, it was to enquire anxiously how the ship fared or how many members of the crew were ill. He hardly even glanced at his islands, which were unfurling in a grey mist to our left as we sailed southwards along the coast. It was as if he had been paralysed by enchantment, by an all-embracing disgust for the world he had discovered. Was it because he could now see with his own eyes the barrenness of his islands and how far they were from the Arcadian bliss he had described in his report to the King? Was it only now that he finally realised the cruel fate that would certainly await him, when he returned to Court and tried to explain away his exaggerations? My only explanation is that the Chevalier de Kerguelen knew he was doomed and withdrew in his own private world of despair.

***

Soon after, the storm calmed and we decided to take the risk of exploring the islands. Your Excellency can imagine the pride and anxiety that I felt as I descended the ladder to the landing boat: it was to be my moment of glory for I was to lead the first party to settle these new lands. Our boat was rowed by a dozen wretches we had prized out of the dungeons. They would also be our workforce when onshore. In case of mutiny, I had taken the precaution of including six well-armed guards and even tucked two loaded pistols under my belt. We had enough rations to last for a few days, expecting to find water from fresh springs and meat from the multitude of seals and birds crowding the shores.

We rowed away from the *Roland*, leaving M. de Kerguelen isolated in his private quarters. The mountainous waves that swelled around us terrified the men and I confess that I was pleased to feel the rosary I had hidden in the lining of my coat. But more frightening than the waves were the huge underwater leaves of strange algae that abound in these seas, fanning the deep like monstrous hands.

Again, we were greeted by a desolate landscape quite unlike anything we had ever seen in the world: league upon league of gravel and stones stretched out as far as the eye could see, and wind-chiselled rocks jutted out like sentinels. Behind, the hills were of a luxuriant, rain-soaked green and there was not a tree in sight. We all knew in our hearts that the land we had discovered was indeed worthless and that our sufferings and privations had been in vain: it was obvious that the south of the island was as barren of life and prospects as the northern parts that we had visited the previous year. Even if the English discovered the islands, they would surely be only too glad to leave them to the French.

We landed under the curious gaze of huge seals that basked contentedly on the beach. Conscious of my historic duty, I proudly carried the flag of France high over the icy waters and rammed it into the sand to claim possession. I then made the convicts line up with the six guards and, at my command, they all took off their hats and saluted the flag which was tossed by the icy winds. We discharged a round of musket shot in the air to tell the *Roland* that we had landed safely, provoking a chorus of snorts and grunts from the herd of seals close to us.

I sent a search party to look for firewood but no trees or bushes of any kind could be found, so we made a fire with some of the wood we had brought with us, as the dry algae on the beach gave out an unbearably thick and acrid smoke.

Everywhere there was nothing but magnificent desolation, a grey immensity of rock under a vast empty sky. Under the curious gaze of a herd of seals that had gathered around us, we hastily constructed a shelter from the biting winds with sheets of canvas and then huddled around our pitiful fire for warmth. We had provisions and food to last us two days, but already it was abundantly clear to us that no settlement could ever survive on this part of the island. I decided that I would lead a party of exploration to search for more hospitable lands over the hills, towards the interior of the island. None of the men wanted to follow me and so I drew lots to select a 'volunteer': the choice fell on a huge fellow of hirsute appearance, whose visibly immense strength was at least some form of reassurance.

Accompanied by my felon, I started to climb the steep, gravelly hills behind our encampment. The going was very hard, as it was difficult for our feet to find a firm grip on the scree. On the way up, I encountered a huge bull seal which had somehow hoisted himself up the slope for some unknown purpose. There he stood, perched on a rocky promontory, surveying his surroundings with a noble air of contempt. He did not seem perturbed by the strange new creatures advancing towards him, but merely snorted a disdainful grunt of warning. I went right up to the beast, moved by a spirit of curiosity but my companion refused to come anywhere near it. I went on ahead regardless and I could hear the low mannered wretch cursing and murmuring a hasty prayer as I advanced towards the animal. I got close enough for the bull seal to swipe at me with its sharp tusks had it wanted to, but apparently it decided that I was no threat but merely a strange and rather intriguing creature. It started to sniff at me with its grotesque nose, which I can only describe as a most ungainly growth on its face in the shape of an upturned trunk. Its huge watery eyes had an almost loving expression, making it look placid, even innocent, and I muttered a few soothing words to the beast, just as would do if advancing towards a difficult horse. I was startled by another grunt from the animal but it meant me no harm: I found it astonishing that it had no fear of my presence. I could only conclude that the gentle monster had never set eyes on the human form before.

The notion that the Islands were barren of human life was confirmed for me when we next came past an albatross rookery. These birds are the giants of the southern skies, as they float majestically across huge distances carried by the winds which they know how to tack as well as any sailing ship. There were perhaps a dozen of them in front of us, some sitting on their eggs, others tottering about using the tips of their enormous wings to balance themselves as they walked. My companion (a fellow called Boulanger, who had killed a man in a tavern brawl) found the birds a source of great amusement. He sat down and bellowed with laughter, pointing to their stumbling gait, his laughter echoing round the rocks and startling the birds who looked up at us. Boulanger was like child with them, suddenly bringing out a playful tenderness that belied his violent past and rough appearance. And then, most wondrous of all, he walked up to the nearest albatross who showed no fear at all when

Boulanger picked it up: the huge bird allowed him to stretch out its wings to their full span and offered no resistance when Boulanger started to perform a grotesque dance with the albatross in his hands. This only provoked further paroxysms of mirth from the rough fellow, who laughed so much that he dropped the bird, which skipped away looking disgruntled.

Suddenly, a skua landed nearby and the albatrosses quickly massed in a defensive formation to protect their eggs. The skua, I should explain, is the predator bird of the Southern Oceans, a bird about the size of a large seagull. It is a redoubtable fighter and a scavenger of great ingenuity. The albatrosses instantly recognised it as a foe and chased him off, much to the hooting and clapping of Boulanger.

One could not want a better proof that the islands are uninhabited: I can understand the bull seal not being frightened by us, as we were but pygmies in front of him, but for the birds to allow us such close contact and then vigorously chase off a recognised enemy must surely be conclusive evidence that we were the first representative of the human race ever to walk on this strange land.

It is indeed an awesome sensation to walk where no man had been before, to tread on virgin land which had been untouched since the first days of Creation. I felt an odd mixture of responsibility and sacrilege as we walked on reaching the plateau at the top of the slopes. I remembered M. de Kerguelen's enthusiastic descriptions of the moral qualities of the islanders and the heated debates I had witnessed in the salons of Paris about the new Continent's noble savages: what is it about the human imagination that we find a need to invent men where there are none? Can we not bear the thought of our non-existence? Is it arrogance or insecurity that makes us dream of seeing our shape in every corner of the world?

At length, we reached the plateau, far above the sea, and we were rewarded by a magnificent sight. To the right towered the snow-capped peak of a huge mountain, surely the highest point of the Kerguelen Islands. To our left and in front of us there stretched a vast plain of blackened rock where tiny lakes were dotted about everywhere, some glinting as they caught the sun's rays. But the most remarkable things were the veritable sentinels of rock carved by the winds, standing like gnarled outstretched hands or the tormented tresses of petrified gorgons. These fantastic shapes populated a wide area and, as we made our way through the strange rocks, my naïve companion looked increasingly concerned.

I realised that he was worried that we were progressing ever further away from our encampment and observed his reactions with great amusement: here was a man, a huge brute of a fellow, who had murdered a man in a fit of rage and experienced the horrors of prison life. From what I gathered from our conversations, he came from a poor family in Normandy and had tried to better himself by volunteering in the army. Boulanger had fought several engagements against the English, but seeing so many of his companions slain on the fields of Flanders, he had taken the first opportunity to escape to a new life in our colonies. His career in the Indian possessions had been as unpromising as his military adventures in Europe and he had soon drifted down to the lowest elements that gather in the ports of these oceans. It appears that his murderous conduct in the tavern was a common event of these parts. Even though the wretch had experienced the very worst that life can offer I grew to like him: there was a strangely amiable and trusting childishness when he talked and I was amused by his superstitious terror of these islands. His fright at the sight of the bull seal was nothing compared to his expressions of sheer horror as we advanced, quite alone, in this desert of monstrously shaped rocks. His eyes rolled anxiously and I could hear him murmuring dimly remembered childhood prayers as he walked behind me. Occasionally he would ask me for some explanation. What was that rock? Did not something move over there? As if I were his guardian. And yet I must confess to Your Excellency that I was not half as reassured within myself as I pretended to be in front of the amiable felon. We were advancing further and further away from the rest of our party: if we became lost the deep crevasses and jagged rocks that make up this land would make it impossible for any rescuing party to find us.

I do not know how long we walked for, but the going was very hard and we decided to settle down to eat some of our rations. We sat down under a rocky promontory carved by the wind like the ruined turret of a mythical castle. The clouds were gathering up for one of the Islands' frequent storms and the lowering sun projected muscular shadows from the crenulated rocks. The wind rose- a low, menacing diapason, like a curse at our desecration of this virgin land. I caught Boulanger making a surreptitious sign of the Cross as he anxiously eyed the sky. We ate our provisions in silence and it was clear that we would have to shelter from the rushing storm in our gothic castle as best we could.

It was under that phantasmagorical rock that I lived one of the greatest moments of my life: this was the oddly pleasurable sensation of being as far from humanity as possible, of being utterly vulnerable to the giant forces of Nature, of being reduced to a tiny speck of conscious life in this desolate immensity- one man humbly face to face with his Creator.

Nothing prepared us for the violence of the storm that suddenly erupted above our heads. As if unleashed by some demonic force, thick black clouds swept across the sky and the winds immediately shrieked to a climax. The heavens opened and a deluge of icy rain crashed down from the sky. Boulanger ducked beneath the rocks, absolutely terrified, while I stood up in an absurd gesture of defiance against the elements. My temerity was soon chastised as the winds nearly knocked me over and giant hailstones started to fall everywhere around us, smashing onto the rocks with terrible force, obliging me huddle behind the same rock as my lowly companion. So harsh was the storm that raged around us that I clutched my felon like Lear holding his Fool in the uncouth tragedy that has become so fashionable in Paris of late.

Then, as suddenly as it had arisen, the storm vanished and we stood up to see the rain-soaked plain, filled with a rising mist. The sea birds came back to fill the sky with their cries and we felt reassured.

It was late in the afternoon and we decided to return to our encampment. I regretted abandoning our lonely exploration: deserts create a peculiar intoxication of the spirit and I hoped that I would be able to go further inland the next day. Boulanger was visibly relieved to be retracing his steps as the brute seemed quite unable to appreciate the beauty of this desolate grandeur. For a moment we feared that we were lost as the grotesque shapes were so numerous that it was difficult to decide which rock was the correct landmark to guide us back to our companions. Impulsively, I fired one of my pistols, hoping for a return shot from the rest of our party. Instead, as if the gods were toying with puny intruders, the sound of my pistol echoed and bounced back across the crevasses, like a magical game, where it was repeated now loudly there and then softly here and again loudly far away. It was as if the sound of the pistol had multiplied into an army of pistols and I could not help laughing as I watched Boulanger turning round and round trying to follow the echo as it moved.

After some anxious moments we did find a familiar escarpment, and I triumphantly led my worried companion in the direction of the sea. It was an exhausting march to reach the edge of the plateau. Finally, we arrived at the end of this veritable forest of nightmarish shapes, but as we approached the brow of the hill, strange sounds began to fill the air. The echo distorted the sounds as if they were the roar of a distant battle, a mixture of shouts and animal groans, coming from the left and then suddenly surging from the right. I exchanged worried glances with Boulanger and drew my remaining loaded pistol from my belt. My companion was unarmed, since he had not been trusted enough to carry weapons, and he therefore picked up a few sharp stones. We both slowly advanced to the brow of the hill from which we would be descending to the shore, ready to defend ourselves if attacked. Perhaps I had been wrong and the Islands were indeed inhabited by savages who had ambushed our companions. I signalled Boulanger to crouch down and we crept forward.

We reached the brow of the hill and looked down to where our encampment had been. It was there that we were to be greeted by one of the most sickening and ghastly spectacles I have ever witnessed.

Everywhere the smell of raw flesh filled the air mingling with the saltiness of the sea breeze, and the sea was red with fresh blood. In the sky, flocks of skuas hovered and dived, scavenging the carcasses littering the beaches. It was not a battle but a wanton massacre: our companions were engaged in a frenetic battle with a herd of seals, killing and hacking with every weapon at hand in an orgy of slaughter. The great beasts lay dead or dying everywhere, their sides gashed open and pouring blood on the shingle beach. The males had gathered in a defensive circle in a desperate attempt to head off this onslaught. It was a heroic but futile sacrifice since the large clumsy beasts were no match for the hunters. The seals lunged forward but our men cleverly manoeuvred out of their range: instead, the hunters jumped around them, hacking at them from the back, slashing at their heads or piercing their sides with their swords in savage ecstasy. Others were shouting with barbaric joy hurling rocks at the defenceless beasts, who groaned and roared at their new enemies in desperate rage. One bull seal decided to shuffle forward with that strange waddling movement of theirs, provoking hoots and cackles of laughter before being cut down by slicing swords. It was a veritable feast of death, the men gladly scything down everything in sight, their shouts of joy filling the air. As I watched the carnage I felt a sickening sensation in the pit of my stomach: mankind had spilled its first blood on the Islands, desecrating the primordial innocence of these new lands for ever.

Slowly we walked down the rocky face of the hill. As soon as the ground became easier, Boulanger rushed forward, eager to join in the massacre. I walked with a heavy heart, powerless to stop the sacrilege. Bodies of the great beasts lay everywhere, their gaping sides covered with skuas busily gorging on their flesh. It was not even as if we could profit from this ghastly work, as we had neither firewood to boil down the blubber that oozed onto the beach nor barrels in which to store the result. The massacre was purely gratuitous, all that blood was being spilled in a ghastly form of entertainment, as a release for the pent-up energies of men caged up for too long in the cramped quarters of our ship.

Eventually the slaughter subsided- not because we ran out of animals to kill but through the sheer exhaustion of killing. Men started to throw their rocks more clumsily, they began to lunge forward with less energy, and gradually sheer fatigue made them abandon the slaughter.

As nightfall approached, the men slumped down on their rocks, contemplating the hundreds of carcasses and groaning animals strewn on the beach with empty and dazed expressions of sheer exhaustion. The air was thick with the acrid smell of blood and the happy chatter of scavenging birds. Gradually, the waves washed the shore clean and the surviving animals retreated into the evening mist.

***

This was to be my last glimpse of the Islands. Soon after, the weather deteriorated once more and the now all too familiar storms returned with a vengeance. For two days, we were tossed on the waters like a little cork, as if we had become the plaything of the gods.

Words can scarcely describe the miseries this inflicted upon the crew, already fatigued beyond endurance by a long voyage, rotting provisions and scurvy. Throughout, M. de Kerguelen behaved even more strangely, refusing contact with his fellow officers and immuring himself with his paramour. It was as if he had travelled halfway across the globe to be overwhelmed with disgust at his 'discovery'. Far from taking the opportunity to explore the Islands that bore his name, the tortured soul shunned his progeny.

On the third day, the weather calmed once more and we advanced into a cove which could have afforded a safe landing site. If ever we had a chance to drop anchor and set up a permanent settlement, it was then.

The court martial heavily condemned the Chevalier de Kerguelen for failing to take this last opportunity. Instead, he literally turned his back on the accursed Islands and declined the chance to explore the mysterious country that lay so tantalisingly close in front of us.

The most extraordinary fact, Your Excellency, is that M. de Kerguelen never once set foot on the Islands that now bear his name.

***

I need not trouble Your Excellency with the melancholy tale of our return home. It may be that M. de Kerguelen feared disaster if he prolonged our explorations any further- at least this is the reason he gave to the court martial. It must be admitted that the *Roland* was badly in need of repair and fresh supplies. We had collected a little fresh water from the Islands but our food stocks were dangerously low: although the seal meat was tough and reasonably edible, there was not sufficient wood to smoke it for long preservation. We had to throw most of it overboard for the skuas to feast on. Perhaps our Captain had gambled on finding sufficient vegetation to replenish our food stores; in fact, the only native plant we found worth eating is a strange type of cabbage which is unique to the Islands: it requires boiling at least twice before eating, producing a flavour not dissimilar to the common radish. A poor harvest indeed after so many hopes, illusions and sacrifices.

Yet our now disgraced Captain was obviously worried at the

consequences of returning empty handed, for he took the unprecedented step of drawing up a report recording the state of our vessel and crew in minute detail, and then asking each officer to countersign the document. This attempt to abrogate his responsibility won him little mercy from the court martial.

Your Excellency knows the rest of our story. We limped home, losing a few more sailors through disease on the way and arrived home to face our condemnation. The court martial was harsh, but those who climb highest must expect to fall furthest: however I think even M. de Cheyron, who testified with all his customary venom against M. de Kerguelen, must have felt a twinge of compassion to see his Captain reduced to the ranks and imprisoned in the Fortress of St. Nazaire at the King's pleasure.

The ultimate irony is that our efforts have been proved to be futile by our greatest rivals: it was recently announced in London that Captain James Cook was blessed with fine weather when he navigated in the direction of the Kerguelen Islands and that he took the opportunity of checking up on the much vaunted French discoveries. Circumnavigating them with ease, he conclusively proved that M. de Kerguelen's islands are no more than a worthless archipelago about the size of Corsica, isolated in the middle of the southern Indian Ocean. If there exists a Great Southern Continent it must lie either even further south, or somewhere in the immensity of the Pacific, many leagues away from the area where we were sailing.

***

I have never discovered M. de Kerguelen's reasons for deliberately rejecting his discoveries. In his place, I would have persevered and sailed further east towards Australia, where new lands are constantly being found.

Only one person knows the Chevalier de Kerguelen's secret, and that is Mlle. Louison. She was the only person to share his quarters and was the only person privy to his thoughts and fears as he navigated around the Islands. But she has taken her secret with her to the perpetual silence of a convent and not even the might and authority of the King's court martial can prevail over the eternal vows of the *clausura*.

THE LORD OF HEAVEN

THE LORD OF HEAVEN

MACAO, DECEMBER 1742

Father Corrado hesitated before answering, looking at the row of implacable faces before him.
'The problem is that the Chinese have no word for God. That is why we had to improvise. We had to take certain liberties.'

The wind rose and the roof shutters slammed violently with a loud clap that echoed round the Seminary Hall. It was as if the Heavens themselves had pronounced their displeasure.

The Visitor's face hardened. His was a rotund and fleshy face, a good Roman face and tension made it ugly. He stared hard at Corrado, smelling heresy and laxity of doctrinal practice.

Corrado took a deep breath and continued:
'When our illustrious predecessor, Saint Francis Xavier, started his ministry in Japan, he was faced with the same dilemma as we faced in China. He asked his native helper for the appropriate term for God in Japanese and the result was that he preached the Our Lord's Gospel using the name of a fertility goddess. It was a full two years before the mistake was rectified, by the grace of God.' He crossed himself rather theatrically, hoping that this would carry the right emphasis. 'We now use the Chinese term *T'ien Zhu*, the Lord of Heaven, but we also recognise that the Chinese traditions also provides a number of perfectly acceptable terms, such as *Shang-ti*, but I shall not divert your Grace's attention with the minutiae of the Chinese language'.

'It is surely the minutiae of that language which should concern us, Father Corrado'.
The Visitor's voice boomed from the raised dais on which the

99

Investigatory Commission was seated. 'It is precisely the use of language that can distort and falsify the true meaning of Our Lord's teachings.'

The Visitor's voice filled the sultry air and no-one dared to stir.

Corrado looked at the Visitor again. He was in his early fifties but had not taken to the Asiatic climate well: his rather corpulent features merely looked uncomfortable and bloated. The Visitor regularly dabbed his glistening forehead with a handkerchief, while a native servant vainly tried to cool his back with a fan. Corrado had long learned that the best way of coping with the heavy monsoon heat was to keep as still as possible. He made a stark contrast with the Visitor, with his gaunt, bearded figure dressed in the plain dark robes of a Confucian man of letters, the literary caste which the Jesuit missionaries had emulated in order to gain an *entrée* into the highest circles of Chinese society. He was older than the Visitor, but the austerity of his life in the tropical missions had given him a certain agelessness, a rather emaciated look of other-worldly wisdom that made him look strikingly handsome in his black robes.

The Visitor picked up a piece of paper and read aloud: 'Once his task of salvation was ended, he ascended back to Heaven'. The Visitor paused and fixed Corrado with his gaze.
'I have read a great many works of Catechism written for the enlightenment of native races in China. Many of these were by members of the Society of Jesus. To my great sorrow and utter astonishment, that is the only reference I have been able to find in these texts to Our Saviour's earthly life'.
He re-read the passage in a voice loaded with contempt: 'Once his task of salvation was ended, he ascended back into Heaven'.

Then he dropped the piece of paper for effect and grunted with disgust.

100

'Kindly explain to me, Father Corrado', his voice thundered in the vastness of the Seminary Hall, 'why there is never a *single* mention of Our Saviour's Passion in your so-called 'Catechisms'? Why is there not a single mention of His crucifixion, of His glorious sacrifice- without which there would be no Resurrection and therefore no Salvation? Why is there no mention of our Lord's Sufferings and of the precious blood He spilled for our eternal salvation? The Cross of Christ is the very symbol of our faith, but I am reliably informed that the only use you and your fellow Jesuits make of the Cross is to invent a pun- yes, a *pun-* based on the coincidence of the shape of the Cross with the ideogram for the number ten in the script of the Chinese! I should be very obliged if you would explain to me why the members of the Society of Jesus find it necessary to indulge in such blasphemous frivolity'.

Corrado had expected this.

Those who were trying to close down the Chinese missions had obviously scoured Jesuit preaching manuals, looking for the most controversial things with which to poison the Visitor's mind. At least, Corrado reflected, he could cite specific Papal approval for the way he and his fellow Jesuits had been preaching the Gospel: almost a hundred years ago, Pope Alexander VII had been persuaded to give his blessing to the Jesuit doctrine of 'adaptation' and, more recently, a Papal Legate who had been sent to China to investigate persistent accusations of heresy had specifically given his approval to Jesuit practices by granting a series of 'permissions'. But Corrado knew that this would not carry much weight with the Visitor: their enemies in Rome would no doubt have played on the fact that the Papacy had been cleverly manipulated by the Jesuits, that the Papal Legate had only been shown what the Jesuits deemed necessary for their cause and that the 'permissions' had been abused, (even assuming that they had been legitimate in the first place).

Corrado instinctively knew that to claim Papal approval would
be a red rag to a bull. Instead, he decided to confront the Visitor
with the reality of preaching the Gospel in China.

'Your Grace is understandably concerned at the manner with
which the Word of Our Saviour is being presented to the native
population of these parts', he began. 'But Your Grace will, I am
sure, appreciate that the Chinese inhabit a very different world
than that described in the Bible. At the very least, it is necessary
to make some adaptation for the different climates and
countries described in the Bible compared to the world which
they know. A catechumen living in Macao will never have been
to a desert, since the only deserts in China are thousands of
leagues away, far beyond Tibet. We are therefore forced to
make certain adaptations to describe the forty days and forty
nights which Our Lord spent in the wilderness. The Chinese
have no knowledge of wine and their idea of bread is very
different: how can we celebrate the Eucharist in China without
making some changes to traditional practices? Again, they do
not have the same animals as are described in the Bible, such as
lions and camels, so that it is necessary to make certain
changes...'

'Father Corrado, I am fully aware that the Chinese do not live in
Palestine', the Visitor interrupted to a ripple of polite laughter
from the rest of the Investigatory Commission. 'Kindly get to
the point'.

Corrado bowed reluctantly and tried to explain.

'Asiatic societies are built on fundamentally different principles
from ours. We Europeans stress the individual and praise the
man who obeys his conscience against the voice of the crowd.
But in Japan, in Korea or in China it is completely different. To
be an individual, to stand out against the crowd is a regarded as
a sign of selfishness, something close to treachery. It is the
group, it is the social order that is sacred not the individual.

Every man has his place. Every greeting must indicate the degree of social distance between the people who are meeting. In Japan, they even have a different language depending in whether those who are speaking are of the same or of a different social status, whether the person being addressed is male or female. Confucius taught that the perfect world is where each man knows his place in the hierarchy and accepts it humbly: he is rewarded by the protection of those above him, but if he defies the hierarchy the consequences are dreadful. Rebellion is a most shameful thing and it is almost impossible to get a Chinese to accept that someone executed by the authorities could possibly be virtuous. It would be disastrous if the Chinese were to regard Our Saviour as a common criminal. That is the problem we face in explaining the Crucifixion.

'In Japan, there were some peasant revolts recently. Corrupt officials had imposed such heavy taxes on the peasants that their lives became unbearable. In the end, they decided to petition the Shogun. Those who volunteered to present the petition were hailed as heroes, because of their bravery in daring to complain to the Shogun and because everyone knew that a horrific fate awaited them. The Shogun's officials duly investigated the complaints and found that the peasants were right and the officials were punished. As for the peasants' leaders, they were boiled in oil or beheaded or even crucified because they had *also* been guilty of rebellion against their superiors and that could not go unpunished. The crowds of peasants who watched the executions did not rebel: their heroic leaders had knowingly broken the essential law of total obedience and therefore their appalling tortures were quite justified. Afterwards, the peasants would build shrines to honour the memory of their martyrs, but nevertheless their leaders had become outcasts and criminals who had broken the order of the world.

'Your Grace will readily see that Our Lord's Passion is difficult to explain to the Chinese or the Japanese. They would regard Him as a common criminal, who had somehow incurred the displeasure of the authorities. This is why we stress the teachings of Our Lord, and concentrate on matters of pure theology, such as the operation of Divine grace or of the sacraments. We only introduce our native converts to the Passion and sufferings of Our Lord *after* they have been baptised, once they are converted and can safely be introduced to the mysteries of the Christian faith.'

'What you are saying to me, Father Corrado, is that you are 'baptising' -if that is the proper word- men and women who are ignorant of the central tenets of the Faith, who make the sacred vows of baptism without knowing the slightest thing about the central fact around which Christianity is built. I find this a quite extraordinary admission on your part, however much you may seek to justify this practice because of the barbaric practices of the native races. It seems to me that the very validity of the baptismal vows of the people you claim to have gained to the Faith are utterly void: as I hope you will remember from your days at the Seminary, the Church does not regard as legitimate marriage vows which are taken under duress. Again, the absolution given after confession is invalid if the penitent is insincere or has hidden sins from his Confessor. How can you possibly allow to the Christian sacraments natives who are wholly ignorant of the most central facts of our Faith? Eh? And you have the misplaced honesty to claim that this ignorance is deliberately fostered and the quite extraordinary effrontery to claim that this is being done for their own good! Father Corrado, I doubt that I have ever heard anything as outrageous in all the years of my priesthood.'

***

Corrado went up the steep steps of the Cathedral. It was terribly hot and his cassock clung to his back with sweat. At least there was a slight breeze when he reached the top of the steps and he was glad to walk into the cool interior.

Suddenly, he was transported back to Europe, to a world of stained glass, of saints' images and the acrid smell of fading incense. Somehow the warm dampness of the tropics never entered the Cathedral and the walls were thick enough to shut out the chatter of the natives.

He knelt down and crossed himself. Then he started to pray rather aimlessly to the effigy of Saint Francis Xavier that stood in the little side chapel. But his thoughts wandered, constantly going back to the events of the morning. Corrado felt a sense of growing unease, even of mounting dread, as if the whole world the Cathedral represented was about to disappear: would they really destroy all that the Jesuits had built up over two centuries of patient missionary activity? Of course it was not perfect, of course they had adapted the Gospel to local conditions, but that was only to create a Christianity which the Chinese mind would understand. Of course it involved compromises- 'permissions' as the Papal Legate had termed them- but that was the price to be paid to translate the glorious message of Christianity into something in which they could believe in...

Lately, he had neglected his devotions, failing to pursue his daily meditations on the life of St. Augustine which he had set himself as a task for Advent. He made a mental note to mark this failing down on the weekly chart of spiritual progress that St. Ignatius recommended to all Jesuits. He said a quick prayer to St. Francis, imploring him to give him the strength to live up to their Founder's example.

St. Ignatius had taught that the first step to spiritual perfection is indifference- indifference that is to whether one's life proved to be long or short, whether one would be blessed with the glory of a martyr's death or whether one would find quiet fulfilment in the obscurity of a convent's ritual... Set against the scale of eternity, it did not matter whether the Empire of China was converted in this century or in the next: the victory of the Lord was a foregone conclusion and it was his duty to be indifferent to the role he would play in the cosmic scheme of Salvation. To do otherwise would be to show personal ambition and the most damnable pride. A true Jesuit was a member of the *company* of Jesus. He would therefore take up his Cross with the same humility and say 'your will not mine', just as Christ had done in the Garden of Gethsemane. He should be ready to obey his destiny, to play his part with his insignificant life in the great purpose of God's providence and find his fulfilment in the mere fact of having made himself available to the Lord. He had sworn an oath of personal obedience to the Pope and if his orders were to abandon the work of a lifetime, then he should have the spiritual strength to accept this.

***

That evening, Corrado went to visit Yu Xie, just as he had done every fortnight for the past three years in an apparently futile attempt to convert the old Mandarin. Xie was interested in the foreigners' strange beliefs: like most educated Chinese, he privately found it puzzling that the foreign barbarians could wield such awesome military power and yet have such extraordinary beliefs, such as, for example, that a man could also be God at the same time, that death could be followed by a mysterious paradisiac existence and that the communal eating of a meal of bread and wine could unleash enormous spiritual energies.

Unusually, it was Xie who had initiated their dialogues, inviting Corrado to his private residence after meeting him at the Governor's Palace in Canton. Corrado's fellow missionaries had been immensely excited at this rare example of a Chinese of the highest class showing interest in the Mission. Corrado had immediately responded, occasionally bearing gifts with a subtle religious message: his most successful present had been a little votive statue of the Virgin encased in a prism of glass, which radiated all the colours of the rainbow when held up to the sun at the correct angle. Xie and his household had never tired of playing with the object and discussing its apparently inexplicable ability to trap all the colours of the spectrum. Of course, Corrado had lost no time in drawing analogies with the way the prism radiated exquisite colours and the power of the Virgin in interceding for the souls of the faithful. Or to point out the way the rays of light significantly shone from the centre of the Virgin's halo.

More recently their fortnightly meetings had become attended by other Chinese dignitaries. Corrado's superiors had been delighted to learn that they were all members of the Mandarin class, and that the prospects of a major breakthrough were excellent. Corrado would be asked endless questions about Europe and especially about Rome, whose antiquity particularly impressed the Chinese. But most of the time, Corrado would be asked whether he could demonstrate that the world must have had a beginning, how it would end, what would happen to souls after death and of what material was the soul made of, what the Christians meant when they claimed that, in a single individual, the Eternal and the Human had been united...

Of late, Corrado had felt that, slowly, subtly and almost imperceptibly, Xie's position was shifting. While he still obviously found it difficult to conceive of a world where a transcendent reality existed behind every moment of time, he had begun to grasp a different way of looking at the world. Corrado persevered, now driven on by a new vigour as he had sensed that he was successfully manoeuvring the old Mandarin towards conversion. Corrado was subtle and realistic enough not to press too quickly nor too hard: he understood that Xie would have to be steered with endless patience and, above all, courtesy. At no point should Xie be made to feel that his ancestral culture was deficient or that European ways were superior: how right, Corrado reflected, the first Jesuits like Matteo Ricci or Adam Schall had been to present Christianity as a purified Confucianism, as an affirmation of all that was noble in Chinese culture but cleansed of the accretions and errors that had accumulated over the centuries.

Xie's mansion was the nearest thing one might find in China to a grand European villa. Set on the crest of a hill, its orientation was south-west, which offered magnificent views of sunsets across the bay of Macao. It was surrounded by pine trees and there would often be a deliciously refreshing breeze, filled with the scent of resin and salty sea air as he rode up to Xie's mansion.

The villa was deceptively extensive, and Corrado had only ever been to the front reception rooms while Xie's family kept their distance from the missionary. He had been formally introduced to Yu-fang, Xie's wife, but only to be greeted by a ceremonial bow followed by a discreet withdrawal to the ladies' apartments. He had also met the eldest son, Yizhi, on a number of occasions but it was evident that the son deeply disapproved of his father's curiosity for foreign ways and that he had decided to confine himself to the minimum civility that would not amount to an insult to his father's guest. Xie had recently delegated the headship of the family to Yizhi, feeling that his advancing years made him unfit for such heavy family responsibility. Xie's decision had been announced quite suddenly, one morning, sometime after his seventieth birthday. His father's retirement had obviously caught Yizhi by surprise, for he now adopted an even graver and more solid demeanour in all his doings round the mansion. In a way, Xie's decision had given him a new lease of life, a sense of release from the constraints that had bound him all these years. Compared to his eldest son's grave formality, Xie now had a spring in his step, even a little mischievous smile as he asked Corrado about the customs of the West. Corrado liked him immensely, for he always enjoyed talking with old men, particularly if they had clear memories of a long life and if they were ready to share them with younger people.

Xie's besetting sin was gluttony- he would laugh disarmingly when Corrado tried to reason with him that a man must eat to live rather than live to eat. But Corrado was fine enough a tactician to know when to press a point and when to maintain a sensitive detachment from human frailty. They sat down and Xie poured out the inaugural cup of 'Iron Buddha', that bitter tea that started and ended meals as an aid to digestion. Corrado politely slurped his tea and enquired as to the health of his son, Yizhi. The meal that followed surpassed even Xie's own extravagant standards of elaborateness. It was to be an unusual mixture of fiery Szechuan and mild Chiu Chow coastal delicacies. Their meal as always, was served by Zhou and Zhentao, a pair of old retainers, who had worked for Xie since his earliest days in the imperial civil service. They also happened to be twins and Corrado always found it slightly comical to see such gravity and pomposity being exhibited twice in an identical way, as the two old servants went about their tasks. Directed by Xie with the smallest signs of the hand, Zhou and Zhentao served an initial series of oysters and clams in a spicy sauce of black beans and chillies. Then came the relieving clear broth leading afterwards to one of Xie's favourites: a cold goose served in chunks of fried goose blood with a dip of white vinegar and garlic. It had taken Corrado some time to develop a tolerance for the liver-smooth texture of the blood, but he dutifully ate with gusto to avoid giving offence.

He waited for Xie to declare which theme he was interested in discussing that afternoon. The two retainers unobtrusively presented freshwater eel served in a brown sauce and a small dish of plain rice as a complement, and Xie raised his cup as a toast. This made Corrado smile involuntarily, as Xie was obviously trying to pay him the compliment of imitating the Portuguese manners he had observed.

Xie sighed as if deep in thought. Then he suddenly asked
Corrado to expound on the origin of the world. How did the
Christian books answer the question of the creation of the
world? Why was the question even important? Why should a
man concern himself with such questions- after all, as the
Confucian Classics said, 'the Heavens do not speak', and the
role of each man was to fulfil his appointed role in the station in
which he had been born. Was it not, in a sense futile, for a man
to ask such questions?
'You say that in the beginning, the Lord of Heaven created the
earth and the sky, and that he maintains all things visible and
invisible in being', Xie said. 'I have not read any such statement
in Confucius, Mencius nor in any of our classical authors'.

Corrado paused before answering. It would have been too easy
for him to respond with the pat answers provided by his
scholastic training- that the existence of God is self-evident,
inasmuch as whatever moves is moved by another and that
motion is nothing else than the reduction of something from
potentiality to actuality (such as fire is wood made hot thereby
changing or moving it). That it is impossible for something to
be moved and at the same time to move itself and that therefore
such things must be moved by Another. Since the chain of
movers cannot go on into infinity it is therefore necessary to
arrive at a first mover... And thus, if everything has a cause,
then the only way of escaping out of the logical nightmare of an
infinite chain of causes is to conclude the necessary existence of
a First Cause, a Being whose existence is not dependent on a
previous creator, a Being who is absolutely *necessary* in every
sense of the word... But Corrado knew from experience that
while such arguments might work in Europe they usually met
with a wall of incomprehension in China. The world existed, it
had always existed and would always go on existing. St.
Augustine's idea that God lived outside time and that the
Creation necessarily introduced the notion of a linear

development through time would have been quite simply incomprehensible to Xie. Corrado would have to present the doctrine in a Chinese way.

Corrado chose his words carefully. For Xie, all the wisdom and knowledge worth having was contained in the Five Books recording the great tradition. It was, of course, crucial to demonstrate that the Confucian Classics were not silent on the origin of the world. The Five Books did indeed deal with the problem of the First Cause, if properly interpreted. Like all Jesuits missionaries, he had been trained to know the Classics of the Chinese canon as well as any Confucian scholar: the Jesuits had quickly understood that the only likely way of converting a hierarchical society like China was to aim to convince the ruling class, and to do that it was necessary to become as much like them as possible, above all to *think* like them.

'Reason exists in a man's mind, like the sun shines in the heavens', Corrado began, 'and I would respectfully suggest that by examining the proper nature of things, one can go back to their original causes. A temple does not build itself, it needs workmen. The workmen cannot be born by themselves, they need a father and a mother. And so everything must have an origin, a cause. And logically, there must be an ultimate cause that is not caused, that is necessary, that is to say a Being or a Cause that is caused, a Being that cannot not exist, a Being that necessarily exists...'

Xie looked at him politely, nodding with masterly neutrality.

Corrado decided that it was time to shift his demonstration more obviously on the Confucian canon.

'The *ying* and the *yang* are joined in indissoluble fusion in the cosmic order, and the Ten Thousand Spirits are born out of them by a process of transformation', he said, hoping that this would be a reasonable quotation from the *Yijing*, the Confucian book of divination. 'But what governs this process? Even the

Masters and the Saints have been unable to give the primal force a name. They call it the *Taiji*, the cosmic origin the source of the universal energy. That surely is saying much the same thing, as our Christian books in Europe. Confucius is not therefore ignorant of our argument for a Necessary Being'.

A warm breeze softly fanned the painted scrolls on the wall, and Corrado admired the way the painter had made the mountain emerge out of the mists by mere hints of inchoate shapes. In his heart of hearts, Corrado despaired of bridging the gulf that existed between him and Xie. However curious and sympathetic Xie might be, he nevertheless inhabited a radically different mental world. As he continued with his scholastic demonstration of causes and effects, he remembered his discussions with the oldest Jesuit resident at the Court of Peking, Father Albert Jacobs. The old Flemish Jesuit had spent a whole lifetime in China and had built up perhaps the deepest knowledge of Chinese civilisation of anyone in the Mission. In his opinion, conversion was ultimately a hopeless cause for as long as the Chinese retained their Confucian culture, for as long as they remained Chinese. The oriental mind, he would say, starts with fundamentally alien conceptions compared to the world as conceived by the classical Greeks and the Christians. For Aristotle, Father Jacobs maintained, the normal state of things is the absence of movement, and the universe of material things must therefore be moved by an outside agent. For the Chinese, movement and change is the natural state of things. The *Taiji* is thus the principle of a universal, all-pervading energy that is a given, a constant state that is the very essence of the universe: 'Tell the Chinese that there must be something to start the whole thing off and they simply cannot understand what you are talking about', he would say with a impish little smile on his lips.

The two retainers came in with Xie's favourite delicacy, the Cantonese *Gum chen gi*, or Gold Coin Chicken: skewered livers separated by pieces of pork fat, roasted red until the liver is soft and succulent and the fat becomes crisp. And then served with the final touch: delicate pieces of orange flavoured bread. Corrado ate with relish, complimenting Xie on the excellence of his kitchens.

***

Even though servants trotted behind them, holding umbrellas above their heads, there was no escape from the leaden heat. The Visitor mopped his face periodically with a lace handkerchief. Corrado could see the sweaty thumbprint on the cover of his Breviary.

The shrine stood at the end of a little path through the eucalyptus and the bamboos. At least there it was cooler thanks to the shade from the trees and the Visitor sat down heavily on a small stone bench. An acrid smell of old incense hung in the air and the ground was strewn with bits of food offerings. The shrine was made of sandstone and felt hot to the touch. Under the canopy stood a venerable seated figure of an old man with a rather complacent expression on his face, dressed in the ceremonial robes of a Confucian scholar. The figure was worn with age and its face was partially covered with red silk tassels and draped with a banner displaying a ritual prayer in beautifully drawn characters.

'This is the family shrine', Corrado said, explaining that each Chinese family was linked to a clan ancestor. There was a restricted number of these, the clan Lee, the Wu, the Wang, the Deng and so on. The Chinese did not owe allegiance to the Emperor so much as to their clans, each name being supposedly traceable back to a single ancestor who had given his name to the clan.
'It is not a shrine in our sense of the word', Corrado went on. 'It is the symbol of the family's virtue, of its identity. They do

113

not so much worship it as pay their respects to it or meditate on the virtues embodied in the figure of the ancestor.'

The Visitor looked at him with a sardonic expression and picked up the half decomposed remains of a food offering on a little tray. A few flies buzzed in the thick, humid air while the Visitor examined the tray with a mixture of amusement and contempt.
'And you maintain that this is not a sacrificial offering?', his voice sounding increasingly irritable.

Corrado chose not to answer.

One of the Visitor's acolytes whispered something in his ear. The Visitor frowned and then turned to Corrado.
'Is it true that this shrine is used by all the family, with baptized Christians and pagans joining in the same ceremonial?'
'Your Grace has been misinformed', Corrado replied sensing danger in the question. 'This shrine is not a centre of worship in our sense. In China, to revere the ancestors is not to worship as we understand it. It is merely an act of civic solidarity. Not to do so would be an insult to the family. China is not our country and we are foreigners here. We must tolerate local customs, otherwise they will feel threatened and reject us. Your Grace will recall that our practice of toleration for such rites was accepted by Pope Alexander VII in his decision of the 23rd March 1656, which stipulated that...'
'We are all very well acquainted with the Holy Father's decision', the Visitor interrupted. 'Just as you are no doubt also aware of the contrary opinion of the Congregation of the Inquisition, issued after the most exhaustive inquiry into the Chinese rites. I had imagined that the Congregation's opinion would have reached these shores by now: after all it was issued in Rome some thirty nine years ago...', the Visitor concluded with meticulous irony.

Corrado bowed instinctively with respect:

114

'Our intention was not to gainsay the rulings of the Church, Your Grace', he said.

'Have you not taken a vow of obedience?', the Visitor thundered before Corrado could continue.

'Yes, Your Grace'.

'And an unconditional vow of obedience to the Pope?'

'All of us Jesuits take that oath'.

'And how then do you explain... this?', he pointed to the shrine with an irritated sweep of the hand. 'This is idolatry, and an idolatry aggravated because the natives you claim to have converted join in these pagan sacrileges'.

Corrado looked round the garden. The crowd of Chinese servants stood impassively, silent witnesses to the heated debate conducted in a language they could not understand. The Visitor sat on the little bench, sweating in the humid air, flanked by his Franciscan advisers. In a sense, Corrado reflected, the whole scene symbolized what was at stake: there, in front of them, was the prize, the vast sea of souls that was China, with its teeming millions. To convert them, to win them over to the Faith would truly be a world shaking achievement- at a stroke it would easily double the number of souls in the True Church. And they were so tantalizingly close to achieving that aim. The Jesuits had totally immersed themselves in the Chinese world, learning their language and their customs. They could debate the subtlest points of interpretation of the classical texts in a way that astonished the leading Chinese scholars of the day. The strange missionaries had become almost indistinguishable from the Chinese themselves, dressed in the robes of the aristocracy, performing astounding feats with their telescopes and their clocks. Most important of all, the Jesuits had won the trust of the Emperor himself, earning the hitherto unheard of right to be buried in the Forbidden City, and being trusted with some of the highest missions of the state. This, Corrado reflected with an inner sigh, was the key: if the Emperor converted, then all China would convert and Asia would become Christian. They had almost succeeded with the Emperor K'ang-Hsi, who had happily surrounded himself with 'his' Jesuits, as he liked to call them. He had even officially ordered that the God of the Christians should enjoy Imperial protection.

But that had only been achieved through the famous 'permissions', which had allowed the Jesuits to respect Chinese ways and to turn a blind eye to so many strange practices. And now, nearly two centuries of ceaseless missionary work, all that carefully constructed edifice of compromise and persuasion was about to be brought crashing to the ground by the intolerance of bigots and fools in the Vatican.

'If Your Grace will allow me some words of explanation', Corrado began. The Visitor nodded with a little grunt of irritation.

'The Chinese are blessed with an all pervasive sense of the spiritual forces that shape our lives', Corrado continued, choosing his words with care. 'Their custom is to represent this sense of the divine with images. To represent it with countless symbols and pictures- symbols, if you will allow me, of the spiritual world they feel all around them. This little shrine is not worshipping the ancestors, it is the manifestation of a high culture, of a sense of virtue which is deeply embedded in their race. You cannot cut away the rites from their faith. And I use the word 'faith' advisedly. The very worst mistake is to lump together a scholar paying his respects to a statue of Confucius with a peasant sacrificing a chicken to get a good harvest'.

That made the Visitor give a little contemptuous laugh. The Franciscans standing behind echoed him politely.

Corrado went on regardless.

'When the Papal Legate came to China some eighty years ago, he saw what we were doing. And he saw that is was good. That we were winning souls. That is our duty: did not Our Saviour command the Apostles to go into the world and 'make disciples

116

of all nations, baptising them in the name of the Father and of the Son and of the Holy Ghost?' Nothing is perfect in this world. We must take the nations we meet as we find them: you could not force the Infidels of Arabia to eat pork or their womenfolk to take off their veils. To do so would be madness and calculated to turn them into enemies. We have to make concessions in those things which do not really matter, where the essentials of the Faith are not compromised.'

'Isn't that exactly the point?'

'Indeed, Your Grace. But I hope that you will allow us to refer to what the Chinese themselves say about the rites you find so concerning. As Your Grace may be aware, the highest authority in the land, no less than the Emperor K'ang-Hsi himself, made a declaration about Chinese customs which was sent to the Pope, the Holy Pontiff Innocent XI, who has been happily declared Blessed by the Holy Congregation and who will soon, I pray, be canonised', Corrado paused for effect and crossed himself perhaps a little too theatrically. 'The Emperor of the Chinese confirmed *in writing* that the honours were paid to Confucius as a legislator and not as a saint, that honours paid to the ancestors were only a demonstration of love and a commemoration of the good works that they had done in their lives. He even confirmed that the sacrifices made in the temples are not made to the visible heavens but to the Supreme Lord, the Creator and Preserver of heaven and earth, the *T'ien Zhou*, the Lord of Heaven.'

He paused for effect.

'We are all well aware of what the natives here think of their practices', the Visitor said, 'but I am sure that you will hardly need to be reminded that only the Church can decide on matters of doctrine.'

'Your Grace', Corrado replied quickly, deciding to shift the direction of the argument, 'look at the city that stretches as far as the eye can see: it may be huge by our standards, but Macao is not an important city in China and there are a thousand such cities in this Empire. An abundance of souls to be reaped. That is what is at stake, Your Grace. I have dedicated my life to our motto: 'To the Greater Glory of God', ad majoram Dei gloriam... At a stroke, by converting the Chinese we will double the number of Christians in the world. What greater prize could there be than this? We are fishers of men. If ever there was case of the end justifying the means, then this is it'.

'No, no, a thousand times no!', the Visitor shouted, getting up with effort. 'The end never justifies the means. I should have thought that the one lesson your Jesuit seminaries would at least have taught you is that the end *changes* with the means. You make concessions- those damnable so-called 'permissions' which you extracted from the church with your lies and your half-truths. Once you compromise on the Faith, all is lost! The Martyrs of the Church did not compromise with the pagans of Rome- that would have been an easy and cheap way to save their lives. But they placed the value of their souls above even their lives. At least *they* understood that it is better to die in the arena, to be crucified or be thrown to the beasts than to lose the true faith. What you are saying is monstrous, Father Corrado, utterly and completely monstrous. You expect me, as a Visitor appointed by the Holy Father himself to inspect the state of the missions, to countenance the sight of baptized believers joining in a crowd of pagans to burn food offerings before the statues of native 'philosophers'? Eh? To bow their foreheads to the ground before pagan images, to profane their baptised heads in an abject show of superstition... And to call all that 'Christianity'? I have never heard anything so ridiculous in all my life. You have been with the natives for too long, Father Corrado. I shall recommend that you be ordered to return to Europe. For your own good and for the sake of what remains of your soul'.

The Visitor stormed past Corrado, kicking the little votive pile of food offerings that stood in his way in the process.

***

Somehow, Corrado knew that the evening would not be an ordinary literary evening at Xie's. For the past six weeks or so, Xie and he had engaged in a friendly debate about the relative virtues of the T'ang dynasty poets. Xie had conservative tastes, praising Li Po and Tu Fu to the skies for their poise and elegance and for the range of their subject matter. By contrast, Corrado much preferred the private torments of Li Shang Yin, with his intimate descriptions of the agonies of unrequited love, for his courage in laying bare his most private emotions in a refreshingly un-Chinese way. Xie protested that to expose the workings of the heart in this way was indecent, and Corrado replied with a smile that he liked Li Shang Yin because he was almost European.

Their good-humoured debate went on evening after evening, and Xie was obviously enjoying himself. Xie's friends who frequented these evenings would happily join in the fray, such as Lu Zhizao, an extremely old but still intellectually vigorous scholar famed for his fine calligraphy, or Yan Guan Xian, with whom Xie had prepared the gruelling Imperial civil service examinations nearly fifty years previously.

Corrado astonished them by the breadth of his knowledge of the classics of Chinese poetry. They would remark on the accuracy of his tones (it was true that Corrado had a particularly fine musical ear) declaring that he spoke Mandarin better than most Chinese. Lu Zhizao would even compliment him on the elegance of his script... Corrado knew that, at last, he had won their respect and that a huge step forward in the patient quest for conversion had been made: his most earnest desire now was to see Xie a baptised Catholic Christian before he died, knowing

119

that it could only be a matter of years, perhaps of months.

Five years ago, he would have dismissed the thought of converting Xie and his circle as pure fantasy. But things had changed recently. Xie's friends listened politely, if only because of their respect for his scholarship and his knowledge of Chinese culture. Gradually, respect turned into a subtle kind of awe, and behind their new desire to find out more about the source of European's power, Corrado sensed a gnawing doubt that their ancestral civilisation might, after all, have something to learn from the foreigners and their strange religion.

Corrado knew enough about Chinese ways to bide his time. But by making himself as Chinese as possible, he hoped to reassure them that the gap between his Christian world and the unchanging culture of China was really not as great as they feared. That they could bridge the gulf with relatively little effort on their part. To adopt Christianity would in fact be a reaffirmation of their Chinese culture, it would be a sort of return to the ancestral purity of the world in which Confucius had lived, a stripping away of the centuries which had come to overlay the original glories of Confucianism with superstition and pointless rituals, like limpets and barnacles on the hull of an ancient vessel... He was proud of that image, although he knew it was slightly *risqué* with its implication that what was old was not necessarily good. Christianity was the natural religion of mankind, Corrado would insist when the appropriate moment would come for him to evangelise in as subtle and unobtrusive a way as he could manage. Christianity, he explained, lay buried in each man's consciousness, if they would only unlock that treasure in their deepest selves they would discover its glorious vision of a transcendent Deity reigning over his Creation... Such a belief, he insisted lay at the heart of all true religion: when the Chinese worshipped, they were merely expressing a universal longing which it was his duty and privilege to guide towards perfection.

That evening, Corrado had arrived early and Xie invited him to walk round his garden to admire a fountain and waterfall which he had just finished designing.

'I should like you to baptise my servants Zhou and Zhentao', Xie said suddenly as they sat in the stillness of the garden.

Corrado repressed a smile of triumph. The signal that he had at long last made headway had finally come: what a moment for the Holy Spirit to choose to descend upon them! Now he had the living proof to demonstrate to the Visitor that the Jesuits' methods worked. Having lived with the Chinese and absorbed their civilisation, the Jesuits were uniquely placed to convert the Chinese and the Visitor would now see their methods at first hand.

For some time, Corrado had spotted Zhou and Zhentao attending the occasional Mass at the Jesuit Cathedral. At first, he had assumed that they were only there because Xie had sent them to observe the foreigners in their home environment, as it were. He had been too polite to mention that he had seen them to Xie. But eventually the rather grotesque twins started approaching Corrado with a host of questions: why was there a statue of a sheep above the altar? Why did the colours of the vestments change throughout the year? Could he translate the mysterious words recited by the congregation? It was clear that they were genuinely interested in the Christianity, attracted by the deliberately gorgeous ritual the Jesuits displayed in their Cathedral. It turned out that they were orphans, sold to Xie's family from their village at an early age and that they had been intrigued by the way missionaries treated the poor differently. Without the support of a family network, orphans in China had no safety net to escape falling down to the dregs of society. By contrast, the Christians displayed their universal charity to the world with triumphant exuberance. The Jesuits would hold processions where orphans and the discarded children of

121

prostitutes they had rescued were paraded round the streets of Macao, chanting Te Deums and Magnificats. The missionaries taught that it was a universal duty to help the poor and the sick: the contrast with the pitiless indifference shown by the Chinese to anyone outside their family structure was glaring.

Zhou and Zhentao's curiosity was obviously genuine. Their enthusiasm was discreetly encouraged, by their master- although Xie admitted that he had had to protect them from the fury of his son Yizhi, who deeply disapproved of the 'new religion' and who was only stopped from having them flogged out of respect for his father. As soon as Yizhi was out of earshot, Zhou and Zhentao would harass him endless questions about Christian doctrine: Corrado began to suspect that Xie was subtly using them as his intermediaries, probing more openly through their questions than he would have ever dared to do face to face.

Corrado pretended not to notice and patiently answered their endless questions.

Sometimes their odd Chinese misconceptions of the Faith would make him laugh: he would entertain his fellow missionaries with their endearingly Chinese interpretations of what they saw. His favourite story was Zhen and Zhentao's 'explanation' for the doctrine of the Son's relationship with the Father. It was quite simple, they said: just as every Chinese belonged to a clan like the Wu, the Lee or the Wang, the Celestial Beings belonged to theirs: it was obvious that the Son was related to the Father, since 'Ye-Zu' and 'Ye-Whe' clearly both belonged to the clan 'Ye'.

Later that evening, Corrado baptised Zhou and Zhentao in a simple ceremony. Xie watched them impassively, thanking

Corrado afterwards as if the ceremony had somehow satisfied an inner longing of his own. The rest of the family obeyed Yizhi and had remained in their private quarters.

***

The day's interrogation had, if anything, gone worse than ever before. The Visitor was obviously relishing the occasion:

'Am I to understand, Father Corrado', his voice echoed across the Audience Hall, 'that some of your converts actually go as far as to describe themselves as Nestorians?'

'None of *my* converts, Your Grace', Corrado replied, 'but it cannot be denied that the Chinese veneration for all that is ancient has led to excesses'.

'Excesses? I am sure that you do not need any reminding that the Council of Ephesus declared that those who denied that Our Saviour combined both divine and human natures were heretics? 'Excesses', you say? I should have thought the proper word would have been heresy, and a most pernicious one at that...'

'I would be the first to condemn that heresy too, Your Grace, and indeed I have devoted my whole life to preaching the word of God. I am sixty two, Your Grace, and I have not seen my family and my native Tuscany for over a quarter of a century. I have done all that so that the true word might be believed and I find it particularly distressing to be accused in having so massively failed in my duty and to have apparently deliberately spread false ideas...'

'No-one is accusing *you*, Father Corrado, of heretical beliefs', the Visitor interrupted, 'but it is the effect of your Order's laxity that...'

'Your Grace, every member of my Order has made a special vow of obedience to the Pope', Corrado countered, this time getting genuinely angry.

'No one would question the commitment of the Society of Jesus'.

'Then why, why do you to believe the worst of every rumour that is fed to you? Especially by those who have never risked their lives to spread the Word?' This time he deliberately pointed at the retinue of Franciscans that flanked the Visitor on both sides. There was an uneasy shuffle in the front row but he took no notice. 'This, Your Grace, this is what the Cross means', he said, tearing his shirt down the front. 'Do you see this scar, gashing the front of my chest? That is what preaching in the mountains of Hunan means, and how many scars do those sitting around you have to show to the world?' he shouted.

'Father Corrado, this unseemly display does not advance the progress of our investigations', the Visitor began, visibly taken aback by the force of Corrado's attack, but Corrado was not going to let him escape so easily. He bared the top of his left arm which had been branded by an overzealous provincial Governor, angered because he thought that the Jesuits had gone further than he thought permitted. He described the beheadings he had witnessed of most of his converts some three years previously. He described how he had been smuggled out in the dead of night before the Imperial troops caught up with him. He spared them no details of the tortures inflicted on those who were not beheaded because of their lowly rank, but rather hung upside down over boiling cauldrons and crucified in front of their families. Knowing he had the initiative at last, he pressed on.

Yes, it was true that the Nestorian heretics had fled to Persia and then on to China. That was centuries ago. Yes, it was true that recently an Imperial inscription had been found recording Nestorian Christians some eight hundred years ago: for the Chinese the antiquity of a doctrine was proof of its truth, and the inscription had been used by some to boost the claims of Christianity generally. What did it really matter that it was the 'wrong' form of Christianity? It had served its purpose. Why should he then destroy that crucial advantage just because of a doctrinal difference which would be totally lost on the Chinese anyway?

'Do you have any idea of the sufferings we go through?' Corrado went on. 'How long have you been in Macao? A few weeks and you think that you can understand them? We have won souls- our Churches are full of them and now you are ready to destroy the work of centuries simply because you fail to look at what is really happening.'

'Father Corrado, I must remind you that this commission of enquiry has received disturbing evidence...'

'What evidence?' Corrado almost shouted. 'Evidence that the Cathedral is packed to the rafters with people rejoicing that we have given them hope and you and your kind are doing everything to destroy that hope'.

'Father Corrado, we are all very aware of the difficulties that missionaries face in these parts. But our task is different. We are here today to fulfil the Holy Father's will. I am sure that you will also want to ensure that the Holy Pontiff's orders are ordered- after all, you have taken a personal vow of obedience to the Pope, have you not?'

'Indeed, Your Grace'.

'Then I am disappointed to have to remind you that this Commission has come to investigate grave charges of heresy, allegations of the grossest doctrinal laxity, and even reports that the missions, entrusted as they are to propagate the word of the Lord, have failed to ....'

But Corrado was no longer listening to the Visitor's long-winded accusations. A glorious sunset filled the windows and he could hear the distant chant of an orphans' procession making its way along the narrow streets.

***

The hour before dawn is the worst part of the night. That is the hour inhabited by nightmares, that is when the imagination is seized by sudden terrors, when the mind is woken by half-realised terrors and when all possible horrors become certainties.

Corrado sat up violently and drew back the curtains, gasping for air. His face was covered with sweat and he was trembling slightly as he gradually emerged from his dream. The moon shone reassuringly across the bay, its rays falling on the waves like a little string of jewels. Corrado breathed in the night air, like a diver who has just come up for air. Gradually, he recovered his composure and his breathing returned to normal.

He got up and doused himself with the pitcher of water on his side table. Then he went out onto the veranda and watched the night scene.

Tomorrow, the Visitor had decided to visit Xie, to 'examine' him, as he had put it- as if Corrado had caught a rare animal to be inspected as a prize exhibit. Corrado shuddered at the thought of the venerable old Mandarin being put through the humiliation of such an interrogation... What on earth had possessed him to tell the Visitor about Xie? To announce that he had almost converted a senior Chinese official, to boast that Xie was living proof that his methods worked? It had come at the end of an interminable day of questioning- attack after attack, insinuation after insinuation, until he could stand it no longer. Until he had shouted defiantly that he had won a soul that day... That while they wasted their time searching for imagined heresies, he Father Corrado, had won a soul for Christ, that he had saved a man from eternal damnation, that one of the most respected figures of the Province had formally asked him for instruction in order to be baptised.

The Visitor had decided that he would arrive in the early afternoon, when the day's heat had begun to fade, 'to inspect the native's understanding', as he had contemptuously put it. Xie would be asked to explain his knowledge of the Catechism in front the Investigatory Commission...

Corrado sat down on the nearby bench and buried his face in his hands. A soul would now be lost and that would be his fault entirely, because of his pride, because of his own lack of humility. Had he kept quiet and simply parried the blows, the Commission would have continued in its futile task and Xie would have been saved. He knew that Xie would feel mortally insulted and that he would immediately break off all relations with Corrado, suspecting that he had been betrayed by his friend, and that this proved the pernicious nature of all the foreign devils that were secretly attempting to conquer China with their religion and their muskets. His son would have been proved triumphantly right and years of patient effort would have been wasted.

Xie's decision to convert had come at the most unexpected moment. That afternoon, Xie had paid Corrado the singular honour of inviting him to participating in the family devotions. Corrado had immediately accepted, sensing that this was the portent of even greater things to come. The whole family came out in the inner courtyard and Corrado pretended to ignore Yizhi loud protests to his father that the foreigner had no business being there. But Xie had insisted, and he saw Yizhi bow his head respectfully to his father. Still, Corrado had had the tact to keep his distance and to stand slightly apart from the rest of the assembled household, behind a pillar. There he was out of Yizhi's sight and he knew that Xie would note and appreciate his friend's sensitivity.

Xie and Yizhi were side by side in front of the rest of the family, standing before the household shrine with its row of statues. The shrine displayed a rather eclectic collection of traditional Confucian, Taoist and Buddhist deities. First, they burned incense in front of the Bodhisattva Gyanyin, a plump figure sitting rather smugly on its pedestal. After a few bows and a few silent prayers, the whole family turned to the next shrine: the Confucian Lord Lin Bei, a third century general who incarnated the Confucian god of war. Led by Yizhi, the whole household recited loud prayers to the fierce looking god, with its splendidly garish fangs and blood-curling weapons. Next, they all turned back to the incense bowl, with its bronze dragon's head belching out thick smoke: again it was Yizhi who led the devotions, acting as if he was rubbing the smoke on his face and arms—which Corrado recognised as a ritual designed to bring good health. But he noticed that Xie stood aside and kept his head bowed, with an expression of deep reverence. Then, when they were done, they all turned towards the Sovereign Lord Zitong, the Taoist god of personal destiny, an elegant figure of ebony with a splendidly impassive smile. Next it was the turn of the Patriarch Lü Dong-bin, and others which Corrado did not recognise...

***

The interview with the Visitor did not last very long.

Xie arrived at the appointed time before the steps of St.Paul's Basilica. Despite his age, he managed to climb with some dignity out of the chair in which he was being carried and then dismissed his servants. The Visitor was standing at the top of the steps, flanked by a retinue of Franciscans, some with their hoods over their faces.

Proudly, Xie decided to climb the steps of the Basilica by himself and refused Corrado's offers of help. Corrado thought it better to stand aside and watch the scene from a distance.

Slowly, Xie ascended the steps towards the Visitor, and Corrado said a few prayers quietly to himself, as if to extinguish any other thoughts. Eventually, Xie reached the entrance of the Basilica and walked towards the Visitor. The Visitor lifted his wide hat with a flourish and Xie responded with a deeply respectful bow.

Corrado knew how anxious Xie had been about his meeting with the Visitor: after all, this would be his first encounter with a person whom Corrado clearly regarded as a superior, and the night before Xie had asked questions about the Church of Rome, how it was organised, how a person became a priest and then a bishop. It was obvious that Xie was discreetly establishing how he should react to the Visitor when he met him.

Corrado watched him advance towards the Visitor. He knew Xie well enough to sense how much the old man was awed by the occasion. At the same time, Xie would make every effort to stress the fact of his own high rank. He knew that to have climbed the steep steps would have cost the old man a huge physical effort, but that he would do his utmost to hide this in order to maintain his dignity. But Corrado also knew that the Visitor would be totally unaware of the subtleties of Chinese comportment.

A very young Franciscan advanced towards Xie and led him respectfully towards the Basilica, but the Mandarin made a point of waiting for the Visitor to go in first with his entourage. As soon as Xie gone inside, Corrado rushed up the steps, his mind in turmoil.

Corrado went in quietly and knelt in one of the side chapels, making himself as inconspicuous as possible. Then he prayed with an intensity that he had never felt before: his eyes fell on the little wooden figure of Saint Francis, and the ornate reliquary under the Cross containing some of the authenticated bones of the Saint. His mind was filled with half-realised fears and sudden rushes of the most total despair. His life had been a total waste, a vast and diabolic travesty of the ideals he pretended to preach, and he would face his approaching death in the knowledge that he had lived a lie. The vast dome of the Basilica was filled with a silence that made him want to scream, to flee, to tear Xie away from his tormentors...

He gazed once more at the figure of Saint Francis, but his prayers were formless, a passionate chaos of half-realised emotions, recited with an utter desperation in his inner voice. Mechanically, as if to bring his raging emotions under control, he started reciting the Pater Noster, the Ave Maria, the Credo-anything to fill the vast and dark void that was opening in front of him.

As he knelt, gradually bringing his convulsed breathing under control, he caught glimpses of the Visitor proceeding with his examination of Xie. The Visitor was nodding gravely as he listened to the old man's answers. Sometimes he would bend forward to Xie and say something privately in his ear. Then the examination would proceed. Occasionally Xie would bow deeply and there would be a moment of silence.

Corrado felt calm enough to stand up now. He stared across the church.

Xie had obviously finished answering the Visitor's questions and was kneeling in front of him. The Visitor rose and addressed Xie whom listened with an expression of awe and total resignation. Then the Visitor made a sign of the Cross over Xie and placed his hands on the old man's head. Xie stood up, bowed once more in deep reverence and the Visitor walked away.

***

It was a full three days before Xie contacted Corrado again.

The invitation came quite suddenly one morning, asking him to come to Xie's villa at once. Fearing that he was ill, or even on his deathbed, Corrado rushed across the hills towards Xie's villa on the fastest horse he could find.

As he turned the corner of the hill, Corrado saw the thick pall of smoke rising from Xie's mansion. After the dry summer months, a wooden house like Xie's would burn up in a flash. He leaped off the horse and ran to the front door and dashed into the courtyard.

The fire was already well advanced, thick smoke bellowing out and high flames darting into the sky. Zhou and Zhentao, now wearing large crucifix necklaces, were busily throwing books into the bonfire in the middle of the courtyard and Corrado could still see the blackened shape of Bodhisattvas and the other votive statues standing in the flames. Scrolls of silk were curling in final exquisite contortions and sheets of paper were thrown up in the air by the force of the blaze, like leaves of ash in the wind. Xie was standing in front of the fire directing the servants which objects should be added to the pyre. The rest of the family watched at a distance while Yizhi stood alone, his head bowed in an attitude of resignation or despair.

Corrado walked forward slowly. Xie heard his steps behind him and turned round. He was no longer dressed in his traditional Mandarin robes, but now wore a long white robe, with a red cross on his chest. In his hands, he was clutching a rosary. He bowed deeply to Corrado and suddenly knelt in front of him, kissing his ring reverentially. Then he asked him for his blessing with a beatific smile on his face.

THE IMPERIAL PROGRESS DOWN THE VOLGA

THE IMPERIAL PROGRESS DOWN THE VOLGA

Ukraine, 1770

'No, my dear Alexander Petrovich, we must go on with this charade. We must go on with it until the Empress either dies' - he made a sign of the Cross theatrically- 'or gets finally bored with the welfare of her devoted subjects'.

He poured himself another glass of hot tea from the samovar which stood incongruously on the makeshift table in the tent. And then he sat back with a satisfied and ironic expression on his face.

The speaker was Captain Mikhael Ivanovitch Voronezh, a young officer of the Imperial Guards, whom all St. Petersburg society was agreed was *un grand succès*. He was the scion of a distinguished family which had faithfully served in the Imperial Household since before the days of Peter the Great. Captain Voronezh had lately returned from Paris and was keen to pepper his conversation with the very latest French expressions- even down to imitating *zézayement*, the slight lisp then affected by courtiers at Versailles. He would, of course, absolutely refuse to count seventy, eighty or ninety in the normal way as *septante*, *huitante* or *nonnante*, but always used the fashionable Parisian affectation of *soixante-dix*, *quatre-vingt* and *quatre-vingt-dix*.

If his companion did not show his irritation at Captain Voronezh's affectations, he certainly felt it. But then it was literally worth more than his life not to humour the young officer of the Imperial Guards. For Captain Voronezh's companion was not dressed in the gold-braided uniform of the Imperial Guards, but instead wore the smock of a lowly Russian peasant, coarse boots and a very worn leather hat: to the untrained eye he was every inch the archetypal Russian *mujik*. He watched enviously with the eye of a hungry man as

Voronezh tucked into another chunk of pheasant. Indeed, he had not eaten anything that day except for a miserable bowl of the traditional Russian peasant's gruel -the ubiquitous *kasha.*

Alexander Petrovich Litvinov knew what pheasant tasted like from the happier days when he had also been a courtier. But that had been a long time ago- before he had killed a rival in a duel and had had the misfortune of being caught, arrested and tried by a new law which had been passed in emulation of all things French- in this case Cardinal Richelieu's law prohibiting duelling. Court wits made the obvious remarks that for the Great Empress Catherine to copy a law dating back over a hundred years to the days of Louis XIII only emphasised the glaring backwardness of the Russians, but to no avail as far as Litvinov was concerned. Disgrace had followed the regrettable incident and the loss of his reputation- or *cachet-* at Court. Nevertheless, his family had enough influence to have him spared the gallows: instead he was condemned to twenty years of hard labour, followed by exile in a remote part of the Urals. Years later, Litvinov had been fortunate enough to meet Voronezh, who miraculously happened to ride through the forest where he was working in a gang of convicts felling trees. Although worn through years of neglect and rough weather, Litvinov's once handsome face had been instantly recognised and he had been rescued by his former friend in the Imperial Academy.

During the long summer evenings, they often had occasion to muse on the vagaries of fate. Voronezh was the same age as Litvinov, his face delicately pomaded and his thin moustache- a rare concession to Russian fashion- exquisitely trimmed, his lips lightly rouged and his soft white hands exhibiting a complete inexperience of manual labour beyond the holding of reins. Litvinov, by contrast, was wrinkled beyond his thirty years of age, and his face bore the marks of several Siberian winters. The notion of him being bewigged and powdered would have been comic unless had been aware of his tragic fate.

'So we dismantle this ridiculous little village *this* afternoon?' Litvinov asked impatiently.

'Yes, my dear friend. This afternoon we dismantle our charming rustic creation: beam by beam, fence by fence, manger by manger. And the day after tomorrow we reassemble it again- but slightly differently- at....let me see...' said Voronezh, consulting a map prepared by his German subaltern, 'at Petrovalsk-Karalkho'. He grimaced ostentatiously. 'These Ukrainian names, they are really quite unpronounceable'. Then he picked up his knife and slowly cut a wafer-thin slice of pheasant breast and ate it, his eyes half-closed with private pleasure.

'Consider yourself fortunate' he continued, 'Petro... whatever it is called ...is only twenty *versts* away, that's a short journey compared to yesterday. If we work quickly, we could have dismantled the whole thing by nightfall and by breakfast tomorrow we'll have reached our destination and built the next rustic little idyll by noon. The Empress will arrive sometime after lunch, and she'll be in good humour if she has eaten well. *And'*, he said with a dramatic flourish of the hand, I have good news for you. The day after tomorrow, Her Imperial Highness intends to spend the night at Donezhk- at Count von Himmendorf's estate- for a day's hunting and lechery. So we'll all have a day of rest.'

At that point, the huge roar of a crowd filled the air. Litvinov went out of the tent. Although he had seen the scene a dozen times before, he could never quite resist the sight of the Imperial passage
.

This time, they had built the village on a hill, on a bend in the river. They had built it there, partly because Captain Voronezh thought it looked picturesque- 'so like one of those charming landscapes by Claude I saw in Fontainebleau'- and partly

137

because, at that distance from the Imperial flotilla slowly making its way down the Volga, the hurried nature of the construction would not be recognised. Litvinov thought that their workmanship had become so routine of late as to be almost slapdash: the Empress would soon discover the fraud.

But this time she evidently didn't.

He immediately spotted the Empress, in her magnificent pink dress, with a pretty display of lace around her fleshy neckline and her elaborately braided hair. She was sitting between Prince Potemkin (all azure blue and gold) and a corpulent official fawning at her side. The official handed her a field glass to examine the village and the villagers. Exactly on cue, as she raised her field glass, the well-trained 'peasantry' produced another magnificent and hearty roar. 'Long live the Empress Katerina! Hurrah! Hurrah!'

On this occasion Captain Voronezh had taken the whole charade a step further by having a traditional Ukrainian welcoming cake baked and brought over in a barge by three suitably rustic-looking convicts. The boat set out, two convict-peasants rowing and a pretty young girl, dressed in a naïve simplicity that would have charmed Marie-Antoinette herself, presenting the cake on a wooden plate. Further shouts of 'hurrah!' and 'long live the Empress Katerina' resounded over the scene, as the boat slowly inched its way up to the Imperial barge.

Yes, thought Litvinov, Captain Voronezh had perhaps taken a risk in building the village so hurriedly. What if the Empress suddenly decided to inspect the village? The Imperial itinerary did not take into account the architectural difficulties of making sure that prefabricated villages would emerge at convenient locations, filled with enthusiastic and prosperous peasantry. Nevertheless, the welcoming cake was a clever touch, ensuring that the Empress' attention would be diverted at the moment when she would have been closest to the village and therefore most likely to notice that the belfry was visibly tilting off-centre.

Suddenly, Litvinov was seized with uncontrollable joy. 'I have it!' he almost shouted in his joy, 'I have it!'

In a flash, he had found a way of gaining his freedom. He would prove to the Empress that she was being elaborately and monstrously duped by her lover and chief minister, Prince Gregor Alexandrovich Potemkin. He would be reinstated, his past misdeeds forgiven by a grateful monarch- who knows, he might be promoted to the post of trusted *confidant*- anywhere but away from this Sisyphean world of make-believe, in which he played an insignificant part.

Then he thought the better of it. No, it would be too risky. He might be misheard, he might be misunderstood, or even stopped.

Better to wait for the appropriate moment, when the Empress would be riding close by. He would then throw himself in front of her, endanger his life to get a hearing by leaping in front of her horse. He would brave the bodyguard of Cossacks to demonstrate his devotion to the Empress.

He watched the Empress's flotilla take a slow turn around the bend of the river and roared with laughter.

***

The journey had been as easy as Captain Voronezh had predicted: the entire contingent of six hundred and twenty three 'villagers' and their cattle- a well-scrubbed herd of Friesland cattle and several splendid shire horses imported all the way from England, not forgetting a few hounds from Alsace- moved

139

rapidly along the easy road to Petrovalsk-Karalkho after dawn. As they advanced towards the little meadow where they were to construct the village for that day, Litvinov felt a heady sense of impending freedom, like a swimmer who sees land at last within his sight. He tried not to show it- convicts must not show enthusiasm if they want to avoid attracting suspicion. Nevertheless, he woke up as the first rays were parting night from day. He got up energetically. Whereas, before, the cold dampness of the ground he had slept on would have extracted a series of oaths and coughs, today he did not curse and he did not cough. He could hardly suppress the smile on his lips.

He went for a walk and breathed great gulps of fresh country air, and thought that the dull undulating landscape before his eyes was the most beautiful sight in the world.

He almost felt like praying.

The other convicts were beginning to get up, and as far as the eye could see, in the half-light, fumbling figures emerged coughing, cursing and shuffling from their makeshift bags and tents towards the few campfires which were still alight and blew on the ashes. Shouts could be heard in the damp morning air, grey with the cold dawn and the wood smoke of slightly damp logs hastily thrown over fires. In the distance, Litvinov could hear orders being bellowed out from the officers' quarters. He paced impatiently, waiting for this miserable mass of humanity to shake itself out of its torpor.

After an eternity, they set off, soldiers posted on either side of the long column of prisoners to prevent escapes- but it was hard to imagine who would be foolish enough to want to do so. After all, here you were at least fed and clothed after a fashion and that was better than returning to the cold wastes of Siberia or worse if you were caught. Besides, Litvinov only had a decade left to serve-just ten years. Next time, if he got into

140

trouble again, he would not be able to use to use what remained of his family influence to save his neck.

It got hot early that morning as they began building the village at a sleepy curve in the river. There was a road on the other bank along which the Empress was destined to ride- Captain Voronezh always taking the precaution of keeping some distance between the Imperial train and the "village" being inspected.

That day, Voronezh had ordered yet another variation on the design of the village. He was clever enough to realise that successful deception relies on playing on the preconceived ideas of the person being deceived. It was an *idée reçue* at Court that all villages exhibited certain fundamental characteristics. 'It is essential' he would explain 'that there be a few neat thatch barns and cottages but they should not always be in the same configuration. We must ensure that the *trompe l'oeil* is genuine. The village water well must be differently positioned every time. The village school must be moved around and the colour of the doors must alternate between red, blue and brown, but not every time'.

Litvinov began to think that Voronezh actually enjoyed his almost daily exercise in architectural fantasy. It never ceased to amaze Litvinov that the Empress Catherine could actually be taken in by the deception. Why did she not talk to the villagers, asking them about their crops or talk to the charming little children who sprayed her with flowers as she went past? The countryside was in a desperate state, worn down by years of war and taxation. Last year's harvest had failed and there were reports of starvation in the western Ukraine. An Empress' Chief Minister always sits uneasily in his office: but it was a mark of Potemkin's desperation that he had to resort to this elaborate stratagem to dupe the Empress that all was well in the countryside.

Sooner or later, she would find out and heads would roll. Litvinov therefore had little time to seize his chance and be the faithful subject who bravely expose the elaborate fraud at great threat to himself - for the ruthless and deceitful courtiers who surrounded the Empress would stop at nothing to save their own skins. He would have to choose his moment with extreme care, he reflected, as he helped to strap a panel of pre-prepared thatch roofing over a barn. The burly Pole who was his work companion shouted at him to watch what he was doing or the whole thing would collapse. He swore back at him but realised that the brute was right: the two parts of the roof were wide apart and the left hand post holding everything up was at a dangerous angle. If he was not careful, the entire barn would come down on the three men working below nailing in the walls.

'Faster, you scum!' a sergeant bellowed at them, pushing an old woman back to her work. He brandished his horsewhip. 'You over there, what the devil are you doing? The whole thing's about to fall down!'

Litvinov prayed that Sergeant Volkdorff was not referring to him. Like all German mercenaries, Volkdorff was proverbially stupid and brutal, and Litvinov's back still had the scars to prove it. Those lashes had been for losing a barrel of apples- a genuine loss, but Litvinov had been blamed for the suspected theft and not even his friendship with Captain Voronezh could save him from the *'passage à tabac'*- an absurd name for an extremely unpleasant French military punishment, consisting of a gauntlet of two rows of whip-brandishing soldiers along which the unfortunate victim was forced to progress, lashed at every step until he fainted.

A tremendous crack of wood was heard and Litvinov instinctively prepared himself to jump off the roof, thinking his precarious edifice was about to collapse beneath him. Instead, it was the church, about which Sergeant Volkdorff had been rightly alarmed. Litvinov craned his neck just in time to see the belfry slowly collapse to the ground, bringing down its hapless assemblers in the process. There were howls of pain amidst the dust and the falling debris, as people rushed to the scene. One man- a thief from Kiev- was badly injured, his leg horribly gashed by having fallen straight onto the railings. There was a great commotion as he was carried off, screaming imprecations to his mother and the Virgin Mary, while crowds of soldiers and 'villagers' milled about heaving beams of wood, examining the damage and clearing it all up hurriedly.

Captain Voronezh now arrived on the scene and went into and incandescent rage at the thought that the village church would not be complete for the Imperial visit. Sergeant Volkdorff was given a monumental dressing down for not properly overseeing the *canaille* under his care: he stood stiffly to attention, reddening deeper all the time until he became almost comical- but none of the 'villagers' laughed, knowing full well that Sergeant Volkdorff would to take it out on them as soon as the Captain had left.

Voronezh bellowed out his orders at the crowd of convicts. The Empress would arrive by noon. If the village was not ready, they would all be sent off to the mines, where few if any would survive a year- a fate they each richly deserved. Not a second was to be wasted in getting the village ready for the Imperial visit. He ordered the church to be removed: if the Empress asked why the otherwise prosperous village had no place of worship, she would be informed that the inhabitants were Ukrainian Catholics and thus subversively dissident of the Holy Orthodox Church of all Russia, of which she was the most glorious Protector and that the heretics were not to be allowed their own place of Popish worship. Meanwhile, Voronezh sent the church to the regimental Sappers to be repaired. They were ordered to work through the night, if need be: on no account was there to be no church in tomorrow's village. Sergeant Volkdorff clicked his heels, his face by now as scarlet as the beetroot soup so prized by his countrymen, and he began to shout his orders so loud that Captain Voronezh would hear his orders being faithfully repeated, however far he might be.

Litvinov looked up to the hills on his left. Tomorrow morning, the Empress was due to come down from there, riding a horse or more probably she would be in a coach. She would have to slow down as she rounded this part of the road, thought Litvinov. That was the only place when he would realistically have a chance of leaping forward and prostrating himself in front of the Imperial Presence and revealing the appalling deception that had been perpetrated on her. He practised his speech mentally, knowing that it would have to start dramatically: he would not be given much time either by the Cossacks or the likes of Captain Voronezh. He would have to grab her attention with the first sentence: 'Your Majesty! You are being deceived!' No that would not do. It had to be something more arresting, he decided, heaving the final panel of the roof into place. How about: 'Stop! In the name of Holy Russia!' No, that would not do either. He would be carted off as a lunatic. Then he had it: 'Empress Katerina! Chancellor Potemkin is a liar!' Yes, that was better. Dramatic. To the point. And effective.

He smiled.
'Looks good, eh?' said the burly Pole, interpreting Litvinov's smile as one of satisfaction at their morning's work.
'What?'
'The barn. Looks great'.
'Oh yes, the barn. It looks splendid'.

***

144

Miraculously, everything was indeed ready when the Empress appeared the next morning.

Litvinov decided to manoeuvre himself closer and closer to the edge of the crowd, near to the road so that he would be able to make a quick desperate dash when the coach came round the corner. The crowd roared louder this time and his heart thumped inside him as he got closer.

Another roar.

Litvinov became intoxicated with the vision of his sudden heroic dash in front of the Empress, perhaps even leaping up on the coach's footrest and grabbing the door handle, shouting 'Empress Katerina! Chancellor Potemkin is a liar!' He would have to be quick, because a Cossack would be certain to take him for a would-be assassin and cut him down with his sword.

In a few moments, Litvinov knew he would either be dead or showered with glory.

Then he caught sight of the coach making its way in the pretty village square they had constructed by the school: from there the coach would have to turn left and go up the street where he was standing. He got himself into position.
'Litvinov!' a voice shouted. It was Voronezh. 'Get that rabble shouting! What's the matter with them? Have they lost their voice?' Voronezh was on horseback with five foot soldiers following him. It was hopeless. The opportunity was lost.
'Come with me', said Voronezh. 'I'll have them all whipped! They'll answer for this!'

Litvinov had no option but to follow the platoon of soldiers. His heart sank in despair as he was forced to dragoon the other 'peasants' into rousing choruses under the watchful eye of Voronezh. At first apathetically, but with a growing enthusiasm based on fear, the villagers roused themselves into a frenzy of cheering at exactly the moment when the Empress' coach turned the corner.

Captain Voronezh took off his wide-brimmed military hat with a magnificent flourish *à la francaise*, as the peasantry boomed out their applause. Litvinov could not be sure that Voronezh's face was red with pleasure or anger, but he cheered on for all he was worth, anxious lest his next opportunity might be denied to him.

'Long live our Empress Katerina!' he roared at the top of his voice during a sudden lull in the cheering. He was lucky, as at that very moment, the Empress was graciously pleased to look out of her carriage and was visibly moved by the naïve devotion of one of her subjects. She gave him a little coquettish smile and pointed out Litvinov to her companion inside the coach. Litvinov's heart leaped into his mouth: he had been marked out by a smile from the Empress. He broke through the crowd, running after the Imperial Coach. Intoxicated by the prospect that his freedom was so close at hand, he ran like a hare after the Empress, shouting 'Long live our great Empress!... Long live Katerina!... Katerina!' like a desperate lover. For a second, the memory of his first cell in the Urals came to his mind: a sudden vision of his shackles being removed as he was dumped on the stinking straw, a fleeting glimpse of that first morning when the cold immensity around him drove home all the harder the vastness of his isolation, a solitude which made the remoteness from his previous courtier's life all the crueller. All this flashed in front of his eyes like a dream and still he was running behind the coach, shouting 'Katerina!' He did not even notice the Cossack who had started his horse after him, feeling for his sword to strike down the impudent wretch who was daring to come near the Empress.

Afterwards, he would always remember the face of the Empress Catherine, suddenly peering through the coach window to look at the devoted peasant who was running so enthusiastically behind his Sovereign. She smiled again, looking at Litvinov's face of contorted agony as he kept up with the carriage shouting her name like a chant. Then she brought out one of the bouquets which a "villager" had thrown to her and tossed a flower to Litvinov.

The coach sped away. Litvinov picked up the flower, mesmerised. The Cossack's horse careered to a halt with a loud snort, as it was reined in by its rider. Litvinov was confusedly aware of cheering and of shouting all around him. He held the flower with a beatific expression, oblivious to the Cossack who swore at him to keep his place.

Now he had caught the eye of the Empress. Tomorrow, she would recognise him, tomorrow he would be granted an audience and tomorrow he would be free...

***

'*Mon cher ami, vous êtes devenu complètement fou*', said Voronezh, offering Litvinov a spiced quail's egg.

Litvinov was suspicious of his friend's attention: Captain Voronezh did not normally share out his gastronomic privileges, as if this stressed his rank further. 'Running like that- you have turned into one of them, a *mujik*- the part has gone to your head', he said, with obvious disgust. His words struck Litvinov like an axe: the thought that the afternoon's incident would remove him from the next day's village building filled him with a desperation bordering on violence.

He threw caution to the winds: 'The Empress appreciated a bit of personal devotion. She must grow tired of peasantry cheering her at a distance. She threw me a flower. She smiled. We produced what she wanted.'

Captain Voronezh produced his most sardonic smile:
'Next, you are going to propose that we assemble the villagers in line for her personal inspection'.
'Why not? Why shouldn't the Empress have personal contact with her subjects?'
'Don't be absurd', said Voronezh, 'she would instantly recognise that they are the same peasants village after village'.
'You think she hasn't already noticed?'
'My dear Alexander Petrovich, you have been a convict for too long. It has probably infected *my* mind as well as yours, all this contact with the *petit peuple*. But then, I rejoice in the thought that in exactly two months' time, I shall be back in St.Petersburg and away from the lot of you'.

Litvinov stood rooted to the spot with fear. The thought that soon his only protector would be gone, that he would be thrown back in the universe of the convicts filled him with an animal terror, a vision of perpetual night...
'In two months' time?' he blurted out involuntarily. 'But...'

He stopped.

Voronezh looked up, genuinely surprised.
'You don't seriously expect me to spend the rest of my days in this absurd charade, do you? I intend to flee this *limbo* as quickly as I can', he said, pronouncing *limbo* with an affected Italianate accent.
'Mon cher ami, ce sera bientôt adieu', he added, carefully shelling another pretty quail's egg.
Litvinov watched the eggshell falling delicately into a heap of speckled brown flakes.

'*Lente, currite, noctis equi*' said Voronezh and then added to Litvinov's impotent anger by providing his own commentary on Horace's line: 'Perhaps the finest line of Latin poetry, I think.
'Slowly, run, ye horses of the night'... Voronezh translated, and

148

then acknowledged that Russian did not allow the economy of phrase of Latin. 'Such a wonderfully alliterative line, don't you think? And so wonderfully expressive of the slow passage of darkness. The Mediterranean mind is much more poetic than the Slav', he concluded.

Litvinov only just succeeded in controlling his internal fury.

Captain Voronezh swallowed his egg and then yawned.

' Come along, mon cher. We must rise at dawn. I must ask you to leave'.

He blew the candle out.

***

The village was now ready. The belfry had been repaired during the night, and now sported a weather vane made of wood. This time, the village was an ambitious construction, with an attempt at depicting a boat station for Volga traffic.

To Litvinov's surprise, Voronezh had accepted his suggestion. He had decided that the Empress might want to come onshore and be saluted by a chorus of Ukrainian peasant girls in full costume.

The weather was perfect, a slight breeze preventing the hot summer winds from the Volga plains from being oppressive. The sky was blue and vast, the low lying landscape making the orb of the sky appear all the vaster.

Most of the villagers stood on the banks of the river, ready to shout their welcome to the Empress when she appeared. A few, however, were posted in front of the houses and, as an extra touch to set the tone, Voronezh had deployed the full herd of Friesland cows on the lush meadow in front of the village.

Litvinov was lucky that day. He was posted in front of the village school, this time positioned next to the church by the

149

quay. Mentally, he rehearsed his speech. He was still trying to perfect it. 'Empress Katerina', he would suddenly declare bursting through the throng of the young village girls welcoming the Empress as she disembarked at the quayside, 'Empress Katerina, you are surrounded by liars and deceivers. Nothing in this village is true. It is all an elaborate lie'. No, that last sentence would not do. 'They are lying to you', he would say, kneeling dramatically in front of the Empress 'we are not peasants at all. I am a convict from Siberia, forced to act out this lie. Empress Katerina, forgive my impudence, but I must speak out against those who deceive you.' That would not do. He must not lose the advantage of surprise after dramatically announcing: 'we are not peasants'. He must shout: 'this is all a lie! This village was built this morning to deceive you'.

Yes, that was good.

Litvinov surveyed the square in front of him. It was no more than twenty yards across. The Empress would go up those steps from the quay and would be met by the young girls just there. He would then shout out the Empress' name and rush forward. Luckily, the square was too small for there to be many Cossacks. At most, it would be only Volkdorff and a few of his German troopers. Yes, his chance was now, if it ever was.

***

A tremendous chorus rent the air as the Imperial ship reached the village. The Volga was not so wide at this point but it was still a mighty river, and the banks on the other side were hardly visible in the haze of the afternoon heat. The ship neared the quayside and a gallant troop of Horseguards cantered along the river bank, saluting with their hats. The Empress was moved to respond with a little wave of the hand, which provoked a series of hearty 'hurrahs!' from the Horseguards. The ship approached further and Litvinov, his heart pounding with excitement,

150

pressed forward. He looked round to gauge the position of the soldiers. He had been right. The Cossacks had been deployed on the higher ground in a semi-circle, suddenly sending out a martial roar of greeting, to which the 'villagers' responded with an even louder roar.

Litvinov spotted Voronezh on his horse, giving instructions to his subalterns. Good, he was far away. Meanwhile, the Imperial vessel made for the quayside and he could see Prince Potemkin helping the Empress up on the gangplank, ready to berth. Litvinov got closer and mentally rehearsed his speech one last time. The girls in front of him raised a shrill chorus.

The Empress' boat was almost at the quay. A strange calm came over Litvinov as he waited to strike. The Empress slowly ascended the steps. She was splendidly attired, in a blue summer *chiffon* because of the heat, while her lover, Prince Potemkin, all in white, looked like a handsome page.

Suddenly, Litvinov spotted Voronezh, pointing him out to Volkdorff, giving him instructions. Obviously, he was determined to prevent a repetition of Litvinov's unseemly demonstration of feudal devotion. Litvinov dashed forward as the Imperial vessel berthed to a tremendous chorus of praise. He knew that Volkdorff and his soldiers would not have time to stop him.

A series of shots filled the air, and the Empress stopped in her tracks, looking in the direction of Voronezh, who was brandishing a pistol. The whole village stood still, and the smoke from the pistol floated as if in ethereal silence. The Cossacks immediately responded in kind and let off their pistols: a tremendous fusillade drowned all other sounds and the troops followed this by a volcanic 'Hurrah! Katerina!'

Before Litvinov could advance, Volkdorff was on him, pinning him to the ground with all his weight. 'Katerina!' he blurted out but another soldier kicked him in the stomach, and sent him reeling down the back of the square.

The Empress smiled graciously as the Cossacks all fired their second pistols in a further patriotic salvo. Then the whole village cheered again.

Litvinov's shouts were drowned as he was led away.

***

'Tell me, *mon cher*, did you seriously imagine that I would ever let you get anywhere near the Empress again?' Voronezh said, as Litvinov stood to attention in front of him in his tent later that evening.
'Why do you think that this was my intention?'
'It was perfectly clear that you were desperate', said Voronezh lighting a clay pipe.

There was a pause.

'She will find out, you know'.
'Find out what?'
'That you have duped her. You may send me back to Siberia, but too many people know. The secret is bound to come out sooner or later and when she finds out, what will you do then? You, a young man of such promise, will be finished. You will be put into the same bag as Potemkin- he cannot last forever. Sooner or later, all favourites fall from favour.'

Voronezh looked at him, and suddenly exploded with genuine laughter.

'I see', he said, and then he burst out in another fit of laughter. 'Now I understand! *C'est délicieux!*' he said, wiping real tears of genuine laughter from his eyes and shook with uncontrollable

laughter again. 'You really believe it is all true?'
'What?' asked Litvinov.
'This. The village. Everything'.
'Well...yes...'.
'*Mon cher ami*', he laughed again. 'I owe you an apology. I thought you knew.' He laughed again: '*C'est parfaitement charmant!*'
Suddenly, his face became serious. 'You do not seriously imagine that the Empress of All Russia relies *exclusively* on her Counsellor, Prince Potemkin? The first maxim of any ruler is to be wary of over mighty subjects'.
Litvinov barely listened as Voronezh continued his explanation. Everything became a blur.
'The Empress knows, *mon cher ami*. The Empress knows. It is a most amusing spectacle seeing the Prince Marshall Potemkin thinking he is so clever that he has duped the Empress with so obvious a trick. The Empress has her faithful servants who inform her of the true position', he said with ill-disguised pride.
Suddenly, Litvinov understood the whole ghastly trick.

There was a long silence, broken only by the sound of a gust of wind outside.

Captain Voronezh looked up, suddenly noticing Litvinov's white face, an expressionless picture of despair. He smiled indulgently.

'*Allons, mon cher.* I promise I shall put in a good word for you! It is about time you returned to the Court.'

Then he roared with laughter again.
'It is really too amusing that you genuinely thought the Empress was taken in by Count Potemkin's villages!'

He chuckled again. Then, overtaken with pity, he invited Litvinov to sit down. He offered him a glass of his finest

English port, a special present from the English Ambassador in St.Petersburg and repeated his promise that he would do his best to obtain a pardon for him.

***

Early the next morning, Prince Potemkin had a meeting with his most trusted aide-de-camp, Captain Voronezh of the Imperial Guards. The young officer was proud to inform His Excellency that all subversive elements among the "villagers" had now been dealt with and that he could guarantee that everything would run smoothly the next time the Empress visited a village, (this time a pretty *kholkoz* set in a charming Ukrainian valley).

'I can assure your Excellency that the imbecile now genuinely believes that the Empress is in the know and that the whole thing is merely one of her elaborate games. But nothing must be left to chance. I have therefore ensured that tomorrow he will be despatched to Siberia.'

THE MARRIAGE OF COUNTESS ISABELLA

THE MARRIAGE OF COUNTESS ISABELLA

Mantua, 1610

He had never been into the private rooms of the palace.

The whole room was a dazzling display of colours, swirling shapes and fantastic creatures. The floor was covered with concentric circles of brightly coloured tiles that twisted and turned outwards from a central point, eventually reaching the four walls of the room. There the *trompe l'oeil* effect continued as the pattern of the tiles imperceptibly changed from squares to lozenges, and then into the leaves of thick foliage painted on the walls. Beyond this, the forest thinned out to reveal a gentle pastoral scene of shepherds and nymphs cavorting gracefully with only a hint of sexual ambiguity. And above that, as the ultimate display of the painter's skill, the ceiling represented the clouds parting to reveal the heavens- a dome receding into infinity. There, set against a background of brilliant sunlight, a flock of exquisite cherubs fluttered around classical gods looking down at humanity with grave expressions.

Arlequino- or 'Quino', as he was known to everyone- craned his misshapen neck backwards to admire these wonders. He smiled his slightly grotesque smile as he noticed Vulcan in the process of throwing down a javelin at the spectators below, the weapon frozen into eternal immobility by the artist's imagination.

He felt oddly ill at ease at having been summoned there by Countess Isabella. The fact that he was a dwarf helped of course. Indeed his good fortune was to be a particularly oddly shaped dwarf, with a hump on his back and an amusing crab-like motion as he manoeuvred across a room. Collecting dwarves was all the rage in European courts these days and, like the Dukes of Mantua, Count Arnolfo had ordered an entire wing of his palace to be built for his diminutive subjects. There his courtiers could amuse themselves visiting the dwarfish apartments on all fours, admiring the miniature apartments, the amusingly tiny glassware on the tables, the infant-size beds. Count Arnolpho's collection included Italian dwarves, French dwarves, even turban wearing Turkish dwarves brought back from a trading mission to Istanbul. Rumour even had it that the Count had positively ruined himself purchasing a priceless Swedish dwarf...

Quino walked across the tiled floor. The whirlpool of red, green and blue tiles made him feel slightly dizzy as it expanded in great swirling circles of colour towards the walls. He looked up again: this time his eye noticed that the dome had a colonnaded gallery, in which the artist had painted passers-by nonchalantly gazing at those down below in the room. It all seemed impossibly high up, so much height, so much space under the vast sphere of an illusory dome that merely existed because of the painter's surpassing mastery.

Countess Isabella was seated on a divan in the middle of the room, directly below the cupola.
'Quino', she said.
The dwarf was uncertain whether the tone of her voice was a cry for help.
Countess Isabella was beautiful, but her beauty was of a rather particular kind: depending on her mood, her angular features could make her look as austere as the faces in those Spanish portraits which were all the rage at court. At other times, she could look fragile to the point of innocence and one would be suddenly reminded of her mere fifteen years of age. But she wore the thickly ornamented dresses of the current fashions with a gravity and poise well beyond her years. It was also said that her conversation exhibited a learning that was really quite astonishing for a lady, and that the real reason why she had rejected the hand of the Count of Valois was that he could not recite Petrarch or Ariosto as passionately as she liked.

All this only made her imminent marriage to the Grand Duke Ladislas of Cracow even more tragic. True, the Polish aristocracy had adopted Italian ways ever since the Medicis had exported their less attractive surplus daughters over there. The Poles were fervent Catholics, built their palaces in the Italian style and even their word for tomato was *'pomo d'oro'*- as Quino had frivolously pointed out to Isabella to cheer her up at the prospect of living through the Polish winter, only to regret his flippancy when he received a sharp thwack of her fan for his impertinence.

That it was a grand match, there could be no doubt. It would create a strong ally just to the East of the increasingly powerful German Empire, and should the so-called 'Holy' Roman Emperor decide to assert his territorial ambitions in the rich valleys of Northern Italy, the Poles could be relied upon to open up a second front. The Grand Dukes of Cracow were of the highest blood, being related to the Dukes of Burgundy and the Princes of Savoy, and having vast estates in the wooden hinterland of southern Poland. Ladislas was a very fine figure of a man, tall, with a sweep of brown hair and clear blue eyes that fixed its prey at the hunt with a steely hardness. He was a fine dancer too, with a real talent for the complicated steps of the Bourre, the Passepied and the Sarabande. He had also seen battle, having bravely fought at several battles in the forests of Lithuania, where the Poles were now rivalling the Muscovites for control of the Baltic ports. He was courteous, well-mannered and spoke good French and very passable Italian. In all respects, the match would enhance the prestige of the House, and yet...

'Yes, my Lady', he answered.

Isabella looked up at him with one of her piercing stares. Although her eyes were slightly too large for such a finely shaped face, their dark expressive colour had enchanted so many suitors.

But not for the Grand Duke, of that Quino was certain: indeed their forthcoming marriage was all the more tragic because these two magnificent beings felt no attraction for each other. They were like two perfectly proportioned statues which somehow jarred if exhibited in the same room. Yet go ahead the wedding must and that in three days' time. Quino felt helpless before his mistress' palpable despair.

'Tonight, there will be a dance', she said, 'and I want you to do me a service.'

Quino bowed respectfully and awaited his instructions.

'I want you to observe the Chevalier de Hierant.'

'Yes, my Lady.'

'You'll easily recognise him. He normally wears a sword with a golden cross on its handle.'

'I think I know who you mean.'

'I want you to observe what he does and report to me.'

'Yes, my Lady.'

Quino bowed respectfully and immediately understood. He was amazed at how quickly Countess Isabella had learned the deadly rules of life at court. Courts were harsh environments and to survive you had to learn all the skills of a dog in a fighting pit. The Countess might only be fifteen but she had already learnt to play the ruthless game of intrigue with a finesse that betrayed the Medici blood she had inherited on her mother's side. The whole scheme was perfectly obvious: if Quino could find out enough about the Grand Duke, she might be able to escape her ghastly marriage altogether. And what better way to do that than to start with the Grand Duke's closest *confidant*, the Chevalier de Hierant? That way, Quino would discover some indiscretion- if he was lucky he might actually catch the thick-set Polish brute in *flagrante delicto*. He suppressed a smile as he said:

'I'll go straightaway.'

***

160

One of the advantages of being a dwarf was that nobody took you seriously enough to be worried if you came into the room. Quino could thus observe people off their guard and, if he witnessed anything compromising, he would produce a little pirouette and a quip, and then roll grotesquely out of the room to echoes of laughter, but with his knowledge intact.

Quino despised the Chevalier, who represented everything he hated about modern courts, with their dashing young men and the latest fashions of the French Court dictating their every movement. The Chevalier de Hierant was indeed one of those dashing young men, a man as famous for his skills as a duellist as he was admired as a horseman. He had seen the Chevalier whoring and drinking; he had seen him brutalising a servant and the next moment producing a flourished bow to a passing dignitary. He had even seen him half naked in his bath, and knew that the Chevalier was not beyond abusing the privilege of his rank with the female members of the local peasantry.

***

A few hours later, Quino took a few hesitant steps in the splendidly lit gardens. He was dressed as a cupid, with little golden wings attached to his feet which made running awkward, and he had been made to carry a ridiculous little bow, painted in gold leaf. His costume as also made of gold coloured cloth so that he positively glowed in the light of the torches that lit the gardens.

The musicians had started to play and everywhere servants were busily carrying trays of cooked meats, elaborately decorated platters of cakes, large baskets overflowing with fruits of all kinds and colours. Gossip from the kitchens had it that the *coup de théatre* of the festivities would be a peacock sculpted from a block of ice which had been kept well hidden in the coldest cellars of the Palace.

He knew he would find them by the Hall of Columns, that magnificent room on the ground floor of the Palace, with its large windows looking onto the gardens. The columns, spaced out at twenty pace intervals, were made of the finest Carrara marble, with a slight pink hue that softly reflected the light of the candle stands. Above the grand staircase, he could see the musicians with their lutes, their theorbs and their viols: in front of them were two young men and a woman dressed in golden silk with green sashes, (the colours of the Countess), singing in front of the orchestra which was dressed in the white and red colours of the Polish Crown, as an oblique compliment to the Bridegroom.

Then he spotted the Grand Duke himself. He was standing in the centre of a group of courtiers: the Chevalier de Hierant stood outside the main group, looking in the distance with a slightly bored expression on his face. When a couple of ladies walked close by, the Chevalier made a slight bow but his expression hardly changed. He had a hard face, Quino decided, the face of an opportunist, the face of exactly the sort of venomous professional courtier whom he would take the greatest of pleasure in exposing as a vice-ridden snake. He watched him for a while from a distance and observed how the *confidant* eyed the oafish figure of the Grand Duke like a falcon homes in on its prey.

Quino decided to get close to the circle around the Grand Duke. And there once again, being a court dwarf gave you a certain advantage: you could go straight into the women's room and no-one would throw you out, and you could even run into the King's bedchamber and all you would risk would be a kick up the arse.

Nevertheless a court dwarf always remained an outsider, he was neither courtier nor servant, neither man or woman: he was only a figure of fun, even if Quino probably knew more about life in the Palace than any 'normal' human.

He pirouetted as grotesquely as he could manage towards the Grand Duke and finished with a little cartwheel deliberately aimed at jostling the burly figure of Countess Isabella's future spouse. The he clapped his hands and produced a particularly raucous laugh which he knew would amuse everyone, and brandished his fake lyre to intone an obscene little ditty. Everyone was highly amused and the Grand Duke lifted him up good-naturedly by the waist, like a toy. He had immensely strong arms which locked onto Quino so hard that he almost cried out in pain. As he was lifted up, Quino winced as he tried to imagine how delicate little Isabella would survive in his embraces. He would have dwelt further on the fate of a woman forced to satisfy the lust of her drunken lord, but his thoughts were rudely interrupted as he was spun twice upside down in the Pole's powerful grip and then gently brought down to the floor to general applause. Quino artfully rolled away and re-emerged through the legs of a courtier and scuttled off. He would only come back after a few moments, as he knew from experience that a court dwarf should keep his mysterious distance.

***

The moment he had been waiting for came unexpectedly early. The pack around the Grand Duke had now reached the main courtyard, where a fountain jutted out of a vast Roman head of Neptune. Its jets glittered in the lights of the hundreds of torches, making the waters sparkle in the darkness like a fantastic display of jewellery. There were many courtiers there, in their finest attire, all crowding around to admire the beauty of the gardens now lit up by so many flames that it looked as if day had been created out of night.

The procession of gallants and courtesans that followed the Grand Duke now came into view and the crowd parted to gaze admiringly at so much youthful elegance. Somewhere inside, the musicians struck up a stately *pavane*. The music wafted into the gardens through the hall's large windows, which had been opened in the evening air. Quino hid behind one of the columns that flanked the outside of the Palace and watched the Grand Duke and the Chevalier like an archer following his target. At first, it was the usual round of empty court frivolities, the courtiers bowing and flourishing plumed hats. There was much laughter at something the Grand Duke said to a lady in a red silk dress, and then- of all people- the Papal Nuncio decided to demonstrate what remained of his youthful vigour by leading an impromptu dance around the fountain.

Throughout all this, the Chevalier appeared distant, even melancholic, as he stood aside and watched the crowd from a distance. It was as if he was observing them on the orders of somebody else. He seemed to watch the Grand Duke with an expression of contempt, even of hatred. But had not Isabella said that the Chevalier was his closest friend? If someone came up to him to exchange some pleasantry, he would nod, or even bow graciously, but somehow always keeping his eyes fixed on the Grand Duke. It was as if he was judging him, as if he was measuring each of his movements for some mysterious purpose only known to himself. Then the Papal Nuncio's dancing party coiled itself around him, making a circle around the Chevalier, who was visibly uncomfortable at the whole business but was doing his best to look amused, but his obvious discomfiture only provoked further laughter. Round and round they went, now making two concentric circles and the Chevalier was well and truly trapped. At last, the partners changed hands and the Chevalier seized the opportunity to dash through the momentarily unjoined arms of the dancers.
Quino watched him looking this way and that, desperately looking for someone. Quino guessed that he must be looking for the Grand Duke. Had he also been sent out on a spying mission? And by whom? By Isabella? By her father, Count Arnolfo? And to what purpose?
Quino looked around for the Grand Duke's burly figure. His attention had been momentarily distracted by the incident of the

dance and now the Grand Duke was nowhere to be seen. Quino scuttled around the garden, his little winged sandals and cape causing much merriment. He adroitly avoided being caught by a gang of ruffians who wanted to show him off to a group of giggling Spanish ladies, but he was both too quick and too small for them, darting behind a statue and under a hedge, clutching his little crown of golden ivy leaves as he did so. Then he darted across the Hall of Columns and made for the Hall of the Seasons, the large and elaborately decorated room with frescoes of the months of the year, a part of the Palace of which Count Arnolfo was particularly fond. Quino had a hunch that the Grand Duke would have gone there, if only to pay his respects to his future bride's father.

It was there that, darting round a corner as fast as his little feet could carry him, he crashed into a thick-set man standing in one of the alcoves in the corridor leading to the Hall of the Seasons. Quino rolled sideways and had almost started running off again until he recognised that the golden hose into which he had collided were those of the Grand Duke himself. He turned back and bowed to present his apologies when he saw that the Grand Duke was not alone. Rather, sitting on a marble bench in the alcove was the same lady in red silk to whom he had spoken a few moments before in the gardens, and the lady was now staring at Quino with a face almost as red as the rich hues of her dress. Court dwarves can expect scant respect at the best of times, but a dwarf who has been indiscreet enough to see something he should not have seen swiftly learns that a quick sprint offers the only real chance of escaping a beating or worse. Quino immediately bowed again and scuttled off, leaving it unclear (he hoped) whether he had noticed anything compromising. He dashed off down the corridor, and ran up the stairs to the relative safety of the dwarves' apartments. There the dwarves were generally left in peace in a world on their scale, a world where they could exist with the spurious dignity that came from living with many others of their kind.

Once inside, Quino breathed more easily. He caught sight of himself in the large mirror by the entrance, all dressed up in his ridiculous costume and angrily ripped off his crown of ivy and his cape. Then he walked past a group of dwarves noisily eating their supper and ignored their questions about his evident state of high agitation. That old witch Martha was particularly keen to know why he wasn't pirouetting around the dance floors but he simply walked past her and didn't reply. He needed time to think. He grabbed a hunk of bread from their table and went to his room. He prayed that Ercole, his room-mate, would not be in, but he remembered that Ercole had been asked to attend at the Chapel that evening.

He went into the simple bedroom with its two miniature beds and sat down with a sigh of relief at being on his own.

Then he began to try and make sense of what he had seen.

***

That evening, Quino entered his mistress's apartments with a deep bow. The ladies-in-waiting made little attempt to suppress their amusement at the grotesque and diminutive figure which stood in front of Countess Isabella, arching his misshapen back into an approximation of a courtier's reverential bow. Isabella immediately ordered them out of the chamber and there was a rustle of skirts and suppressed laughter as the girls went out.

'Well?', she said to Quino when the girls had left the room.
Quino examined her face for an indication of what she thought, so that he could formulate his answer in such a way as to avoid a beating- after all, there could be few more foolhardy things than to accuse the Countess' future husband of infidelity, unless he was absolutely sure of his ground. But all he saw was Countess Isabella's young but austere face, those firmly drawn lines and deep brown eyes. Yes indeed, the Countess was old beyond her

years, Quino reflected, with a sudden surge of pity towards Isabella for being a victim of the destructive results of an aristocratic birth.

'My Lady', Quino began, adjusting his posture, 'I have been out in the garden as you instructed me...'

Then he broke off, suddenly hesitating. Surely he could not construct evidence of the Grand Duke's infidelity merely from what he had seen. After all, what had he actually *seen*? Merely a blushing and very young courtesan sitting in an alcove in the corridors of the palace. There could have been a thousand reasons for the Grand Duke being with her. And if he had the misfortune of being wrong in his suspicions, then no power on earth would preserve him from the rack or worse. He needed to go back and spy a little while longer.

'There is little to report, your Ladyship', he said with a broad smile which he hoped would look convincing. Then he explained how he had observed the Grand Duke's circle, how they appeared to pursue their innocent pleasures in the gardens or in the Hall of the Columns. Throughout Quino's explanations, the Countess looked at him anxiously, as if there was something particular she was hoping to hear.

'And what about the Chevalier de Hierant?', she asked.

Quino replied that the Chevalier appeared to be very much one of the Grand Duke's intimates, but that he seemed to keep his distance, as if he found the festivities somehow distasteful. At this the Countess's usual composure failed her and she visibly tried to repress a smile of intense pleasure. Quino pretended that he hadn't noticed and carried on describing the Papal Nuncio's enthusiasm for dancing.

Isabella succeeded in reverting to her previous rather imperious expression:

'So, in the end, you have found nothing?'

'*Found*, your Ladyship? I was not aware that your Ladyship had instructed me to find anything.'

'Never mind, Quino. I am pleased with your services.'

'Thank you, your Ladyship.'

'I should like you to go on observing the Grand duke and the Chevalier de Hierant. As you know, the wedding is the day after tomorrow.'
'Indeed', said Quino mechanically, 'and we all wish your Ladyship every happiness and...'
She interrupted him:
'It is important that you observe them closely and that you report to me tomorrow evening.'

This time Quino produced a particularly deep bow and since Countess Isabella didn't say anything more, he assumed that he was being dismissed and scampered off.

As he closed the door, he was certain that the Countess had deliberately turned her back to him to prevent her favourite dwarf noticing the sobs which now convulsed her graceful body.

***

There were jeers when Quino returned to the dwarves' apartments. Ercole and Count Arnolfo's favourite dwarves- (three Turkish dwarves now dressed in full islamic costume), were drunk- no doubt on the wine they had stolen from the banquet. Ercole was standing his full height on a miniature chest of drawers bellowing a disgusting song he had learned in Naples about an 'actress' whoring her way through the courts of Italy. He had just got to the Court of Mantua when Quino appeared and there was a chorus of drunken clapping and whistles as Quino came in.

Quino was immediately besieged with questions as to why he had spent so long with the young bride-to-be, and any answer he gave was inevitably twisted into something prurient by the drunken dwarves. Quino gritted his teeth and played along with their jeering and whistling. The other dwarves spent their days scampering round the Palace and if he stayed and shared their drunken gossip, he might glean some interesting information about the Grand Duke. In particular, they might have seen or heard something about that Polish brute which might be used to prevent the marriage. Court dwarves, eunuchs and convicts have one thing in common: standing at the margins of society, they take an obsessive interest in the lives of 'normal' people - the eunuch will have an inexhaustible thirst for gossip on the sexual prowess of his master, the convict for any story about his jailers and the court dwarf for the intimate life of his full bodied owner.

Quino therefore swallowed his pride and sat down, laughing and carousing with the Turkish dwarves as they described the Count's sons and their escapades in the stables.

Predictably, Ercole played hard to get. Quino had to use all his inventiveness to cajole, flatter and sweet-talk out of him the gossip he had heard about the Grand Duke and the Marquise de Rocheblanche- for that was the name of the blushing courtesan in the alcove. Finally, Ercole swore him to secrecy and produced a whole catalogue of night-time meetings of the Grand Duke and copious details of what he really did when out in the woods hunting. There could be no doubt about it, the Marquise was the Grand Duke's mistress, and Ercole produced extraordinary detail, even the fact that the Marquise had a birthmark on her left shoulder- a detail he could only have extracted from one of her dressing maids. Quino tried to press Ercole to find out what he knew about Isabella but Ercole had learned the fundamental lesson of all court intrigue, namely that information was even more precious than gold and that it should be shared out very sparingly: if asked to reveal anything, then you should only reveal *part* of what you know to enable you to stay one step ahead of the others. Ercole therefore chose to play the daft laddie, which intensely irritated Quino, but he knew that he would not get anything further out of him that evening, and that Ercole obviously knew something which Quino did not. Quino would have dearly liked to know which

169

of Isabella's maids was untrustworthy, but at least he had achieved something by promising not to reveal anything about Ercole's theft of a barrel of fine wine from the Palace cellar yesterday.

Quino wondered what to do next. He had now had hard evidence that the Grand Duke was unfaithful. The wedding was the next day and today would be spent in making the final preparations, parading the happy couple through the streets to be acclaimed by the populace and so on and so forth. That Ercole's stories were all true there could be no doubt, and his blood boiled at the thought of the burly and oafish figure laughing and carousing in the palace while the young Countess prepared herself for a life of childbearing and married exile. Did she have any inkling that hers would be a loveless match, tarnished with adultery even before it started? He knew Isabella better than most, having played with her as her companion ever since he had been bought for the little Countess on her eighth birthday. He had watched her grow up, and grow taller than himself, as they played and she matured from a girl into a young woman. He had always been one of her favourites, reading poetry with her, discussing ideas with the freedom that can only exist in a relationship where sexual union is unthinkable. He had grown to love her deeply, partly for her intelligence but more for her vulnerability, for the way she could be so hurt by a malicious rumour or the sudden fall from favour of a courtier. After all, she was only fifteen, and at that age no girl should be forced to devote her best years to a drunken womaniser, even if he was the Grand Duke of Cracow. And what would her sacrifice achieve? Nothing, probably. In a few years' time- earlier even- the political alliances would shift and there would be no need for a Polish counter-balance to the German Emperors. Countess Isabella would have devoted her beauty and her youth for a transient political advantage. She would then languish in the faraway court, breeding the Grand Duke's heirs while he fornicated elsewhere and her life would have been utterly wasted.

No, Quino decided, rising suddenly from his little couch, he would do everything in his power to stop the whole ghastly business. Even if it meant exposing himself to grave personal danger.

To the astonishment of the three Turks, he kissed Ercole fondly on both cheeks and rushed out of the dwarves' apartments.

***

There is a wistful look which all mothers have when they are about to lose their daughters in marriage. Countess Matilda was still a handsome woman for her forty three years, and that motherly expression of grief mingled with joy suited her.
Isabella sat next to her mother while the Grand Duke of Cracow, sitting next to Count Arnolfo, displayed a true hunter's appetite as he polished off partridges and quails with generous draughts of the Count's finest wines. The four of them sat at the 'Table of Honour', as it was called, facing the rest of the court which was sitting at long tables that filled the Great Hall. There was the usual series of speeches, recitations of classical authors and then music. Everybody was agreed that the celebrations were splendid- indeed, many said that the festivities had been as lavish and as wonderful as the Count's own wedding celebrations twenty years before.

Quino positioned himself on the bridegroom's side and he had a good view of the Grand Duke's muscular shoulders adorned by a epaulettes of gold thread. The Chevalier de Hierant was sitting at the nearest table to the Table of Honour. He managed the unusual feat of looking both bored and suave. An ironic smile on his lips occasionally evolved into one of subtle contempt but otherwise he watched the celebrations with stony contempt. He would cast a glance at Isabella, and Quino noticed how something would evidently pain him and how the smile would momentarily vanish as a terribly serious expression came over

171

his face. Did he suspect the Countess of something, Quino wondered, as he watched the Chevalier. Did he hate her for some reason? The Chevalier was a good actor, however, and he would quickly bring his emotions under control and that little ironic smile would soon reappear.

It was a fine June evening and the heat of the day was now being blown away by a cool breeze. Count Arnolfo proposed that everybody should move to the formal gardens, where a disciple of Palladio had recently completed a replica of an antique Roman theatre. There the court would sit on the marble steps and be entertained by singers and actors reciting appropriate passages of Petrarch and Ariosto. The chief glory was, of course, the theatre's proscenium, a vast facade of two storeys, with doric columns at regular intervals and little alcoves from where statues of classical gods peered at the audience. The centre of the stage was an elaborate arch, leading backstage, while the arena of seats was surrounded by more columns, which were ideal for gossiping behind.

Quino stood aside behind one of the columns, trying to think of a way of attracting his mistress' attention. He saw her sitting in the front row to her father's right, exchanging little waves of the hand with members of the audience, looking carefree and happy. Could it be that he was wrong? What if Ercole had lied? Telling him about the Marquise de Rocheblanche might have been a trick, played to unseat Quino from his privileged position as the Countess' favourite dwarf. After all, once Isabella was married, there was no guarantee that his future would be safe: his mistress would follow her husband to Poland but what if he was not taken with her and had to remain behind? Whom would he serve?

The singers had just finished singing a series of madrigals and there was a burst of applause. Quino winced as he saw the Grand Duke clapping too loudly, and he noticed the Chevalier de Hierant looking away as if disgusted by the Pole's vulgarity. His thoughts turned once more to his future and he hardly listened to a word of the sonnets of Petrarch being recited.

The recitations were soon over and the guests started getting up for the interval. He caught Isabella's eye as she turned, and she produced one of her radiant smiles, beckoning him to her with a little wave of her hand.

As quickly as he could, Quino scampered down the steps of the amphitheatre, carefully manoeuvring past the billowing skirts of courtesans and the ornamental swords of knights. At last he reached Isabella, who greeted him with an affectionate little kiss on the head, as if he was just a favourite pet. Quino produced another of his amusingly grotesque bows and the guests nearby duly laughed.
'My little Quino', she said, with an odd tenderness in her voice, 'what am I going to do without you?'

Quino's heart was sliced in half. So it was true that she would not take him with her to Poland.

In that tiny moment, Quino's mind was filled with mounting panic and despair. He imagined himself abandoned by her, and abandoned by the court who would then have no further use for him. He was now nearly fifty and there were younger, prettier dwarves than him looking for employment. He knew exactly what fate had in store for him: he would be thrown out onto the streets and he would be lucky if he didn't end up begging in front of the Cathedral. His eyes filled with tears, he tugged at Isabella's dress- a thing he had never done before. She turned round startled, looking more beautiful than ever. He loathed the Grand Duke of Cracow with a passion made all the more intense by the desperate situation that he was in.
'My lady, I must talk with you. Where no-one can hear us. I have the news you asked me to obtain.'
Isabella looked pensive and merely nodded. Then she followed him behind one of the finely cut hedges where there was a little

bench to sit on.

She sat down and looked at him with that austere expression that made her look so much older.

'Well, what have you got to tell me?', she said simply.

Quino did another little bow, thus filling up another moment while he thought of how to begin. This time Isabella didn't smile at his crooked body's attempt to bow, but looked at him fixedly.

'Your ladyship asked me to keep an eye on the Chevalier de Hierant. This I have done as assiduously as I can. But, as your Ladyship is well aware, the Chevalier is a close companion of His Grace, the Grand Duke of Cracow.'

Isabella's expression became harder. Quino nervously took in a little breath before going on.

'Your ladyship', he started, 'we all give thanks and prayers that the noble house of Cracow will now acquire the gracious addition of your presence. Marriage is a sacrament blessed by the church and, like all sacraments, must be entered into with a pure heart and the will to fulfil the designs of Our Creator for his flock.'

Having prepared the ground sufficiently, Quino now slowly inched his way towards making his revelation.

'Bearing false witness is a grave sin, as Our Lord taught us. But equally great is adultery. And when the two are combined, they are sins that cry out to Heaven...'

There was a rustle of leaves from the hedge as he spoke and, to his horror, he saw the tall figure of the Chevalier de Hierant standing at his side. Instinctively, Quino did as deep a bow as his twisted frame would allow without falling to the ground. The Chevalier didn't even acknowledge his respects but looked at Isabella intently, as if he had been struck by some devastating news.

Isabella got up to greet him, her face suddenly blushing with embarrassment- or was it joy?- by his arrival.

'Quino, leave us', she said with fear in her voice.

Quino scuttled off as fast as he could. But then he changed his mind and, as carefully as he could, he slowly walked back towards the bench where Isabella was now engaged in a heated conversation with the Chevalier. He crawled behind the hedge, the sound of his footsteps covered by the noises of the audience returning to their seats. He found a gap in the hedge just big enough to fir his small body and then listened.

The Chevalier was standing in front of Isabella, who was sitting on the bench. Quino could see him clutching the handle of his sword as if to control his emotions. Isabella was crying, and tears trickled down her cheeks speckling the green velvet of her dress with little dots. He winced as he heard her utter a muffled cry of despair.

'There is nothing else for us to do', he heard the Chevalier say. 'I cannot continue to live a lie. And I cannot compel you to do the same. You have a whole life to live. My own life is now over.'

Quino craned his neck to listen as the Chevalier leant forward to say something to Isabella, but his voice was drowned by the first blast of the orchestra's trumpets and sackbuts. Isabella got up suddenly, her face contorted by an expression of sheer terror. Quino instinctively wanted to rush to her aid but managed to control himself by a superhuman effort of will. Isabella paced up and down, twisting her hands with violent despair. The Chevalier went up to her and, with infinite gentleness, took her in his arms. Isabella immediately collapsed on him, her body shaken with tears.

And then Quino understood.

He watched as the Chevalier kissed Isabella's head, as she clutched him with desperation. Her body shook violently with her sobs but Quino could only hear the clapping of the audience and the triumphant sound of the choir intoning some joyful cantata in celebration of the imminent wedding of the young Countess. Then he watched the shaking subside and a sort of immense peace seem to descend on the couple. Perhaps the sheer impossibility of their situation had overwhelmed them, crushed the will out of them, and the peace that now came over them, gradually stilling her still trembling body, was a peace of resignation and acceptance.

Slowly Quino got up and walked away, as the orchestra reached a triumphant climax.

**

The next day, the Countess was married to the Grand Duke of Cracow in a magnificent ceremony which all agreed was one of the most splendid the Cathedral had ever witnessed.

The Chevalier de Hierant died several years later, a model of Christian chivalry while defending the citadel of Rhodes during the siege of that city by the Turkish infidel.

ENTERTAINING MONA LISA

ENTERTAINING MONA LISA

Florence, 1494

Lady Mona Lisa del Giocondo came in, accompanied by her maid, Francesca. She was late but she did not apologise. Leonardo bowed without speaking and straightaway sat at his easel. She did not say anything either, as if their movements were controlled by pre-ordained rules. Instead, she went to her appointed place by the window, where Leonardo had decided that the afternoon sun would best catch her angular features.

Leonardo fixed her with his eyes. There was total silence.

She had got used to this ritual. At first, she had submitted to it because it was her husband's wish and she could see no point in defying him over something as trivial as a mere portrait. Every night, he would ask her about the progress of the painting, and she had long since given up complaining about the interminable slowness with which this strange man, with his bizarre collection of animals and his high-pitched voice- all the more laughable in a man of his athletic build- continued to paint interminably day after day, applying wafer-thin layer after wafer-thin layer to produce what was only a simple portrait. Francesco del Giocondo apparently was as obsessed by the painting as Leonardo and never listened if she ever dared to complain.
She had also long since lost the ability to be flattered or embarrassed by the fixity of Leonardo's gaze, by the way he seemed to want to peel you alive, to penetrate to the innermost part of your mind. 'The eye is the window of the soul' Leonardo would explain when she asked him why he insisted on staring at her so intently. Then he would begin to paint and she had to sit still, absolutely still, 'like a piece of jewellery in a box', as he used to say.

She had returned every day since that morning nearly four years

179

ago, to sit by the window on the left hand side, to sit for interminable sessions, until the portrait sessions became part of her daily routine, like having her hair elaborately plaited by Francesca- only to have it undone that same afternoon on the Painter's orders, who insisted that such artifice was an act of sacrilege, of desecration of nature's gift of a magnificent cascade of hair, and other such nonsense which he no doubt thought was flattering.

The first months had passed quickly, through an unusually warm spring when abundant flowers had made the Florentine hills seem alive with colours. Then the summer had come: a hot, stifling summer, where the air seemed heated in a huge furnace, when even the abundant waters of the Arno had been unable to wash away the smells of the streets. She had sat through that cauldron in the dark blue velvet dress chosen by Leonardo, almost expiring every morning when Francesca tied her corset strings. Only the evening brought any relief- relief that is, from both the oppressive heat and the endless sitting sessions in front of the strangely abstracted man with whom she spent so many hours of her life but hardly knew.

He frightened Francesca. Her superstitious peasant mind had endowed him with supernatural powers because of his immense strength, because of the way he could produce hundreds of drawings of impeccable quality only to throw them away in disgust, as if such beauty could be produced at will, like water from a fountain. Lady del Giocondo told her maid not to be so silly, but deep down Francesca's fears might have been right. She knew so little about him, except for rumours: how he had travelled to the Orient to work in the pay of the Grand Turk and designed war machines of awesome power; how he had covered the walls of a priory in Milan with paintings of exquisite beauty, working at extraordinary speed; how he wrote in a mysterious way that could only be read if you held the paper up to a mirror; how... But there were a hundred such stories about him, each more improbable than the last. Perhaps that was inevitable for a man like Leonardo da Vinci, who habitually dealt with kings and princes, who confided in no-one, who had never married, who seemed beyond the constraints of ordinary mortals with his almost infinite talents. He seemed to transcend gender with his feminine voice and graceful movements, contrasting with his muscular build. He was beyond normal humanity, conversing with animals, and surrounding himself with grotesque examples of deformed men and women, as if further to highlight his own perfect physical grace and looks.

They were one of the most difficult things to bear, those weird misshapen figures which he drew or invited to his house from the backstreets of Florence. He was like a wizard conjuring up his worst fantasies from the deepest recesses of his imagination and then materialising them in front of your very eyes.

The first time it happened, she thought that she had suddenly gone mad. She had entered the studio with Francesca in a state of considerable distress, having just been attending a memorial mass for a distant relative. The face that she was confronted with was female, a fact that she guessed from the absence of facial hair, but her eyes looked at you from deep within cavernous sockets, veritable wells sunk deep into a face grotesquely contorted to accommodate a twisted nose and a chin as convoluted as a gnarled root. The door had opened: the gargoyle face was staring at them, framed in the doorway by the sunlight behind the head. Francesca had screamed at the top of her voice. For a terrifying moment, Mona Lisa thought that she had been plunged in Hell, that the priest's terrifying sermon on the afterlife had suddenly become reality. She had dug her amethyst ring into her palm to prevent herself from uttering a small cry of her own and had somehow succeeded in maintaining her aristocratic composure.

That was the first time she had heard Leonardo laugh.

***

'In the total absence of light, is a green leaf still green?' said Gianni, doing a somersault and landing just in front of Leonardo's easel.

'Be careful, you idiot, that paint costs money'. But Gianni didn't take any notice and pirouetted again in front of Mona Lisa. She laughed, but more at Leonardo's irritation than at Gianni's jokes. 'Why are there four horsemen of the Apocalypse?' said Gianni, his dwarfish head appearing through his legs.

'Let me guess', she said. 'Because there are not five of them?'

'Yes!'

Gianni uttered a squeal of delight and pirouetted like a doll across the room and landed kneeling in front of her. His eyes were so infinitely sad, she thought: the eyes of a dwarf, who knew that despite his intelligence and infinite jest, he would perpetually seem ridiculous to other men simply because of his freakish size.

Gianni sensed that Leonardo respected him and Gianni therefore worshipped him like a god. Indeed, Gianni was one of the few people who seemed able to come close to him. Often, as she came in for a session, she would find them deep in argument about philosophy, about art, about theology, and her entry would break the spell. They would immediately break off from their discussions and the interminable sittings would resume. It was as if an entire world existed beyond her grasp or understanding, where that prodigiously gifted man conversed with physical freaks and grotesques, who congregated around him like the priests of a mysterious deity.

She would sit patiently, wondering if Leonardo regarded her as more than just an object of interest. The possibility had dawned on her that, for him, she was simply yet another of his human freaks, being merely unnaturally beautiful rather than unnaturally hideous. She knew that she was beautiful: ever since she had

182

been a little girl she had been secretly flattered by the exceptional attention adults would pay her, knowing in her heart of hearts that they regarded her as different from other girls. Like every truly beautiful woman, she had a deep consciousness of her good fortune in having been born with beauty, of how her destiny might have been different had her face been differently shaped. Her less fortunate friends had taken longer to be found husbands or had even been despatched to the cool obscurity of a Tuscan convent. But for him, for this man with the strange piercing gaze which seemed to contemplate humanity from an Olympian height, perhaps she was just another human archetype, a face which interested him for a different reason than that old woman's gargoyle face.

'Would your Ladyship like to stand? Your Ladyship has been sitting for over two hours'.
Leonardo's question broke her reverie.
'Yes', she replied, 'it would be a relief to stand'. Silently, she got up, her limbs grateful for the freedom to move around at last. The autumnal chill had made her back stiff. She went to the centre of the studio, that confined she had visited almost every day of the past four years. Behind her, there was the large window with its magnificent view of the church of San Miniato on the hill across the river. In the corner was the ornate wooden chest where Leonardo kept his drawings and notes. On top there was a collection of clay pots where he kept his brushes and behind them, a shelf with a neat row of bottles where he stored his paints. The wall was decorated by a large Ottoman tapestry, with convoluted Moorish letters: they always made Francesca do a little sign of the Cross as she came into the room because she knew the strange letters spelt heretical words from the Saracens' holy books.

Mona Lisa shut her eyes. She knew every sound in the room. She could even recognise the voices of people in the street outside. There was the loud laugh of the butcher whose shop

183

was on the corner as you turned left out of the house; the shouts of the old women who leaned out of their windows, trading insults with the merchants whose prices were always too high; the voice of the little boy across the street who had been born in the first year she had started sitting for Leonardo and who was now playing in the street. And behind that wooden contraption rested the canvas which recorded all those hours: if it were to burn in a sudden fire, four years of her life, four years of silently endured tedium to satisfy her husband's vanity at having married a beautiful woman, would vanish without trace- except, that is, for the image in Leonardo's mind. And that would eventually die with him, too.

She seldom asked Leonardo about the progress of the painting, treating it all as a routine to which she dutifully submitted with the silent patience of a wife. Over the years, she had built up a private world, a sort of cocoon within which she shielded herself from the boredom of these endless afternoons of inactivity, in which she retreated into a personal universe of dreams and fantasy, away- far away- from everything but herself and her thoughts. She would imagine herself transported in one of those mythological countries from the romances she read so avidly. Or her dreams would be a haphazard mixture of thoughts about her children, her childhood, or even a face she had glimpsed at one of the recent extravaganzas of the Medici court. Gradually, she had begun to look forward to these moments of enforced contemplation as she sat in the studio as still as a statue... They were a welcome release from the daily routine of a Florentine Lady of her standing, with its obligatory courtesy calls, and its futile conventions, its stifling formality. For a few hours every day, the world and its empty routine was forced to stand still in suspended animation, as it were, while her natural, living self was being copied in an absurd but disturbingly inanimate likeness. This transmutation of her living essence into a lifeless copy had never struck her as odd until that afternoon: now it was surely nothing less than a futile attempt to catch reality, to constrain a living person within manageable bounds. If anyone were to look into the room, they would see a tall man concentrating on some tiny detail of the painting with the patience of a Jewish jeweller form the Ponte Vecchio, while on the chair sat a young woman, her hair loose over her shoulders, looking fixedly in front of her, with a dwarf at her feet and a maid sitting in the corner. There would be no sound except for the occasional stroke of the painter's brush. The whole process would be laughable if there was not a heroic aspect to it.

But today was different. Perhaps it was the humiliation implicit in so much enforced passivity or perhaps it was the accumulated frustration of the years of constrained liberty. She did not really know. Afterwards, when she would remember that afternoon, she could never decide whether it was anger or pride that had made her decide to ask to see the portrait, something she almost never did. She was suddenly overpowered by a desperate desire to see the result of all those hours of enforced stillness. For a second, the nightmarish thought came to her mind that it had all been an elaborate trick, where someone had only pretended to paint for all those hours. Perhaps it had all been the diabolical device of a jealous husband anxious to occupy every hour of her life. Perhaps it had all been a dream, perhaps...
'I should like to see my portrait', she said simply.

Leonardo lowered his brush and looked at her. If he was surprised by her request, he did not show it. Instead he bowed impassively and he turned the painting round for her to see.

She knew that Leonardo's technique was unique among portraitists. Leonardo painted in minuscule layers, each superimposed one on the other, until the face on the canvas shone with life, until the infinitesimal layers of colours acquired a depth and a subtlety which made the two-dimensional face seem almost alive. But Leonardo was never satisfied with the result; there would always be some tiny detail he wished to correct 'to make the face breathe'.

She looked at the painting. It had taken almost four years to get to this point.

It was an odd sensation to see her own face emerging, unformed, undefined but still recognisable from the original blankness of the canvas. Her own eyes stared out at her from a face in the process of being created. Her mouth did not yet completely exist, being drawn out only in outline: it was impossible to tell whether the final portrait would describe her as solemn or joyful. Her head occupied the centre of the painting, set in an undefined but conventional landscape of distant hills and meadows divided by the twisting curves of an imaginary river. But what caught her attention was the living quality of the nascent face, the way her body seemed to live in the idealised world of the canvas, her hands folded with an impossibly natural grace. The whole seemed to be already alive, were it not for the absent curvature of the lips. She was seized by the terrifying notion that it might be many years before the portrait was finally completed, and she would have finally earned her freedom.
'Your Ladyship looks concerned. Is your Ladyship displeased with the result?'

The question shook Mona Lisa out of her thoughts.
'No... It's a very pleasing likeness... It is wonderful', she answered almost mechanically.
Leonardo looked at her with his searching eyes. He produced a few compliments, with a courtier's instinct for finding the sort of soothing words that would reassure her that the portrait was going to be the talk of the Ducal Court and so on and so forth. Mona Lisa merely smiled back to humour him, because she remembered how Leonardo had always said that her smile was the most intriguing thing about her. He had made several

attempts at painting her smile, but had always given up with a cry of disgust, hastily covering his work with a layer of paint. But, inside, her mind was in turmoil, reeling with the perspective of an eternity of never-ending sessions to create an impossibly perfect portrait...

***

A few weeks before that day, Leonardo had introduced Gianni. He presented the comically misshapen dwarf with a sober bow, declaring that this would help 'to chase away', as he put it, 'the melancholic expression painters give to their portraits'.

Ever since that day, Gianni and a team of musicians had entertained her while she sat during these endless hours. They had all suddenly appeared one day, bursting with an inexhaustible repertoire of songs, riddles and jests. Gianni would regale her with improbable stories from his days in the dwarves' apartments at the Court of Mantua, how he had danced with ladies at the Gonzaga court, how he had even been presented to the visiting King of France and so on. But Gianni would take a particular joy at frightening Francesca, using his small size to hide and suddenly pop out of the most unexpected places. He would mercilessly play on her superstitious fears, inventing bloodcurdling stories about Leonardo's experiences in the Near East, until even his master had to intervene and reassure the terrified maid.

But it was Mona Lisa for whom he reserved his true affection, so much so that she would sometimes think the dwarf was in love with her, a love made all the more pitiful by the cruel distortions that fate had imposed on his body. The bizarre entertainments went on, and even acquired a certain notoriety in the neighbourhood. Even the old women in the street outside ceased barracking passers-by and listened to the sunny tenor voice of Michele, a young Adonis from the private chapel of the

187

Medicis, a loan from the Duke who admired Leonardo beyond measure.

The strangeness of her daily existence had, if anything, increased from that date. She would compare her daily life with that of other Florentine Ladies of her standing. Their lives were organised by a strict code of conduct based on narrow notions of womanhood. They offered few opportunities for exploring a world beyond a routine dictated by court etiquette or the now fast decaying rules of chivalry. While the wives of her husband's circle- the bankers and merchants that had made Florence the Queen of Europe- spent their days organising the household staff, attending court or interminable religious ceremonies, she had been sent to pose in this studio, year after year. For two hours a day, she entered a world which few of the women she knew would even be capable of imagining, a totally different world where she sat as rigid as a column of marble in front of the unsettling presence of her husband's chosen portraitist, her mind entertained by the bizarre combination of a dwarf of infinitely fertile wit, a singer of extraordinary beauty and musicians of surpassing skill...

***

Today's session had begun with the usual ritual. She had come in with Francesca and found Leonardo drawing a complex geometrical pattern on the floor, explaining an astronomical problem to Gianni. The dwarf was sitting in the centre of a square drawn within a circle on the dark floor- like a fantastic goblin in one of the Flemish tapestries that adorned the Ducal Palace. She had hardly crossed the threshold, ushered in by the grotesque old maid, when their conversation stopped abruptly. Gianni did a gravity-defying leap, then led Mona Lisa to her sitter's chair with a deluge of riddles and puns, as if desperate to divert her attention:
'You use it from roof to floor: the more you use it, the thinner it

188

grows'.

'I give up. What's the answer?'.

'Paint!'.

A quick impish chuckle.

'It's as long as a hundred men and its stronger than a hundred men, and a thousand men can't force it to stand'.

'I don't know', she laughed, kissing him lightly on the head. 'I never know the answer to your riddles'. She tickled Gianni playfully under the chin. 'I give up. What is it?'

'A piece of rope'.

And so on and so on, until she sat down.

Francesca untied her elaborately curled plaits and her hair flowed down over her shoulders, exactly as Leonardo had directed. Gianni got hold of a flute and played a few notes. Then he started taking off Michele in a falsetto voice. Mona Lisa pretended to be amused and smiled. But her mind was on the pattern drawn on the black floor, with its circle impossibly surrounding the square.

The square was drawn in red chalk while the circle was traced in blue. Gianni was now standing in the middle of the square again: standing on the black stone floor, he looked like a mysterious elf suspended in a dark sky. She noticed that there were some letters written at the four cardinal points round the square, recognising them as letters from the Greek alphabet.

Leonardo was carefully preparing a mixture of the colours to be used for her cheeks and neck, the colours which he said were the most difficult to get right. She knew it was useless asking him what their conversation had been about: Leonardo would simply not answer, and Gianni was now subtly doing his best to erase the pattern with his feet by doing a little dance imitating the notorious walk of a corpulent banker of her husband's acquaintance, wiping off the chalk in the process. Soon the delicate geometrical drawing would be totally effaced and their secret would be safe.

For the first time, she decided that she wanted to know. Indeed, she had a right to know. With mounting anger, she felt that she wanted to share their secret, that she should be allowed to enter their world. If they refused, she would suddenly announce that she would no longer co-operate. She would leave this terrible prison and refuse to come back: she would defy her husband, she would run to her father's estates and beg his protection. She would... But she knew that such rebellion was unthinkable: the habit of obedience was so deeply ingrained in her since childhood that she instinctively knew that she had no choice but to submit.

She began to hate the walls of the room, the prison she had been forced into by her husband's vanity. She suddenly felt the heat of the day bearing down upon her like a lid, as if the walls were closing in, even the serene summer light in the window became oppressive, like a wall of sharp stinging brightness.

She breathed in deeply, hoping that this would clear her head, but instead the feeling of imprisonment grew stronger. The four long years of enforced stillness on that little chair were now four terrifyingly sterile years, years when her life had been ebbed away by those accursed hands reproducing a monstrously lifelike representation of her.

She got up suddenly, inventing the excuse of a sudden cramp in her side. Francesca fetched some water; she could hear the patter of Gianni's little feet behind her, with predictably ribald jests about her 'condition'. She stood in the middle of the room, breathing as calmly as she could.

She knew that Leonardo was watching her, but she avoided his gaze.

For a moment, she had the strange thought that perhaps she had always lived in this room, that this perpetual inactivity was a peculiarly devilish circle of hell... Everything had been a dream: her children, her husband, her childhood in the hills around Florence. And it would end one day with her death, when her beauty would vanish as her face and her harmoniously proportioned body would slowly rot in her grave. She mentally recited a quick prayer, comforted by the soothing familiarity of the *Ave Maria*: 'Holy Mary, mother of God, pray for us sinners, now and at the hour of our death'. She might easily die there and then, in this room. She would die and all that would remain of her would be a fading memory in the minds of those who had known her. A name recited by nuns in her sister's convent paid to recite masses for her soul by a grieving husband. Her jewels would be worn her daughter when she would become of age, as she now wore those once worn by her own long dead mother.

Like a suffocating wave, an overwhelming sense of her own uselessness swept over her. What was the use of her beauty? What was the point of recording it in that absurd square piece of painted cloth? What was the use of her life? She felt the heat rise to her throat. She felt for the lace-knots of her bodice and untied them with quick movements of her hands. She walked nervously around the room, with a mounting sense of panic, the ample movements of her long dress making the drawings strewn on the floor flutter away with the sound of dry leaves.

Strangely, it was a comfort to know that Leonardo would die too. So would Gianni with his jests and Michele with his honeyed voice, and the grotesque old maid. In the grave, they would all look the same, distinguished only by the state of their souls. 'Pray for us sinners, now and at the hour of our death.' The phrase sprung up from nowhere, from deep inside her mind but she felt comforted by the mechanical words, words which she had whispered since her earliest childhood, which now came back like a soothing caress. She said the words of the Hail Mary again. She was breathing more easily now: standing up had done her good.

She looked out of the window: the trees around San Miniato had that deep, deep green of the Tuscan afternoon, when the thickest parts of the leaves become almost black. Everything was still, as if transfigured in a silent moment of eternal peace. Heaven, she decided, must be something very much like this: a perpetual moment of beauty caught in mid-movement, like a perfect painting.

And then, she understood.

She understood the reason for this endless painting and repainting. She understood why he had said that painting is like frozen music, where people are transported into an ideal world of silence, of beauty and of perfection... She looked at him now: she didn't know whether Leonardo had been watching her all the time. Perhaps all those thoughts and emotions had raced through her mind in a few seconds.

She saw him looking at her, with his wise, knowing eyes, and his smile, that strange smile she could never decide was of contempt or joy.

Gianni and Francesca were back now, carrying a tray of glasses and a jug of water. Gianni was laughing. She ignored Gianni's obscene hints at the imminence of her delivery and sat down slowly in her sitter's pose, while Francesca adjusted the folds of her dress.

Suddenly she desperately wanted Leonardo to finish, for him triumphantly to show her the finished painting, to see herself subtly idealised in a likeness of her living self, something which would survive her death. Yes, now she understood why it had taken so long. Francesca poured her a glass of water. She sipped the cool, clear water and felt revived. The room had become imperceptibly different, as if now suffused by the golden light that came through the window. Everything was still, suspended in a perfect moment of blissful, translucent peace. She desperately yearned to belong to that world of silent beauty. 'Be still and know that I am God', said the Psalm. Yes, perhaps that was it: beauty brought you nearer to God, to eternal life.

She smiled. Leonardo was looking at her intently. It was the first time that he had ever looked at her face in this way.

Her mind was filled with a sense of overpowering joy: she felt serene, transported into a perfect world where her own inevitable death, the transience of her own existence was an irrelevance. She suddenly felt inexpressibly free, and she could not restrain a smile, a smile of joy at her liberation. She noticed that Leonardo had started painting, his eyes hardly looking at the canvas as he concentrated on her face. Before, she would have found his piercing gaze unsettling, but now she felt that she was his equal.

Leonardo was painting quickly now, as if desperately trying to catch something before it vanished for ever. She smiled back at him. It was a strange smile, a smile that hovered between joy and mirth, like a line drawn against eternity.

A PERFECT WORLD

A PERFECT WORLD

ROME, AD 295

To C. Marcus Volusenna Rogatianus from his friend in the spirit of our master, greetings, all health and good fortune
Porphyrus of Tyre

I write these lines, dear Marcus, in the almost certain knowledge that I do not have more than a few months to live.

My doctor was trained in the best schools of Athens and I therefore have no reason to doubt his competence. He tries his best to reassure me by discussing possible new remedies, but he and I both know that this is but a meaningless charade.

In my darkest moments, I take heart from the example of Plotinus, our Master. At least he died a death full of nobility. You, my dear Marcus, were too young to know him, but your father was one of his most ardent disciples. For years, your father sat at the Master's feet and he was rewarded with wisdom. Plotinus had one of the greatest minds of our age and anyone who diligently followed his teachings was effortlessly transported to the highest Empyrean.

And yet Plotinus' death was a squalid affair. Racked by open wounds and disease, he was shunned by many of his closest disciples who could no longer bear the sight of his putrefying sores. He eked out his remaining days in the property lent to him in Campania by Zethos, where his wants were furnished by the estate. At least Eustochius, his one faithful friend, was there at the final moments.

When the time of his death finally came, Plotinus declared: 'I have been a long time waiting for You. I am striving to give back the Divine in myself to the Divine in the All'. As he said this, a snake crept under the bed where he lay and slipped away in a hole in the wall: our Master died at that very moment.

***

When I first met our Master I was a lost soul.

I mourn our Master's passing as bitterly as if I had lost a father. The irony is that I thirsted after death as a man thirst for love. It was Plotinus who taught me that true wisdom is to know how to accept death.

For me, death had become a source of hope: it became a goal, a termination for which I yearned as passionately as a lover waits for the arrival of his beloved. I began a morbid and yet systematic reading of all the great suicides of our civilization: Socrates, Cleopatra, Brutus, Cato and many others paraded before my eyes in their noble contempt for life. I admired Socrates for the calm fixity with which he outstared the approaching darkness, holding up his cup of hemlock while discoursing a point of philosophy with his disciples. I read and re-read Plutarch and his description of the Egyptian Queen cheating Julius Caesar of his final victory. I envied Brutus the political misfortune which allowed him to demonstrate contempt for worldly glory if it meant dishonour. I applauded the despicable Petronius who, having pandered to Nero's most perverted desires, nevertheless ended his life with a studied elegance, smashing his priceless collection of vases to deny his Emperor the pleasure of owning them after his death. I even acquired a healthy respect for the Christians whom I saw joyfully embracing death in the Coliseum...

And yet, I had no reason to yearn for self-extinction. I knew that my own death would pass unnoticed, that it would move nobody to tears, still less that it would be offered as a sacrifice to an ideal. I would simply die as uselessly and aimlessly as I had

198

lived my life. Philosophy disgusted me when it did not actually bore me: what was the use of all those arguments and all those scrolls of learned discourses if they could not prove to me that life was actually worth living? The rest was so much empty verbiage and posturing.

Seneca says with disdain that suicide is the easiest thing in the world since opportunities for self-murder abound everywhere: each precipice and river, each branch of every tree, every vein in our body will set us free. And yet I both lacked a real reason or the strength to do it. Each day sunk me deeper into self-disgust and despair. Every day started with the nagging refrain 'I wish I were dead', like a song perpetually ringing in my ears.

I owe my life to Plotinus.

That simple bald statement does nothing to express the huge and towering debt that I owe to our Master. Quite literally, he saved my life by giving it meaning. Even after his sordid death, after he had been abandoned by all his friends- I live with a fervour and a passion that is the noblest advertisement for his philosophy. He taught me that while the Muse of Philosophy may teach us how to die, to be a philosopher is to be wise and that to be truly wise means knowing how and why one should live.

***

They say that today we live in happier times. Diocletian has now reunited the Empire. Our frontiers are safe again, the legions are on duty in their forts, keeping the unspeakable savages of Germania at bay. They prowl deep in their forests while we Romans enjoy the fruits of civilisation. Nobody now need be afraid while travelling on the imperial roads and I can look on my children's children in the reasonable hope that they will die in their beds.

The world of my youth was different. You cannot imagine, my dear Marcus, what it meant to spend the best years of your life in a world torn by war and utter lawlessness, to see your youth pass by in a world when it is impossible to watch the sun set and feel be confident you will witness the next dawn.

The tide of calamities that fell on the Empire started when the Persians captured the Emperor Valerian in battle. It was maliciously said that Gallienus had fled from the field of battle like a cowardly young girl or- even worse- that he had deliberately allowed his adoptive father be taken prisoner so that he could seize the Imperial throne. Valerian was to endure several years of captivity in Persia, humiliated at every possible opportunity. Shapour, their Emperor, made him kneel and grovel to the ground in the shape of a footstool every time he climbed on his horse. They even say that after his death the Persians had Valerian skinned and that his stuffed effigy was exhibited at every banquet, to be humiliated even in death.

Meanwhile, the Roman Empire was torn by civil war as usurper followed usurper in grim succession. Most were quickly killed off either by rivals or by Gallienus' loyal legions. But some remained defiantly in control of huge areas of the Empire. Posthumus controlled Gaul and Spain and even minted his own currency, calling himself 'Emperor of the West'. As for the East, Gallienus had no alternative but to recognise Odenath, the Palmyran, as his co-regent of Syria and Egypt. The Empire which Augustus had built was being reduced to a miserable rump of Italy and the North African provinces. To add to this catalogue of misery, a huge earthquake shook the cities of Asia and even Rome felt tremors. A plague then decimated Italy and Achaia, which frantic libations of the temples were powerless to quell.

I thank the gods that I was not fated to be an Emperor: I will not die foully murdered like Gallienus or almost every wearer of the imperial purple. I did not have to fill the empty minds of the *plebs* with sacrifices, processions and copious libations of blood in the amphitheatre. In another life, had Fortune willed it, Gallienus would have been a fine thinker, a seeker after eternity like Our Master. But instead he had to abase himself to placate the depraved tastes of the populace.

I remember the time when the chaos of the Empire and the devastations of the plague created such popular discontent that Gallienus was persuaded to appease the Roman people with a display of unparalleled magnificence. It happened during my first days at court and I can still remember the overwhelming impression which the Imperial procession made as it advanced towards the Capitol. The entire Senate marched with Gallienus, preceded by legions of soldiers dressed in shining white tunics. They were flanked by countless slaves clearing a path through the crowds, carrying huge candles and torches of scented wood. A hundred white bulls, their horns decorated with gold and covered in multi-coloured coats of silk were led to the sacrificial altars. The Emperor even donated ten elephants to the ritual slaughter. A thousand gladiators followed them, dressed in female robes, darned with gold thread. Then came wild beasts of every conceivable species, chained or caged, some even dressed in sumptuous garments. A series of chariots carried actors, mimes and jugglers who jeered obscenely at the cheering crowds, acting out the legend of Polyphemus falling in love with the drunken nymph Galatea. The people of Rome drank in the spectacle with open mouthed stupefaction, clapping and cheering the mad procession as it ascended to the temples and palaces of the Capitol, as if the horrors of the past years had been but a dream.

Gallienus led the whole monstrous pageant, wearing an exquisitely embroidered toga and a laurel crown of gold leaves. The insignias of all the legions were held high around him, while representatives of all the subject races of the Empire paid him homage- Goths, Numidians, Samartians and countless others...

The next days were dedicated to extravagant feasting and particularly blood-curling massacres in the Coliseum. Thus was the devotion of the *plebs* purchased by Emperors during those terrible years...

***

In his private moments Gallienus took refuge in a different world. A world of philosophy, of poetry and of beauty. The Empress Salonina gathered the finest minds of the time around her in the court and it was to that world that I was introduced by Plotinus, when Our Master chose me as a disciple and presented me at court.

It was my good fortune to have attended the schools of philosophy and rhetoric at Alexandria and Athens. I knew, therefore, that one must set no store in worldly success and that the courts of Emperors are certain to exhibit mankind's blackest capacity for vice and intrigue. But nothing could have prepared me for the atmosphere of Gallienus' court. It was in a state of near war between two opposing factions. One represented traditional Rome, the other the new clan of career soldiers from the Illyrian coast.

On our side were the philosophers and poets who surrounded the exquisitely beautiful Empress. Their natural allies were the noblest Senatorial families haughtily displaying the antique traditions of Rome. With them were the court officials who went about their business with the accumulated deviousness of generations of imperial service.

Ranged against them were their sworn enemies, the brutally uncouth Illyrians, ambitious soldiers who made no secret of

202

their contempt for the refined ways of the Roman courtiers. There was Heraclianus, the Prefect of the Guard, a huge man with devious eyes; Cecropius, the general of the cavalry, who was at his happiest spearing animals on horseback or demonstrating his skill at hand to hand combat; and Aureolus, a barbarised Roman (if there can be such a thing), whose naked ambition was only tolerated by Gallienus because of the desperate state of the Empire.

The Empress Salonina immediately took to me. I know you will smile indulgently at the thought of a young man, fresh from the Provinces, suddenly catapulted into the court and then confronted by the sight of a woman of such extraordinary beauty. To my youthful eyes, she seemed to float rather than walk into a room and her every movement radiated indescribable grace. Nevertheless, her beauty had a certain severity, that peculiar sort of hardness that comes from great classical beauty: when she stood in her ceremonial robes, her statuesque poise was almost inhuman. There were also times when I used to find her kind of beauty almost verging on the ugly, but it was redeemed by a tragedy that gave her expressions an odd pathos: her only son, Saloninus, had been left by Gallienus in command of the imperial garrison of Trier. When that despicable usurper Posthumus conquered the town, he had Saloninus cruelly put to death along with all the Imperial officers he could lay his hands on. It is said that a parent never truly recovers from the death of a child and the Empress' beauty would cloud over whenever she spoke of her son. But more often, her pain was left silent: I used to notice the way her eyes would become strangely distant when she watched a spectacle at court, when she looked at a beautiful landscape or when she heard musicians playing in her private apartments. Then I knew her son was still alive in her thoughts.

Gallienus never displayed his grief publicly. Like all Emperors, he had to live with the thought that assassination could come at any moment. We ordinary mortals can reasonably expect to die in our beds, or, if we are lucky, to die quickly in an accident before the slow and squalid onset of old age. We are simply not worth killing. But Gallienus was perpetually surrounded by the possibility of a sudden and violent death: his every waking moment was guarded by hand-picked Praetorian Guards; and every dish was first tasted by a slave against the possibility of some hideous poison. He could never walk alone in the privacy of his gardens without the fear that somewhere, somehow, a dagger might be poised to pierce his heart.

His only refuge was in the realms of the spirit and there he found a guide in the Our Master, Plotinus. Perhaps it was more than a way of escape: perhaps he genuinely believed that the soul was eternal and able to survive the sordid and brutal death which he somehow knew was bound to come to him. Gallienus relied on Plotinus and drank at the fountainhead of his philosophy like an infant suckles on his mother's breast.

His death was, as you know, a particularly savage death, but I will come to it later in this letter. For the moment, let me return to the first months when I was brought to the court, when my world was still one filled with hope and beauty. It is a world which will never come back, now that the Empire is ruled by the victorious Illyrian generals and every province has been turned into a military encampment.

***

When I said earlier that Gallienus withdrew into a private world of philosophy and art, I meant this quite literally.

During his discussions with Plotinus, the Emperor became increasingly fascinated by Plato's concept of an ideal City of Philosophers. Soon the idea completely took hold of his mind: at first it may have been an elaborate whim- one of those sophisticated courtly games which the Illyrians despised- but gradually it became a passion that dominated Gallienus. He ordered the Aristarchus the architect to design an Ideal City- with an *Agon* where the philosophers could meet, with barracks for the young to be trained for a martial life and temples where the populace could worship and be awed. But it soon became simply too expensive to build an entire city from scratch. Aristarchus suggested that it would be possible to convert the old temples and ramshackle buildings on the Esquiline and build the 'Platonopolis' in the heart of Rome: but the idea was thought too dangerous as it might provoke the *plebs* who swarmed around these buildings to civil disorder.

Plotinus suggested that the most 'authentic' thing would be to build 'Platonopolis' in an ancient Greek city. It would be comparatively easier to restore an old city to its former glory and it was also more likely that the buildings would have been of the kind envisaged by Plato. The ruins of Greek cities in Sicily were rejected because the Emperor could hardly take the risk of absenting himself so far away from Rome. Then someone- I forget his name- mentioned that there existed the ruins of an ancient city in the countryside south of Ostia.

Gallienus rode out to inspect the site the very next day. The city was indeed in ruins and completely abandoned, but it was not so ruined as to be beyond repair. Columns still stood out in the dense forest that had grown inside the ruins and there was a reasonably intact temple on a hill which gave the Emperor the idea of what he could do with the site. He sat silently on the top of the monumental staircase, wrapped in his thoughts, the wind swaying the lush forest that allowed only hints of once magnificent buildings. Then suddenly he stood up with a radiant smile and fondly embraced Plotinus.

Despite the crumbling state of the Empire, all available resources were deployed in the grandiose scheme. The finest marbles, the rarest woods and the most skilful artisans were pressed into service. Arsitarchus was only given a few months to prepare the Platonopolis in time for the feast of Janus, at the Winter solstice.

***

The atmosphere at Court became worse by the day. These events are now so far away from me that I remember them as in a dream, a vision in my mind where the overwhelming feeling is one of menace, a brooding darkness enveloping the world around me. A few incidents stay vividly in my mind, memories made all the more sinister because I only half understood what was really happening behind the scenes.

I remember Gallienus, standing a few hundred feet away from me, in front of the Palatine. His guards kept themselves at a respectful distance while the Illyrian generals were having a heated argument with him. I could not hear what they were saying as I was on a balcony, looking down on the courtyard where they were standing. I can still clearly see the small group crowding ever closer around Gallienus, every gesture filled with that stiff formality of high anger. Eventually, the Emperor's patience snapped as he drew his sword with an angry sweep and brandished it in front of him. The Praetorian guards immediately sprang forward to protect their Master, their weapons at the ready. But this time the Illyrians knew how to bide their time: they raised their arms slowly, with only a hint of reluctance, and each placed a hand on the blade of the sword. Then they swore an oath that I didn't quite make out, but it was no doubt yet another empty promise to defend the Empire and its noble Emperor to the death -something quickly thought up to pacify the Praetorian guards but which would be just as quickly forgotten when the propitious moment came to rebel.

At other times, when I attended the Empress I could sense the underlying tensions that were poisoning the Imperial household. She would return from the apartments of Gallienus and retire with her women to weep inconsolably. Once I distinctly remember her taking my hands- I was one of her favourites- and imploring me to escape while I was still alive, telling me that I was still young with a whole life still ahead of me to devote to a better purpose. She urged me to shun the empty glories of the world and to devote myself to the pursuit of Wisdom. I attributed this rather incomprehensible advice to her Christian leanings- which I despised, as I had no time for the fantasies of that absurd and barbaric cult.

But still the tension grew. Gallienus was never without an escort of Praetorian guards wherever he went and I should have read the signs of the horrors that were fated to come. All young men have a natural tendency towards boundless optimism and the thought that I would one day witness the senseless destruction of all that I held precious never even entered my mind.

***

It was about that time that the building of Platonopolis began in earnest, spurred on by Gallienus and Salonina. It was as if they wanted desperately to build a lasting monument to the ideals they stood for, something eternal and noble that would outlive them, something that would speak across the centuries to future generations, something to defy the death they somehow sensed was advancing implacably towards them.

We travelled from Rome in the tightest security: reports had come of marauding bands of Franks and Alemanni pillaging the area around the Alban hills. We advanced steadily towards the flat plains south of Rome, a long imperial procession surrounded by several cohorts of Praetorian guards, an interminable cloud of dust hovering over the endless coaches filled with court dignitaries.

We reached Platonopolis by nightfall. We were greeted by the tall stumps of columns, standing in groups of threes or fours, silhouetted against the darkening sky. We walked through the streets, the houses and decayed temples barely visible through the sprawling vegetation. Shrubs grew out of once ornate doorways and the paving stones of the streets jutted out at odd angles, where they had been displaced by the roots of the thick forest growing in the middle of the ancient city.

But in what had been the forum or its equivalent in those far-off days, the mark of the Roman engineer was beginning to manifest itself. Scaffolding stood everywhere around a well preserved temple, like a monstrous climbing plant, clinging to every wall and hugging each column. The square in front of the temple had been cleared and overlaid with new dales of shining marble. It glowed a warm red hue in the sunset, and the gold ornamentation freshly painted on the roof of the temple caught the rays of the dying sun.

Workmen were everywhere, swarming like insects clearing up the debris and generally preparing the next day's work. Everywhere there was a sense of purpose, an air of quiet determination as the thousands of artisans and painters and joiners went about their tasks: even the slaves appeared better dressed and better fed than usual.

I am now over ninety years of age. My eyes are so weak that I can hardly make out the letters that I am dictating to my slave. I can only hope that my words reach you accurately: in a sense I no longer care, for it is the vision that my words express that matters. A window has been opened for me through which I can see the brightest and most colourful garden the mind's eye could ever hope to see, and nothing- not even death- can destroy that image. Isn't it an odd thing- for a man to be happy merely because of a mere vision? Because of an indescribable and insubstantial thing that lives in his dreams and makes life worth living? Other men need an ideal or a crowd of healthy children playing around them to spur them on to active life: all I have is a fleeting vision, a picture of ecstasy towards which my mind stretches like Orpheus grasping at the image of his vanishing Eurydice.

***

Our Master Plotinus not only taught us how to philosophise, but he opened up entirely new areas of experience to his disciples. He taught us to be indifferent to this world's notions of success. He taught us how to face the prospect of our death, of our own physical annihilation with that calmness of mind that is the source of true wisdom.

One evening he even made us feel as if we were inhabiting Paradise. You may find that last claim exaggerated but the events of one extraordinary evening in Platonopolis will haunt my imagination as long as I live.

We were in a garden somewhere in the half rebuilt city. We had been debating the existence of the soul and the nature of the afterlife. Eustochius had argued that the body had a natural span of existence and that the worst cruelty would be to impose on it a life measured in centuries rather than years. Everything has an appointed place and role: death is therefore as much a part of the pre-ordained scheme of things as birth or love. Plotinus agreed but the debate led our discussions to consider the nature of the spiritual aspects of our earthly existence, the nature of the soul. Zosimus then asked what evidence was there that the soul existed after the death of the body? What sort of world it inhabited after death and how we could even begin to know anything about the world of the hereafter?

What quality of life would our souls have? Zosimus asked. Would they feel pain? Could they experience joy? Could they go on loving the souls of those whom we had loved in the earthly life?

Outside, the day was dying in a glorious display of warm colours and the darkening sky made the branches of the pine trees on the hills turn a deep black, silhouetted against the horizon.

Plotinus' answer lives on in my mind like a bright flame in the centre of a fire.

We sat together in a hushed silence and then Plotinus began to answer.
'Beauty is around us everywhere. Beauty can be felt mainly and above all through the eyes and by our ears. It exists when we admire eloquence or when we are entranced by exquisite harmonies. But there is a realm beyond the realm of sensations: we can abandon the mere material world of sounds or shapes and move to a higher level where we can sense that certain actions or even lives can be beautiful...
'What is it that makes our bodies seem beautiful? How is it that our faculties are able to feel the presence of beauty? How can a thing of beauty touch our souls? My friends, is it the case that one and the same Beauty renders everything beautiful or must we conclude that the beauty of physical bodies is of one type and the beauty of souls of another?
'Our bodies are not beautiful in themselves but acquire their quality from their union with the Ideal which shines through the cosmos. Other things are beautiful in themselves, such as the virtues or Love. Even our bodies can appear beautiful at certain times and then suddenly appear ugly: a face can be perfect at one time and then deformed on another occasion, according to the direction in which beauty fires its symmetry... It is as if there is a distinction between having a body and having beauty.

'Let us list the emotions that beauty provokes in us. When our eyes come into contact with beauty, the result is admiration, a joyous exultation, an intense longing passion, even a subtle terror which mingles with the pleasure inspired by the beauty. 'This is the world to which we must strive, touching our minds with the infinite, the sublime and the eternal...'

I was enthralled.

On he went, weaving almost a spell with his voice so that we followed him up through the heavenly spheres, to the purest Empyrean, although we were crowding around him in the heat of the Roman summer. Somehow, all the squalor of Rome, the teeming city and the sordid brutality of its mass pleasures vanished as we continued our discussions through the sultry night.

We listened with our mouths wide open, drinking in the purest waters of philosophy, our minds soaring in the sky as they were guided by Plotinus' magnificent imagery. However much our senses might experience the pleasure of the body, he said, however delightful a sensation might seem in this world, it would be as nothing by comparison with the life of eternity. His words breathed a passion of pure fire as he guided our thoughts ever higher, up to the highest sky, towards the Eternal Being itself. Step by step we climbed up beyond all corporeal objects to the heavens from where Sun, Moon and the stars shed their light on Earth. We moved up into a new realm, where life is wisdom and perfection, where all is stillness, beauty and perfection.

For a brief moment, Plotinus transported our minds to the highest heavens and kept us there for as long as our imaginations could stand the burning light of pure beauty... For an instant, our minds touched something eternal. We held our breaths, gasping with astonishment and exhilaration as all our intellects were somehow fused into the contemplation of the same wondrous vision. We remained there for what seemed an eternity of bliss, as if suspended in the air by our ecstasy, by this certain knowledge that our earthly lives were not even worth a speck of dust compared to the beatific vision that we were presently experiencing.

Everything became impossibly still.

At last, the deep, deep silence could no longer be endured. Gradually, the world invaded our thoughts again and the vision vanished from our minds and flew back to the eternal spheres from which it had come. Slowly we left that empyrean and returned to the noise of our human speech. We recognised each other in our earthly bodies and a cruel sense of being in exile from paradise overwhelmed us. Some of us wept openly, others contained their grief with heart-rending sighs as they breathed in the warm evening air.

***

The next day, the Illyrian Generals came to Platonopolis. Even the brutish Heraclianus was in awe when he stood under the portals of the largest temple, his massive frame looking puny between the huge Doric columns. Cecropius galloped along the recently paved streets, visibly impressed by the sheer scale of the enterprise. They would turn to Aureolus for explanations in their barbarous tongue: even though none of us could understand what they were saying, it was obvious that they were fascinated, even if they probably secretly despised the refinement that was everywhere around them. Plotinus warned Gallienus to fear the Illyrians, but he merely laughed it off, affectionately tapping the shoulders of the nearest Praetorian guard, declaring that he always travelled with his trusty shield.

The idea of the Platonopolis was apparently not new: Apollonius, the Imperial Archivist, informed us that some centuries back Herodotus had sought to rebuild the city of Sybaris, the city devastated by neighbours jealous of its luxury. Hippodamus of Miletus was commissioned to rebuild the fallen palaces while Protagoras was given the task of drawing up the City's constitution. The whole court listened with fascination as Apollonius described how the rebuilding of Sybaris came to grief through intrigues and jealousies. If only they had learned from the past follies of men!

***

Everything around me became oppressive and overlaid with a brooding sense of menace. Slowly the Illyrian generals increased their sway over the Court. Nothing could be done without their say, and the Emperor had to suffer the indignity of having to obtain the agreement of that crowd of thugs before making the slightest decision.

I suppose we were fortunate at having Aureolus there: at least he had been brought up in the Illyrian tribes and understood their savage ways. He once described how the recruiting officers would scour the mountain villages, picking out the tallest and sturdiest young men with promises of riches and fame. They joined the Roman army in clans and it was not unusual to find a whole cohort from the same valley.

Unusually for a soldier (or perhaps because he was after all more a Roman than an Illyrian) Aureolus was a man of considerable poetic gifts. He would describe the tall rugged mountains north of Greece where the Illyrians come from, their bitter winters and the awesome beauty of an eagle flying high above a deep green valley. He would regale us with descriptions of the warlike contests by which these half-savages would select the bravest youths: gruelling endurance tests of forest survival, days spent without food or water, long trials of brute strength. Those who survived to the end were declared fit material to make their fortunes in the Empire, and you will imagine, dear Marcus, what they must have thought as they arrived in Rome. They must have both envied and despised the rich and gorgeous clothes worn by the refined courtiers. They must have looked with amazement at the strange foods the Imperial kitchens invented to please our jaded palates. They can only have had contempt for the supine indolence of our rulers and their total failure to subdue the usurpers that were tearing the Empire apart.

***

Our idyllic peace was short lived. News came of a fresh barbarian invasion. This time it was the Heruli, a tribe savage even by the standards of the Gothic hordes. They crossed the Black Sea, devastating the Roman provinces at the mouth of the Danube. Gallienus wearily set out for the East, leaving Aureolus in charge of Northern Italy.

Once more the Imperial troops were successful or, more precisely, they managed to contain the marauding bands to Greece where the barbarians indulged in an orgy of destruction and sacrilege. The Goths even reached Athens but were beaten back by its citizens, organised into a disciplined fighting force by the historian Dexippus: even the ghost of Plato must have smiled at this show of martial valour by an inspired citizenry! Gallienus' army then chased and cornered the barbarians near the river Nessus where they were duly slaughtered like vermin.

The Illyrian generals could not forgive the man they despised for beginning to outshine their military prowess. Aureolus declared himself Emperor in Milan, where he was based with a few legions guarding the entrance to Italy from the Alps.

Gallienus returned to Italy to deal with this latest usurper, accompanied by Heraclianus, Cecropius and the other members of the Illyrian clan. Probably he already suspected them of being in league with Aureolus: but the Empire was in a desperate state and he could not afford to doubt the loyalty of his generals

The legions moved from one battle to another, successfully repelling Aureolus until he was besieged in Milan.

There is nothing heroic about that sort of warfare. I endured many long months at Gallienus' side, sharing the miseries of the troops. You must imagine, my dear Marcus, a whole army bogged down in the rain and mud of Northern Italy, an encircled city with its grey walls standing in the morning mist, surrounded by thousands of fires lit by soldiers huddling for warmth, wondering how long it will go on. A stranded army attracts disease and disorder: the swarms of prostitutes that descended upon us were only matched by the swarms of insects and carrion birds that turned our lives to utter misery. Soon the dreary flat plain became a cesspit of foul vapours, the whole area was turned into a field of indescribable squalor. And yet, for months on end, Aureolus held out and defied the Imperial besiegers.

Gallienus could not do without 'his Philosophers', as he called us. Plotinus brought me with him to write down his thoughts during moments of inspiration. We were there to remind the Emperor of the possibility of another life, as we watched defensive towers being engulfed in flames in the middle of the night and soldiers vainly leaping from the top storey to avoid a horrible death. We were there as symbols of a purer world as we watched a cohort of Aureolus' soldiers who had been captured that morning being pitilessly slaughtered at the foot of the besieged city's walls. The shouts of defiance from Aureolus' troops hardly managed to drown the cries of the unfortunates who were being butchered as an empty warning of the Emperor's vengeance. As if to a father, Gallienus would turn to Plotinus with a look of utter disgust on his face as we saw the cartloads of bodies being carried off for burial at the end of yet another day of the senseless brutality.

Plotinus could give him no explanation for the world's cruelty and it was then that I sensed Gallienus had given up the will to live.

***

None of us realised, of course, that Gallienus' end was to come so soon.

That evening, there was a splendid sunset, with the snows of the distant Alps fired with deep, rich scarlet hues. The fires from the soldiers' encampments already glowed all over the surrounding hills like so many fireflies in the heavy heat of the dying day. The towers of Milan still stood dark and defiant in front of us, as we watched the whole scene in silence. We could just make out Aureolus' soldiers patrolling the battlements, hurling insults at the imperial troops standing nearest to the walls, their voices echoing in the darkness. We had now been stranded in front of Milan for almost six months: the war seemed to have lost all direction and the troops were known to be increasingly restless.

Slaves lit torches around the Imperial tent and the night meal was served with as much pomp and luxury as the austerities of warfare would allow. Gallienus and Plotinus started discoursing on the theme of death and the immortality of the soul. Gallienus asked his favourite poet, Empidorus, to recite the noblest descriptions of death in our literature. It was as if he somehow sensed the possibility of his approaching end, as he stared at the last rays of the sun glowing sombrely in the enveloping night sky while listening to Empidorus' golden voice.

'Alone of all the gods', the poet began, reciting from the Emperor's beloved Aeschylus:
'Death has no love for gifts,
Death despises libations and sacrifices.
Death has no altar and is deaf to hymns.
From him alone Persuasion stands aside.'

Plotinus gently chided the Emperor for his fear of death. 'Death is the most terrifying of illnesses, but it is nothing to us. So long as we are alive, death is not with us. But when death comes, then we do not exist. Death cannot therefore concern the living or the dead since it cannot exist for the former and the latter are no more,' he said, quoting from Epicurus.

I remember Gallienus turning round to Plotinus then, his eyes filled with a longing and almost pitying expression. He commended the philosopher for his strength and his serenity, but confessed with a hollow laugh that he now counted himself one of his failed disciples. Then he got up suddenly and left the spacious tent.

A hushed silence fell on the court.

Early the next morning, there was a commotion from the forward trenches nearest to the besieged city. There were shouts that Aureolus was attempting a sudden breakout. In a few moments the whole camp was in uproar: Gallienus immediately shouted for his horse and gave orders for his generals to assemble. Heraclianus and Cecropius suddenly appeared in full armour and accompanied the Emperor as he went out, unarmed, to watch the movements of the rebel army at close hand.
I saw him riding out towards the besieged city, in the rapidly clearing mists. Gallienus quickly reached the top of a treeless hill, at a slight distance from the Praetorian guards who were hastily assembling for their morning parade. His only

companions were Heraclianus and Cecropius with a dozen Illyrian horsemen.

It was then that I understood the diabolic machinations that had been going on. We were powerless to help as we watched the Illyrians surrounding the solitary Emperor: a forest of swords suddenly appeared and fell on Gallienus, hacking him to death. For a second, I saw his outstretched arms begging for mercy and then all was darkness.

Moments later, the gates of Milan were opened by Aureolus' troops who poured out of the city, no doubt responding to a prearranged signal.

***

We were lucky to escape with our lives as we galloped away from the pitched battle that ensued. I was at least spared the sight of the Emperor's corpse being dragged round the field by his triumphant murderers. Within a few hours, the Illyrians reigned supreme.

***

Fifty years later, my dear Marcus, all this is but a dream- a fleeting vision lingering in the memories of an old man.
The gods have given me a longer life than I deserve. One of the consolations of old age is to watch youth, because in youth we can see traces of our own past. I look at your face and I can make out the outlines of your father's face: in an odd way, that brings me inexpressible comfort. It reassures me that there is continuity after my death- perhaps even that someone will recognise my own long-dead features in someone alive years after I have passed away.

That, somehow, the joys and sufferings I have endured in my

life have a continued existence and meaning.

At least I am a philosopher and I live in a world of thought and eternal ideas. I have the consolation - or if I am honest the illusion - that the achievements of my life can outlive my earthly existence.

But what of Gallienus? The empire he ruled and tried to salvage no longer exists. At least not in a form he would recognise. We now live in a universe created by military rulers who have regimented the Roman world like soldiers' barracks.

The men who wear the purple today would not even be able to understand the simplest discourse of Our Master, Plotinus. It would not even occur to Diocletian and his henchmen to discuss the nature of the Soul or to speculate of what material the Heavenly Spheres are made of... Certainly, to decide to build an ideal City of Wisdom would have struck them as proof of final madness.

They loathed us then, dear Marcus, and loathe us still. We represent a world they could never inhabit.

They therefore had to destroy us.

RELIGIO ILLICTA

RELIGIO ILLICTA

Rome, AD 40

The toga, Quintus Publius Anicius reflected, was a poorly designed garment: you had to fold it without the aid of pins, it was made of heavy linen cloth, and it constricted your movements -even if it did lend an indisputable dignity to a patrician's walk.

He would often argue with his Greek slave, Parthenius, as to the relative value of the Roman toga compared with the Greek *himation*. Parthenius, an educated scribe, always insisted that the *himation* was superior because the Greeks had had the sense to retain the straight edges and the right angles which the cloth had in the loom: when wrapped round the body and tied by a belt, the *himation* produced admirable effects from these elementary forms and simple folds. It was typical of the Romans to have cut the toga cloth on a circular plan: when folded and wrapped round the body, the toga produced richer and more majestic folds, a garment fit to exhibit the arrogance of Roman power to the outside world.

As he adjusted the purple diagonal stripe reserved to members of the senatorial rank, Publius reflected that Parthenius probably had a point: tying the toga required real skill and only an artist like Parthenius who had the eye for the correct folding pattern could do it reliably. It might be majestic, but it was also majestically impractical to walk in: preserving the loaming dignity of its folds required a constant effort of balance, which the slightest jostle in the crowd would inevitably disturb. No wonder the average Roman seldom wore the toga and that the *plebs* only wore them on the occasion of their own funeral.

Quintus Publius quickly checked his appearance on a polished bronzed mirror. It was not the passage of years that depressed him: it was the notion that, after his inevitable and fast

223

approaching death, there was little assurance that the world which had created him would survive. 'But what has the future ever done for me?' his friend and fellow Senator, Longinus, used to say, knowing that his quip would irritate him.

Indeed, what would there be left of the world that he had loved? What would be left of the Rome that had created the Legions, defeated all its enemies and spread the *Pax Romana* over the whole of the known world? These victories were not won easily: they had been won with blood and steel, only now to be systematically violated by the ridiculously named 'Pontifex Maximus', the Emperor, the most recent specimen of which decorated the walls of his Caprian villas with obscene Priapic figures, in a vain attempt to stimulate his geriatric member into activity... Last week in the Senate, rumours were making the rounds that Tiberius even had young slave boys trained to swim underwater and peck at his genitals while he bathed. His 'minnows', he called them apparently. The nobility of the *Res Publica* was being reduced to the vulgarity of an Oriental despotism!

He grunted in disgust and looked again in the mirror: his toga looked respectable, and he was glad that at least *that* emblem of the glory of Rome was properly exhibited. As for today's day's 'vote', the absurd charade which the emasculated Senate was being asked to perform concerning the new *religio licta*, the new authorised religion- the answer was no! a thousand times 'no': he would not be coerced by this Emperor into voting to legitimise a new religion simply to please the eunuchs and slaves of the imperial civil service. Either the Senate signified something or it did not: he would do his utmost to ensure that the others voted like him.

He knew, of course, that the vote was only symbolic: whether or not a new *religio licta* was accepted by the Senatorial vote was really rather insignificant. There were far more important things on which Tiberius might have to ask the Senate for support, and Publius' fine political nose told him to hold his fire. If all you have is the shadow of power, it is sensible to exercise this power only on insignificant issues. Whether the obscure Levantine sect would become a permitted religion was not a decision of great importance- goodness knows, Rome had more temples and more gods than any other city in the world!- but voting against it was at least harmless way to remind Tiberius and his cohorts that the Senatorial Order was not to be reduced to the status of performing apes.

He heaved himself into the sedan chair and gave the order of departure.

***

The sky was a perfect blue but there was a cold northern wind. Publius wrapped a shawl around his shoulders and sat back. He liked to keep the front curtains of his sedan chair drawn: keeping his eyes shut, he could savour the gentle rocking movement of his chair as it was carried by his slaves.
The sun shone through the fawn material of the curtains, bathing the interior with a soothing golden light. Outside he could hear the busy crowd being rudely pushed out of the way by Epaphrastus, the chief slave of his household. Those who dawdled to gape at the passing Senator were shoved off with a stream of abuse in that marvellously coarse slave Latin that always amused him. But he sighed as he thought of that swarming crowd of malodorous humanity: where was the noble bearing of the *populus romanus*, when men gave their best years in service in the legions, when the gods were worshipped with fervour, when the name Roman was a byword for manly virtue? There were so many different peoples converging on Rome that you could seldom see a good aquiline Roman nose: too many northern slaves, too many Greeks and too many Syrians with their fleshy noses and their unscrupulous tricks, and all of them debauching the noble Latin language with a barbarous vulgate fit only to be satirised by playwrights. And even the playwrights were daily losing their audience to the depraved sensations of

225

the amphitheatre...

Soon he would be in the Senate.

His mind quickly took a more sombre turning. He had to think of a sure way of stirring that collection of degenerate aristocrats into showing their teeth. The Empire might now be an unavoidable political reality, but the Senate still had the right to be consulted on all new laws proposed by the Emperor: if they did not exercise this right seriously, the Senate would quickly fade away into a shadowy and irrelevant assembly, a mere puppet show... What would the glorious heroes of Republican Rome think of the *Urbs* now? He blushed as he thought of Cato who had preferred to fall on his sword rather than be captured, or of Lucius Brutus who had ordered the execution of his own sons to demonstrate his impartiality. Which of his fellow Senators would even begin to have this degree of manliness? None: they were only fit to be corrupted by luxurious living and privileges. This wasn't even the silver age of decline, it wasn't even an age of stone: it was an age of dust.

He knew, of course, that he had unpromising material for his proposed demonstration of Senatorial strength against Tiberius: the vote today was on the proposed legitimisation of some obscure oriental sect whose leader had been executed as a common criminal -which only went to show how debased the whole majesty of religion had now become. The report was lamentably vague on the 'practices' of this proposed *religio licta,* save that he could dimly remember something about nocturnal secret meetings of slaves and other inferior social classes where they chanted in unison before dawn.

People should be allowed to believe what they wanted, but personally he had always liked his worship to have a sense of occasion, even of awe.

There were two types of worship which created in him that indefinable sense of touching infinity. There was the public worship in the temples. He particularly liked the Sacred Fire in the shrine of the Vestals, watching the Priestess in her white robes standing out against the ritual flames. He loved the moment when she would sprinkle a handful of incense on the embers, the smoke curling slowly upwards to the ceiling. He would stand quietly at the back of the temple, watching these shrouded women floating past in the darkened aisles, the semi-darkness always giving him the delicious feeling of participating in some arcane mystery.

Or there were those rare places which seemed to breathe a peace that transported him into a different world. He particularly loved the springs near a little village set in a densely wooded part of the Alban hills, covered with ancient cypresses whose branches made a soft sound in the evening wind. He would walk to the little pool fed by mountain springs, its water as clear as glass, with the coins left by the faithful glinting among the pebbles at the bottom. The water was as cold and sparkling as fresh snow, and he liked running his fingers in the water. There was a little shrine of great antiquity, its wood now sadly worn with age where someone had erected a statue of the local god. All around there was a profusion of little shrines, each containing a god and numerous votive inscriptions written in a simple, honest Latin that made him smile despite his respect for the devotion that had inspired their authors... He would go there whenever Rome became too much for him, whenever he felt overwhelmed by its filth and noise.

Epaphrastus tapped respectfully on the ledge and informed him they had arrived at the Senate.

Publius emerged out of the Sedan chair with as much dignity as his heavy garment would allow. The sunlight reflecting on the marble made him blink a little.

As luck would have it, the first person he met was Gaius Livius Aemilius, a close ally, who was talking to another man, a tall, gaunt Senator who seldom emerged from his provincial estates and whose name he could not remember.

Gaius greeted him with a fervent handshake. He introduced him to the other Senator, who acknowledged him with a taciturn nod and gave his name as Regulus. After ritual enquiries as to the health of his family and the crops on his estates, Publius went straight to business:

'You're going to oppose it, aren't you, my dear Gaius?'

'Of course'.

'There are enough charlatans and bogus astrologers around in Rome for us to add to them by voting in favour of a religion of slaves and Jews.'

'And not just slaves and Jews, my dear fellow', Gaius said with a generous smile. 'If my spies are right, this pernicious nonsense has spread to the ranks of the nobility, and even' -his expression became suddenly sombre- 'to the ranks of *your* distinguished family.'

Publius winced at Gaius' little quip. His friend was quite right, of course. One of his nephews had affected an interest in the new cult, much to the delight of his circle of dissipated youth who were predictably impressed by anything which was new and exotic. He had even spoken passionately of the persuasive oratory of a Jewish tent merchant- of all things!- by the name of Aquila. When Publius had contemptuously retorted that the name was obviously a freedman's name, the arrogant young pup replied that social rank did not matter and that he now felt free for the first time in his life, and other such nonsense no doubt delivered solely for the benefit of the elegant ladies surrounding him, who evidently found him so refreshingly unorthodox. Publius had got so angry that he had left the room.

'The gullibility of some of the members of my family makes me all the more determined to vote against it', he replied coldly.

'I'm sorry, my dear Publius', said Gaius, with a chuckle. 'Your nephew is an impressionable simpleton and I've been very rude to remind you of the fact.'

'Not at all. As you say, the young man is a half-wit and we've got more important things to worry about than whether he drinks wine with slaves or gets excited by slitting the throats of young bulls.'

'Indeed. Like the vote today?' Gaius' expression suddenly turned to anxiety. 'Tell me, are you quite sure we *can* afford to

228

oppose it?'

'Why not?', Publius replied loudly. 'After all, if we succeed in declaring the new cult a *religio illicta*, it's not going to shake the world is it? It's only a vote legitimising a new cult or not. We'll simply give Tiberius and his hangers-on a warning that the Senatorial Order is still a force to be reckoned with. After all, the 'Empire'- (he almost spat out the word) - was only supposed to be a temporary expedient to restore order to the Republic. And what, with the Emperor and his court, and the traditions of Rome being flouted daily, we're getting pretty close to restoring the old kings of Rome, if you ask me. And I'm sure Tiberius will not be toppled from his throne if we refuse to legitimise a new Jewish cult.'

'I'm sure you're right, but even you would admit there is a risk', said Regulus, suddenly coming into the conversation with his slow and measured way of speaking. 'We'll be marked out. We'll have shown ourselves to be capable of standing up against the Emperor. His henchmen have a long memory and they have every incentive to manufacture enemies of Tiberius in the Senatorial ranks to increase their hold on the Emperor.'

'If you want my opinion', said Gaius, 'I think it's a pity that we don't have something more important to vote against. Something more dramatic than legitimising a cult that is largely venerated by slaves. Like a vote for a new aqueduct. Or an allowance for a foreign ally. For us to turn that down *would* be a slap in the face. But instead we're reduced to getting worked up over trivia.'

Publius laughed:

'My dear friends, do you seriously imagine that we could galvanise the others into voting 'no' on something which really matters? They are all terrified of Tiberius- all, that is, except those who were quickly bought off and corrupted with villas and privileges from the imperial coffers. You're not being your usual astute self, Gaius. We must first get the Senators used to opposition. We get them to vote against the new cult. If we succeed it won't make a jot of difference to the rest of the world, but the Senate will have tasted blood. They'll want more. Next time they'll vote against something more important. Soon Tiberius will start to realise that he has to start negotiating with the Senatorial Order rather than bullying it around as he wishes.' `Well, I hope you're right', Gaius replied. `I think we should go in, the debate is about to begin.'

***

The Senate was crowded and Publius breathed an inner sigh at the thought of spending the best part of the day in the austerely decorated hall, with its floor of rare marble and that high ceiling which made the voices of speakers echo uncomfortably. There would be that smell of too much humanity packed together, the continuous bustle of messengers bringing news to clusters of Senators intriguing in a corner. There would be the tedium of Classicus' interminable speeches followed by yet another self-important windbag.

He sat down in one of the back rows and listened to the opening speeches and to the procedural announcements for the day's session. He was pleased when Gaius and Regulus went off to look for a mutual acquaintance, leaving him to his thoughts.

With half an ear on the proceedings, Publius mentally rehearsed the speech he was going to make later that afternoon. He enjoyed watching the play of light on the marble and his thoughts started to drift. His attention was then caught by a particularly interesting face in the crowd: it was a new face, the earnest face of a young Senator making his first appearance. He spent some time studying the man's features according to his rather fastidious notions of proper classical proportions. Then his heart gave a start, for he noticed a group of imperial dignitaries advancing towards him. He immediately recognised the leading man among the officials- Narcissus.

Narcissus was of medium height, but with a tendency to go to fat, like so many eunuchs. It was not his beardless face and the thin high voice- utterly unlike a woman's but also completely unlike a treble's- that gave him a look of corrupt weakness: it was rather Narcissus' perfectly bald head, shiny from much oiling with scents, the wide blue eyes that stared at you with a sinister false innocence, and the way his fat, carefully manicured fingers exuded an infinite corruptibility. A more generous man would at least have had pity for a creature so cruelly mutilated and forced into an incomplete existence, but Publius could hardly suppress a grimace of contempt as the eunuch advanced towards him.

With an almost visible effort, the Senator greeted the powerful Imperial counsellor. Narcissus replied with a polished greeting of impeccable courtesy.

'I had not appreciated the Emperor cared so much for Jews', said Publius.

'The Emperor cares for the welfare of all his subjects', Narcissus replied without any change of expression.

'Of course', said Publius with a slight bow of respect, 'but the Jews are hardly the easiest of people to rule. I should have thought there are more deserving cases of imperial favours. The Spanish tribes, for example, who so loyally supported Rome against the Gauls.'

'No doubt the Emperor has plans for them too', Narcissus answered mechanically, 'but it is the wish of the Emperor that the new cult of the Jews should be granted the status of *religio licta*'.

'Subject to the Senate's approbation', said Publius staring hard at Narcissus.

'Subject to the Senate's approbation, of course', the eunuch repeated, suddenly examining Publius with more interest.

Publius ostentatiously readjusted the senatorial sash to its proper angle across his toga.

'Tell me', said Publius, determined to lose no opportunity of asserting his superior rank, 'isn't the Emperor concerned about legitimising a cult whose leader was executed?'

'There is evidence that he may have been innocent', Narcissus replied, his large eyes fixed on Publius.

'But he was nevertheless sentenced to death as a common criminal after due process of Roman law.'

'That appears to be the case.'

'Doesn't that, at least, cast some doubt on this so-called 'religion'?'

'The manner of their leader's death does not necessarily detract from the value of what he preached. Think of Socrates.'

At that moment, a tall young official appeared, bowed respectfully towards Publius and then took Narcissus aside to whisper something in his ear. Narcissus appeared concerned at the news, muttered some perfunctory excuse to Publius and left. Publius was enraged. He was more determined than ever to defeat this preposterous new law. A slave he had sent to find out what he could about the new cult had reported that it apparently allowed Roman citizens, freedmen and slaves to mix on equal terms. Urbanus had also confirmed that they met in private houses where women had the same rank as men, and that Jews freely mixed with Romans during their meetings-although Publius had always understood that these strange Levantines refused to eat with any foreigners whom they regarded as 'impure'. No wonder Narcissus appeared keen on the new cult- he was both a slave and a eunuch. If slaves were allowed to mix on the same footing as free men, then eunuchs were probably allowed in on the same status as real men: he would not be surprised if Narcissus were a disciple of the new cult as well! The whole thing was quite intolerable.

'Gaius!' he cried out, so loud that people turned round. 'I must have a word.'

He led Gaius down the corridors to the clearer air of the Forum. As he stood on the steps of the Senate, gazing at the spectacle of the Temple of Juno, and beyond, the Temple of the Vestals nestling at the foot of the Palatine hill, he momentarily took heart: Rome had conquered the world, it was triumphant, and it would survive this momentary eclipse of its glorious destiny. The glory of Rome was for all time.

232

He stood on the steps for a long time, lost in his thoughts until he noticed Gaius waiting patiently at his side, the gaunt figure of Regulus behind him. He turned and looked at them in a new light, as if he had never realised what they looked like before. Somehow they both looked small, almost vulnerable, standing as they did beside the huge bronze doors of the Senate. For a second, Publius had a sense of them all being crushed by the relentless march of history, of the world belonging to new forces beyond their control, beyond their understanding. How pitiful the pair of them looked in the background of such magnificence! Why had the gods seen it fit to make him live in an age of moral pygmies? He was an old man now, and he did not see any good reason to sacrifice the autumn of his life in defending the values of an age which everyone seemed happy to consign to the dust of history.

Suddenly, he announced to his two friends that today he would be making his final speech in the Senate.

He ignored Gaius' protestations that he was their only hope, or Regulus' insistence that without his courageous stance the Senate would become a mere ghost. No, his mind was made up. Today, he would make one final speech. He would defeat the motion. And then the future could take care of itself.

***

The first of the speeches in the debate started. By convention, the supporters of the motion had the floor first. Publius suppressed a snort of contempt as he saw that the first was no less than Varius Metellus.

Varius could be depended upon to speak in support of the Emperor's motion. A more astute tacker of the political wind could not be found. It was said that during the Civil War, he had at first offered his support to Pompey, then to Mark Antony when the going had become rough, only to scurry back to Pompey at the first hint of impending defeat. Somehow, he had managed to convince each of his new masters that his 'conversions' to their causes were sincere. The scoundrel had now obviously succeeded in becoming a devout supporter of the imperial cause.

The speech was polished, Publius grudgingly admitted, but it was clearly not written by Varius. It bore all the signs of having been written by Narcissus' henchmen: smooth, reassuring, offending no-one, the speech almost managed to convince you that the Emperor actually cared about the adherents of the new cult, although anyone who knew how Tiberius operated must have realised that the whole thing was probably designed to placate some political pressure group in Palestine, or even that it was a clever way of perpetuating the divisions among the Jews under the time-tested Roman principle of divide and rule.

Varius concluded that the new cult fulfilled all the criteria to be declared a *religio licta*. It was not a danger to the civic order of Rome as its adherents did not preach rebellion and indeed made it a point to obey the laws of the State and even enjoined its followers faithfully to pay their taxes; it had its own recognisable ritual; it was strictly monotheistic, but then so were other cults in the Empire, like the cult of the Jews or the Persian followers of Zoroaster; its moral teaching was not contrary to *bonos mores*, and generally the cult, after due investigation by the Imperial Government, was felt safe and proper for recognition as an allowable cult. He called on the Senate to approve the new religion and declare it a *religio licta*.

***

Publius rose. At first he said nothing. He decided to scan the countless faces that surrounded him before speaking, using the age-old but effective actor's trick of waiting for the audience's expectations to build up until it was firmly in his grasp. Then he spoke.

'Senators of Rome', he began- he liked a grandiloquent beginning. 'What is the essence of Rome?' he asked, with as contemptuous an expression as he could manage. He tossed the last fold of his toga over his shoulder with a curt but dignified sweep of the hand and proceeded to answer his own rhetorical question. The foundation stone of Rome's majesty was the dignity of its citizens, yes, their dignity. What, after all, distinguished the Roman from the barbarian? The Roman from the slave? Nothing less than the Roman's consciousness of his own superiority. The Roman did not need to go into battle covered in paint like the Northern Savages. (There was a ripple of approving laughter from the audience). The Roman died at his post rather than face the ignominy of slavery as a captive. Lucius Scipio had preferred to return to Carthage to meet certain death by torture rather than break his word as a Roman. The dying Julius Caesar had taken care to rearrange the folds of his toga rather than die without dignity. Cato had chosen to fall on his sword rather than betray the ideals of the Republic. (There was a murmur of astonished approval, at the daring reference to the Republic that preceded the Empire, but Publius persevered regardless). To die with dignity: that was a Roman virtue, not to wallow in blood and suffering like the followers of that detestable cult of a Jew who had been executed as a common criminal, which the present assembly was now being asked to declare a *religio licta*.

He built up his oratorical effects slowly, invoking the names of the Roman gods, and there was a further ripple of applause. Then he praised the Emperor with as much rhetorical irony as he felt he could get away with: the Emperor had consolidated the peace brought to the Roman world by his illustrious predecessor Augustus, he had proved himself a worthy choice as successor to the highest public office, he was a distinguished member of the *gens Claudia* that had contributed so much to Roman public life and so on and so forth. But these achievements were built on the solid rock of Roman tradition, where public office was held by Roman citizens- (he watched the grimace of Narcissus from the corner of his eye, relishing his success at obliquely attacking the eunuch's status of a slave)- the acts of the Emperor were for the greater glory of the gods of

Rome, and no important decision would be taken without consulting the augurs. The ancestral traditions of Rome had created the Empire, they had even created the Senate where they now sat, their very prosperity was the gift of the gods: they had a duty to ensure that the Senate of Rome would continue to act for the greater glory of Rome.

Having established his traditionalist credentials, he calculated that now was the moment to strike.

The new eastern cults were spreading through Rome like wildfire: he even had a neophyte in his own intimate family, his nephew having been converted to the very cult they were debating today! His sister had bitterly complained of her impressionable son's weakness for whichever outlandish fashion was currently in vogue. He ignored the chuckles of the crowd and continued. Always intrigued by human folly, he had sent one of his better educated slaves to infiltrate the new cult. The reports he received were alarming and depressing in equal measure.

Before revealing his discoveries, Publius decided to add one more rhetorical flourish.

Compared to the sublime formality of the ancestral Roman religion, he went on, he openly confessed to feeling a sense of disgust at the sight of obese cattle having their heads gently raised for a knife wielded by a white-robed virgin. He shuddered at the bestial drunkenness of the *plebs* as they progressed along the Tiber during the Saturnalia. And even worse was the bizarre initiation rites of the Syrians- or was it the Egyptians?, he forgot which (further laughter)- where young proselytes emerged trembling and blushing from the dark caves in which the absurdly garbed 'elders' had initiated them to the secret mysteries. He winced theatrically at the thought of corrupted, gullible youth, and was duly rewarded with more laughter and a burst of applause.

He then went in for the kill.

The new cult being proposed for the Senate's approval also came from near Syria. That was not a coincidence. Their gods might be fit for a foreign climate, but the serene azure of the Roman sky demanded a more wholesome religion. This infection of the Roman psyche had to be stopped! There was another burst of applause, but stronger this time.

He warmed to his theme. The most remarkable thing that his spy had reported was the nature of the rituals. The adherents of the new 'religion' were clearly as cunning as the foxes on his estates. Obviously, they had quickly spotted Urbanus as a spy since all they showed him was a particularly insipid little show, where there was no slaughtering of animals, no plunging of hands into still warm entrails, no sudden outbursts of frenetic dancing. Instead, it was all remarkably tame, even dull- if the cult was not downright anti-social with its insistence on meetings in the semi-darkness before dawn, and that in the respectable anonymity of a town house. But the thing which puzzled him the most- and made him all the more suspicious of the cult- was the total absence of any statues of the gods. The slave had reported that even they did not know what their god looked like! Apparently, the room was bare and the faithful merely chanted in a circle before eating a frugal peasant's meal of plain bread and wine. It was all so inherently improbable that he had ordered the slave to be soundly whipped for telling lies. No doubt, instead of doing an honest day's spying, the wretch had used the money he had given him in one the brothels of the Via Cassia rather than bribing his way to find the truth.
That last witticism earned him a thunderous round of applause, and Publius paused for effect.

But he was not deluded by the Senators' obvious approbation- that crowd of degenerates would clap their hands at anything which entertained them... Publius had an indefinable feeling of

237

growing unease about the whole proceedings. Afterwards, he would remember how the gradual sense of nausea had increased as he continued with his speech. Perhaps it was the heat in the airless marbled hall, perhaps it was his failing health- but in his heart of hearts he knew that his mind was gradually filled with disgust. All at once, his accumulated contempt for the spinelessness of the Senatorial Order, for their despicable compromises, their cowering at the 'Emperor's feet, rose within him in a mighty wave of revulsion. He looked round and he saw the corpulent face of Placidus Galba, who was notorious for his passion for deflowering new slave girls; he saw the half-dozing expression of the Senators to Placidus' side; he saw the foppish elegance of Junius Aquileus and his fashionable set of young followers sitting in the row behind.

Was this the Senate of Rome, were these degenerate specimens of humanity the only safeguard for the values he so passionately revered? With an immense effort, he continued his speech, his inner heart sinking into the blackest despair as he did so.

Had the Senate ever been called upon to vote on anything more absurd and degrading than a foreign cult whose god was a crucified Jew? Apparently, the wretch had met his fate within living memory and so the cult didn't even have the weight of respectable antiquity behind it.

Publius sighed theatrically. His gods were gods who inspired awe and wonder: he vividly remembered his emotions on his first visit to Olympia. There he had admired the crushing majesty of Phidias' statue of Zeus. The gold and marble in the semi-darkness, the head of the awesome god under the huge vault of the ornate ceiling, the distant sound of the sea giving a sense of infinite space... That was a cult which winged the soul and pointed it to the sky, a vision that made the mind of man touch the divine, a religion which gave man a sobering sense of his own insignificance.

Then he caught sight of his cousin Petronius looking distantly through the large windows with a bored expression. The distinguished *rhetor* Marcus Fortunatus, next to him, had his eyes shut with a solemn look of stern contemplation. Publius' pride was bitten to the quick by the general disinterest of the assembly. Only Gaius sat in the front row, with an expectant air. He realised, then, that his instinct had been right, that the whole thing was a waste of time. He was fighting the battles of yesterday, with people who didn't remotely care if the Senate backed the wish of the Emperor or not. Publius paused for what seemed an interminable time, and even Marcus Fortunatus opened his eyes, as if startled by the silence from the speaker's platform. Publius felt a terrible longing to rush out of the hall, he suddenly longed passionately for the cool evenings of his country estate near the sea, where he would soon retire from a world running headlong into madness, to its own self-destruction. He was overwhelmed by such a wave of contemptuous revulsion that it nearly choked his voice. He realised that everyone was looking at him, with concerned faces as to his evidently failing health. Somehow, he found the inner strength to continue, if only to live up to his ideal of himself one final, memorable time.

Yes Senators, he cried out loudly, as if the strength of his voice would somehow drown the inner turmoil in his mind. 'What is being proposed to the Illustrious Senate of Rome?' he cried out, so loud that his voice reverberated under the huge vaulted ceiling. A 'religion' where slaves and Jews skulked away before dawn to chant ecstatically in incomprehensible tongues, in secret hideaways where women were treated as the equal of men and men were treated the same as women, where slaves addressed freedmen as their equals, where Romans were regarded as no better than Scythians or Germans. Had the Senate forgotten that to become a citizen of Rome, a man had to serve twenty-five years in the Legions? Was the Senate to remove, at a stroke, the laws that decreed that a slave - even if freed by his master-was still only a better class of vermin? Did the Senators of Rome propose to forget that the gods, who had brought them power over the known world, would not forgive this most pernicious defilement of their illustrious past?

'No, Senators of Rome', he concluded, 'seven centuries of history are observing you and judging you. You stand before your ancestors. You will be judged by posterity if you flinch from your sacred duty now. In the name of Rome, I call upon you to reject the motion before you.'

The whole assembly responded with a thunderous burst of applause. Publius sat down, exhausted, only just managing to take his seat with appropriate dignity. He tried to convince himself that he had done his duty, that centuries of history had been vindicated in this trivial little vote. He caught sight of Narcissus, high up, in the officials' row, behind the crowd of clamouring Senators, looking at him with an expression of amused contempt. He sat back and shut his eyes as the hollow sound of the applause filled his ears.

***

'Well, my friend, what do you make of the vote? An overwhelming rejection. *Religio illicta*!' Gaius said, savouring the resounding words. '*Religio illicta*', he repeated, 'the Jews will not have their new religion!' He laughed and put his arm round Publius affectionately. 'Did you see Narcissus' face when the Senate turned down the new cult? I thought he would faint! A magnificent speech. Worthy of Demosthenes...'

Publius didn't listen to the rest of his friend's compliments, lost in thought, realising the futility of his victory with crushing clarity.

'No, my friend', Publius replied, placing his hand on his friend's arm. 'This is a tiny twitch of revolt. The sting of a horsefly on a mule: we'll simply be brushed off with a swish of its tail', he said, smiling at his own metaphor.

He stopped in his tracks and looked at Gaius straight in the eye.

240

His friend seemed older, his face jowlier and more evidently corrupted by luxurious living, the face of an older man who has reconciled himself to the fact of his own mediocrity, who has learnt to live with the knowledge of his own failure.

'My dear Gaius', he said, 'I thank you most sincerely for your support, but we both know that today's vote means nothing. Soon we'll be dead. Nobody will care that those who worship a crucified Jew didn't have their religion legitimised. Those gullible fools will vanish as quickly as they have appeared. Our vote today will soon be forgotten. We should realise what we are. We are yesterday's men, Gaius. We are only the dust of history.'

SOURCES AND MATERIALS FOR THE STORIES

THE CONVERSION OF HANS FRANK

The spiritual conversion of the various Nazi leaders during the Nuremberg trials is described in Jean-Marc Varaut's 'Le Procès de Nuremberg' (Perrin, 1992).

PLAYING POKER WITH BERIA

Beria's confrontation with Evgeny Varga over the poker table is recorded by Arkady Vaksberg in his '*Hotel Lux: les partis frères au service de l'Internationale Communiste*', (Fayard 1993).

Material on the purges was drawn from Robert Conquest '*The Great Terror: a Reassessment*' (Pimlico 1992) and Sheila Fitzpatrick '*Every Day Stalinism- ordinary lives in extraordinary times: Soviet Russia in the 1930s*' (OUP 1999).   It is also a pleasure to acknowledge my debt to A.Alvarez' description of professional poker-playing '*The Biggest Game in Town*', (Penguin, 1979).

THE ISLANDS OF DESOLATION

The most comprehensive account of Kerguelen's life is Rear-Admiral de Brossart's '*Kerguelen*' (Editions France Empire, 1970), but it has to be read with caution as it is rather partisan.

I have also drawn from the memoirs of other Kerguelen Islands explorers such as Edgar Aubert de la Rüe '*Terres françaises inconnues. L'Archipel des Kerguelen et les possessions françaises australes*', Railler du Batty *15000 miles in a ketch*, Nelson, (1910) and André Migot (1956).

No-one interested in these remote and outlandish islands should miss '*L'arche des Kerguelen*', Flammarion, 1993, the wonderfully evocative travel memoirs of Jean-Paul Kauffman, the former Beirut hostage who sought solitude in the Kerguelen Islands after his release.

243

THE LORD OF HEAVEN

The Jesuits' attempt to evangelise China in the 16th and 17th centuries is well documented. This story uses material from the *'Tianzhu Shiyi'* or *'The True Meaning of the Lord of Hea*ven' by Matteo Ricci, the first successful Jesuit missionary in China. This famous work, published in 1603, is an account of the Christian faith adapted to fit into Chinese conceptions of the world, mainly by trying to prove that Christianity, if properly understood, is purified Confucianism. E. Ducornet's *'Matteo Ricci'* (Editions du Cerf, Paris, 1992) helpfully quotes large extracts of the 'Tianzhu Shiyi'.

The world of Matteo Ricci (and to a large extent that of his fellow Jesuits in the Chinese missions) is admirably described by Jonathan D. Spence's *'The Memory Palace of Matteo Ricci'*, (Faber and Faber 1984).

The Chinese reactions to the Jesuits' endeavours were puzzled and often hostile. I have relied in particular on material quoted in Gernet's magisterial *'Chine et Christianisme'* (Gallimard, revised ed. 1991) for some of the scenes in this story.

I have also used the entry on the Chinese Rites Controversy in the *'Catholic Encyclopaedia'*, Guillermou's *'St.Ignace de Loyole et la compagnie de Jesus'*, (Maîtres Spirituels, Seuil 1960) and Stephen Neill's *'A history of Christian missions'*, (Penguin, 1986) for material on the Chinese rites controversy that raged at the time in which this story is set.

THE POTEMKIN VILLAGES

Count Potemkin's deception on the Empress Catherine has achieved proverbial status in Russia, perhaps because its cynical manipulation of reality is an archetype of Russian political life. Some of the materials on Catherine were drawn from Henri Troyat's lively biography *'Catherine the Great'*.

THE MARRIAGE OF COUNTESS ISABELLA

Collecting dwarves was a fashion in the sixteenth and seventeenth century courts. A good example is Velasquez' *Portrait of the Infanta*, showing the Princess' favourite dwarf posing next to her.
The well-preserved dwarfish apartments built by Count Vincenzo Gonzaga can still be visited in the fortress-palace of the Gonzagas, the Regia dei Gonzaga in Mantua. Some of the descriptions of the palace decorations are based on the paintings of Giulio Romano in the Sala dei Giganti in the Palazzo Te, Mantua.

ENTERTAINING MONA LISA

Leonardo da Vinci's attempts to amuse Mona Lisa while painting her portrait is described by Vasari in his '*Lives of the Artists*', (Penguin Classics). Some materials for this story were drawn from Leonardo's Notebooks, (World's Classics, ed. Richter, 1952). For biographical details on Leonardo and Mona Lisa, I have used Kenneth Clark's Biography, (Penguins 1959) and Pietro Marani Complete Catalogue, Cantini Edizione, Florence, 1989.

A PERFECT WORLD

The Emperor Gallienus had the misfortune to reign during the worst period of third century anarchy. For the historical background of Gallienus' brief period as Emperor I have relied on H.M.D. Parker's '*A History of the Roman World AD 138-337*' (Methuen 1935) and P. Petit's '*La crise de l'Empire*' (Seuil 1974). For anyone interested in the period, André de Chastignol's magisterial edition of the '*Historia Augusta*' (Laffont 1994), is essential, not least for the more scurrilous details of Gallienus's reign.
Perhaps as a refuge from the brutality of the times, Gallienus surrounded himself with a court of aesthetes and philosophers.

The most prominent was, of course, Plotinus whose work represent the last brilliant glow of Hellenistic culture before the transformation of European civilisation by Christianity and the Dark Ages. In chapter 12 of his *'Life of Plotinus'* Porphyry records the Emperor Gallienus' ill-fated building of a Philosophers' City. Unfortunately, the precise site of the City has never been found. I have used the text of Porphyry's biography and the translation of Plotinus' *'Enneads'* by Stephen Mackenna (Penguin 1991). For Plotinus' dialogues on the platonic concept of Beauty I have relied on the translation of Books I,6 and V,8 of the Enneads by Paul Mathias in *'Plotin: Du Beau'* (Presses Pocket 1991).

RELIGIO ILLICTA

The Senate's vote on the proposed legitimisation of Christianity is mentioned by Tertullian in his *Apology*, Part V. Details of Roman aristocratic life under Tiberius were drawn from Jérome Carcopino's *'La vie quotidienne à l'apogée de l'empire romain'*, (Hachette).

A NOTE ON THE AUTHOR

Philippe de Felice is of Swiss origins and was born in Zurich in. 1954. He received a cosmopolitan education in Swiss, French and English schools, and then studied at Florence University and Oriel College Oxford (where he graduated with First Class Honours in History and French in 1976). He later qualified as a Barrister and followed a career in international law, working on aid projects for the United Nations, on EU affairs for the Commission and the UK government, and most recently in private practice.

He has travelled widely in Asia, Europe, Africa and the Middle East.

He now lives in London with his wife and three children. "*Entertaining Mona Lisa*" is his first collection of stories. He is currently working on a novel and a series of studies on how humans have chosen to express themselves throughout the ages, from prehistoric caves to the internet era.